"I've been

"...unofficially, as far as the commissioner's office is concerned."

"Undercover?" Cops assigned to protective duty, should *not*, Devon decided testily, be allowed to have sexy bodies, mysterious gazes or tousled hair that skimmed their shoulders. It made women think of dark princes with troubled souls and needs that few if any females could ever satisfy.

Riker kept his fists jammed in his jacket pockets. "I'm listed as 'on assignment.'"

"That's nice and vague." He smelled good, like leather and some intriguing brand of male soap. She would have stepped away if she hadn't seen the shadows under his eyes and the stubble on his jaw. He looked troubled—not in the manner of a dark prince, but rather like a man with a host of problems surrounding him.

He felt his teeth beginning to grind and knew it was time to leave. Past time if he were truthful. Guilt and a beautiful woman whose scent brought to mind woodsy Irish flowers were not mixing well in his system. There was, however, one more thing he needed to do.

Kiss her senseless...

ABOUT THE AUTHOR

Jenna Ryan loves creating dark-haired heroes, heroines with strength and good murder mysteries. Ever since she was young, she has had an extremely active imagination. She considered various careers over the years and dabbled in several of them, until the day her sister Kathy suggested she put her imagination to work and write a book. She enjoys working with intriguing characters and feels she is at her best writing romantic suspense. When people ask her how she writes, she tells them by instinct. Clearly it's worked, since she's received numerous awards from *Romantic Times Magazine*. She lives in Canada and travels as much as she can when she's not writing.

Books by Jenna Ryan

The Stroke of Midnight
Jenna Ryan

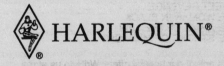

HARLEQUIN®

TORONTO • NEW YORK • LONDON
AMSTERDAM • PARIS • SYDNEY • HAMBURG
STOCKHOLM • ATHENS • TOKYO • MILAN • MADRID
PRAGUE • WARSAW • BUDAPEST • AUCKLAND

To everyone I love—the ones who matter most.

ISBN 0-373-22543-1

THE STROKE OF MIDNIGHT

Copyright © 1999 by Jacqueline Goff

Visit us at www.romance.net

Printed in U.S.A.

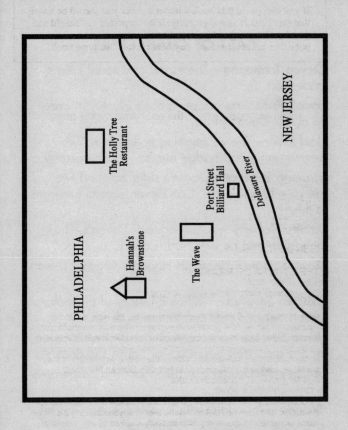

CAST OF CHARACTERS

Devon Tremayne — The target of a serial killer's obsession.

Jacob Price — He adopts a cop's identity in order to obtain Devon's trust.

Joel Riker — The vacationing police detective whose name and badge number Jacob borrows.

Hannah Wallace — Devon's sister has had two nervous breakdowns. Can Devon protect her from a third?

Jimmy Flaherty — A colleague of Devon's. The only girlfriend he ever had is dead.

Roscoe Beale — He wants Hannah, whether Devon likes it or not.

Warren Severen — He has a history of alcoholism and a dubious past connection to death.

Alma Severen — She controls her brother, Warren, and a successful business — or hopes she does.

Andrew McGruder — A neighbor who desperately wants Devon's love.

Brando — An addict with knowledge; but was his overdose accidental or intentional?

Prologue

"You're listening to the Wave, WWAV FM, in Philadelphia. I'm Devon Tremayne. Join me again tomorrow on *City Life*. Oh, and by the way, to the listener who sent me that lovely Christmas angel pendant, I want you to know that I can't be bribed. Have a great afternoon everyone, and be careful on the drive home. It's snowing awfully hard out there...."

The man surged upward from a black pool of guilt, weariness and too much red wine. The woman's voice penetrated the murky layers as if they'd never existed, jerking him awake in the space of a single second.

His dark eyes registered snowflakes dancing outside the curved apartment window and a handful of newspaper clippings scattered across the floor. He got gloomy at Christmas time. He didn't remember hauling out the clippings, but then he'd drunk too much wine and whiskey last night to remember much of anything—and what the hell had the woman just said?

Devon Tremayne's words echoed with eerie clarity. She'd received a gift. A Christmas angel pendant. He hadn't dreamed the remark, he knew that as surely as he knew his name. The host of WWAV's daily talk show, "City Life," had acknowledged her gift openly.

A dull throbbing started at the base of his skull. Shoving the hair from his eyes, he squinted at the swirling snow, then over at the radio he hadn't bothered to turn off last night when he'd stumbled through the door and straight into his punching bag. Devon Tremayne. A voice on the airwaves to her ever-increasing Philadelphia audience. But what else might she be?

Something in his stomach twisted unpleasantly. Forcing himself off the rumpled bed, he stepped carefully over the clippings.

He didn't need to look to know that every headline began with the same chilling phrase: 'The Christmas Murders...' there for all to read in bold black print. And the city was creeping toward the Christmas season yet again.

The sour taste of bile rose in his throat. Halting at the frosted window pane, he let his head drop forward. The throbbing intensified to unbearable proportions.

He closed his eyes, fighting it. He'd wanted to believe it was over. He'd needed to believe it. Seven women dead in eight Christmases. Seven Christmas angel pendants sent to them before they died. Death at midnight where possible, and always by strangulation.

His fingers tightened briefly on the white wood jamb. It should have been over, but it wasn't. Morbid experience and grim instinct told him it had only just begun....

Chapter One

"It's the men, Devon, always the men who treat a woman like a wayward child."

Alma Severen, co-owner of WWAV FM, leaned forward in her padded chair and jabbed a plump finger at the woman standing across from her.

Nine months at the radio station had inured Devon Tremayne to Alma's no-nonsense attitude. People usually summed up and quickly assumed their proper place around the opinionated sixty-four-year-old businesswoman. Apparently, one poor soul had missed his cue.

Taking the window seat, Devon raised inquiring brows at her boss. "Does this have anything to do with that angel pendant I got yesterday?"

"It has everything to do with it, my girl."

Alma's tone made Devon frown. "I thought the police caught the Christmas Murderer last year. A man named Casey Coombes, wasn't it? That's what Hannah told me last night."

Alma sighed. "Your sister's a kind and trusting individual, Devon."

"She's also right, isn't she?"

"Yes. But that doesn't alter the fact that the male portion of the Philadelphia police force is comprised ninety percent of condescending fools who wouldn't know east from west if the females in their lives didn't explain it to them every day at breakfast.''

Tired of Alma's man-bashing, Devon leaned an elbow on the walnut filing cabinet, propped her chin in her cupped palm and blew the wheat-blond bangs from her eyes. ''I wish I'd never gotten that pendant, or mentioned it to anyone when I did. It was a prank, Alma, a stupid hoax.''

''Could've been a copycat,'' a chipper voice inserted.

''I didn't hear you knock, Jimmy.'' Alma tapped an impatient fingernail on her blotter.

The young, curly-haired man grinned. ''I did knock, Ms. Severen. Your secretary wasn't at her desk. You got a new one, didn't you? What's her name?''

''Brian.''

Devon hid a smile. Jimmy Flaherty, older by seven or eight years than his fresh-faced appearance suggested, shrugged and returned his attention to the original topic. ''Roscoe contacted the police as per your instructions. You know, about the pendant.''

Devon slid her a sideways look. ''Alma...''

''A prudent precaution.'' Alma folded her hands. ''You're brushing this off, my dear, but I assure you, it isn't a matter to be taken lightly. Innocents have gone to prison for other people's crimes before and will again.''

Exasperated, Devon drummed her slender fingers on the cabinet top. ''Coombes confessed, Alma. How innocent can he be?''

Ignoring the perfectly reasonable question, Alma pinned Jimmy with a stare. ''What did the police have to say?''

He handed her a sheet of paper. ''It's all there. They told Roscoe they'd look into it, time and officers permitting. But they think they have the guy who killed those women, Ms. Severen. I, uh, doubt if they'll bother much about a copycat gift.''

Devon's fine brows lowered in mild consternation. When she'd first received the gift, she hadn't given it much thought. Now, with the fuss Alma was creating added to the story she had dragged out of her reluctant sister last night, she was tempted to think it through again.

Alma waved an arm at Jimmy's last remark. "That's bull. You tell Roscoe to get in here pronto."

Unperturbed, Jimmy let his grin return. "I can't, ma'am. He's gone to lunch with our top sponsor." He glanced shyly at Devon. "I, uh, could drive you home if you're nervous."

Was she nervous? Devon considered and decided she was not. "I'll be fine." She stood and ran a hand through her layered sweep of blond hair. "I've dealt with weirdos before in L.A. The man behind the Christmas Murders is in prison, end of story. But unfortunately not," she glanced at her watch, "end of day for me. I told Hannah I'd buy a tree from McBean's on my way home."

Clearly put out, Alma offered a stiff, "A live one, I hope."

Now Devon grinned. "Sorry, no. My parents are dyed in the wool environmentalists. They'd disown Hannah and me if we so much as cut a branch off a living tree."

"Hmph. Well, don't forget tomorrow morning. We've scheduled a pancake breakfast here at the station. We're going to discuss those radio Christmas story readings we talked about. Such self-sacrifice on your parents' behalf will earn you 'The Gift of the Magi,' I think. Or maybe 'The Bishop's Wife.' Teddi can be the Grinch."

"She'll love you for that," Devon said with a laugh. "See you tomorrow. And, please, stop worrying about me."

Jimmy tried to follow her, but out of sheer perversity, Alma forestalled him. Devon knew there was a very kind woman beneath that layer of crusty disagreeableness, though one might have to scrape for quite some time in order to fully expose it. Certainly, Alma meant well where Devon's Christmas angel pendant was concerned. Unfortunately, her good intentions were having an unpleasant effect on Devon's resolve not to be disturbed by an obvious crank. Hannah was a worrier by nature, and she'd been only moderately concerned by her sister's disclosure the previous evening.

They'd talked about it over dinner preparations in Han-

nah's high-ceilinged apartment, one of eight in the unit left
to her by their maternal grandmother, Sinead, six years ago.
Management of people, places and things was Hannah's forté
and their shrewd-minded grandmother had known it. They'd
also received Sinead's midnight-blue Jaguar, her emeralds
and her prize Monet. To Devon's parents, Sinead had be-
queathed a large acreage of forest land in northern Pennsylvania. The pair currently resided there, in a large wood and
brick house complete with a craft barn full of hand-made
collectibles.

"We should leave for Mom and Dad's early on the twenty-
fourth," Hannah had said last night in her gentle, practical
way. Her waist-length blond hair had glowed fiery gold in
her kitchen of painted wood, tile and oak parquet flooring.
"You know how Mother fusses."

"Tofu turkey," Devon had murmured. She'd disguised a
shudder as she'd browned the ground beef for her famous
spaghetti sauce. "I'm not sure I'm up to it this year."

"You'll manage." Hannah had reached over to touch her
sister's shoulder. "You're worried about that pendant you
got today at the station, aren't you?"

Devon shook pepper onto the beef. "I'm not fond of
cranks, if that's what you mean. You've told me that the man
behind the Christmas murders is safely behind bars, so what's
to worry about?"

"Nothing." Hannah's competent hands had begun tearing
up lettuce for the salad. "I checked three times and Casey
Coombes has not escaped. Neither has he confessed to having
any friends or family willing to carry on his macabre tradi-
tion. I think you should throw the pendant away and put the
entire incident out of your mind. I assume you've called the
police...."

Devon released a sigh at the memory. Yesterday, she
hadn't thought there was a need to call them. Today, Alma
had rendered the point moot by ordering the station's PR
person, a handsome slickster named Roscoe Beale, to do it
for her. Roscoe, who had undoubtedly followed orders not

because Alma had issued them, but because he'd been hoping
to score a few badly-needed brownie points with Hannah.

Giving her silky layers of hair a shake, Devon dislodged
the worst of the falling snowflakes. She locked her car then
strolled along the busy South Street sidewalk, past boutiques,
galleries and crowded cafés.

Three street-corner Santas rang bells, and she stopped to
give money to each one. Hannah's late husband, Tony, would
have offered a few cynical remarks, but then Tony had hated
Christmas with all its commercial trappings, its constant demand for good cheer and its numerous social functions. Roscoe might be a trifle too smooth for Devon's personal taste,
but at least he wouldn't spoil Hannah's enjoyment of the
holidays.

They were in the same line of work, as well, which helped
his chances. While Hannah functioned in a managerial capacity at Hare and Woden, Roscoe was on Alma and Warren
Severen's payroll. He could hustle clients with the best of
them. Devon only wished he hadn't been so quick to follow
through on Alma's instructions.

A familiar shop window, glittering with clear lights, caught
her eye. It was dark, and motorists on their way home
crunched along over a layer of freshly fallen snow. 'White
Christmas' played Irish-style on the window speakers. She
spotted the tree she wanted instantly, a blue-green spruce,
seven and half feet tall with hundreds of tiny branches waiting to be decked out with ornaments, bows and sparkly garland.

"I feel like I'm living 'The Bishop's Wife,'" she said
twenty minutes later as the shopowner endeavored to stuff
the boxed tree into the trunk of her Jaguar. "Thanks, Mr.
McBean, and tell your wife if she wants some new holiday
recipes to listen to Thursday's show. We've got two cookbook authors scheduled."

The man, a rotund grandfather with a shiny bald head,
gave the box a final, grunting shove. "Forget the recipes,
Devon Tremayne. You find out who sent you that pendant.

We took the Christmas killings very seriously in this part of the city. Seven women dead over eight Christmases. All radio personalities. Four murdered at or near midnight, if that means anything. You watch yourself, you hear me?''

"But Casey Coombes—"

"Confessed to the murders, I know. We all know. But you should know that sometimes crimes get copied. It's not a healthy world out there, Devon. Take my advice and guard your pretty throat."

Forcing a smile, Devon thanked him again and slid into her vehicle. Who'd have thought one little on-air remark would have generated such a fuss?

Hannah and Devon's small but lovely apartment building was constructed of mellow red brick. Its wooden shutters and tall windows hinted at the seventy-five-year-old architectural style within. The building had been erected in 1925 when high ceilings and spacious living quarters were a must. So were elegance, archways and design variation. No two apartments were alike. Hannah made her home on the first floor; Devon had opted for a vacancy on the second. Two of the units were currently empty, scheduled for refitting in early January.

At the curb, Devon opened the trunk and sized up the box inside. "Not likely," she decided. Closing the lid, she started up the snowy walk to the front stoop.

"Ms. Tremayne?"

She instinctively sidestepped the male speaker, who'd appeared like a magician out of the blackened shrubs. Pressing a hand to her stomach, she controlled her start of surprise. "Yes—no." Her eyes narrowed on his shadowy face. "Why?"

Still some distance away, he moved into a pearled beam of porch light. With his hands jammed into the pockets of a winter leather jacket and his dark hair tumbling in disarray to his shoulders, he brought to mind Devon's image of an informant. Only on closer inspection did she realize that his gaze was too somber for such an unsavory occupation, his eyes too focused, his narrow face too intense.

Without removing his eyes from hers, he drew a hand from his pocket. "I'm Detective Joel Riker, Ms. Tremayne. Philadelphia South Side. You mentioned a certain gift you received at the conclusion of your broadcast yesterday afternoon."

Devon wasn't so disconcerted by his appearance that she neglected to inspect his badge. "All right," she agreed, lifting her gaze. "But you needn't have come all the way over here, Detective Riker."

"Just Riker. And there was every need."

She hoped it was the chill in the air that caused her to shiver. "Maybe we should go inside." She started to walk, then halted, vaguely suspicious. "Why were you lurking in the bushes? You must know that this is my building."

The tiniest of smiles flitted across his lips. "I've spoken to your sister. And I wasn't lurking. I saw you pull up and stopped to wait."

"You blend into the shrubbery very well, Detective."

"Riker. It's a cop's best defense." With a faint movement of his head, he motioned her forward. "Can we keep going? I'm not big on snow."

"No? I'd have pegged you as a northern type. The Dakotas, or maybe Wisconsin."

"Don't ever say that to my grandmother. She was born and bred in County Cork." Reaching around her, he held the front door open. "Do you have the pendant in your apartment?"

"Yes." Though she sincerely wished she'd tossed it out with the morning trash. "Look, Detective…yes, fine, Riker." She paused at the foot of the carpeted stairs, hands on the polished newel post, eyes on his face. "I really don't understand this. I'll agree there may be a copycat crime involved here, but do you honestly believe that the person who sent the pendant would go as far as murder?"

"We don't know what he might do, Ms. Tremayne." He

shrugged. "I don't imagine you'd feel any better if I told you my feelings about the case."

Tendrils of unease curled in her stomach. "My grandmother taught me not to avoid unpleasant truths. What do you think?"

His mouth, which Devon suspected would be extremely sensual under more favorable circumstances, compressed. A glitter akin to fury worked its way through his dark brown eyes. "I never believed that Casey Coombes was the guilty man. His confession was a sham. I think the murderer is still out there, and he's getting ready to kill again."

HE WAS A LOW, rotten bastard.

The man, whose real name was Jacob Price but who'd identified himself as Joel Riker, acknowledged that bitter truth with a knife thrust of guilt and discomfort. The guilt he dealt with swiftly; the discomfort he would have to endure.

Devon Tremayne was a vision, beautiful in a manner reminiscent of graceful gazelles, fine china and the Princess of Wales. He hadn't expected her to look like an American Royal. He'd thought…what, he wondered, easing his head from side to side as they climbed the wide staircase. That she'd be like Laura?

The tension thrumming in his neck muscles refused to abate. The lingering pricks of his conscience did so the moment he pictured Laura's vaporous face.

She'd been a delicate beauty in life. In death, she was reduced to a ghostly image, a headful of disjointed memories. He'd loved her—and God help him, he'd failed her miserably. Maybe he'd even helped to kill her.

Laura was gone forever. So were several other women. But Devon Tremayne was very much alive.

Enter deception. Reporter turned publishing editor transformed with frightening ease into cop. For one day or two, ten or twenty if need be.

With the real Joel Riker booked out of his precinct until after the New Year, Jacob felt confident that he could pull off an impersonation—with a little help from his irascible Uncle Rudy, that is.

His own work could wait. The *Philadelpia Beat* was a trendy, upscale newsmagazine these days. He'd built it from a foundation of dated, ex-beatnik groans and criticisms of life as it failed to deliver in the nineties. He hadn't shed all the groans, but while he might prefer to wear black, the color did not dominate at the *Beat*. During the ten years since he'd bought the magazine, Jacob had seen to that.

Devon didn't utter a word as she ascended, but then what was there to say? A man she believed to be a Philadelphia police officer had just informed her that he believed the Christmas Murderer was still at large. Worse, she had almost certainly been targeted as the murderer's next victim.

Oh, yeah, Jacob thought darkly, he was a bastard all right. At the top of the stairs, she studied, first a strand of holly twined with colored lights, then, more covertly, him. "What makes you think that Casey Coombes' confession was a sham?"

Jacob considered lying. "Gut instinct," he admitted at length. "Coombes was nobody until he was picked up as a suspect."

She babied both lock and deadbolt. "Don't murderers often fit that mold?"

She had beautiful hands, elegant and long-fingered. Slender. Drawing his eyes away, Jacob moved a shoulder. "Sometimes; not always. I don't believe Coombes has it in him to kill anyone in reality."

"Meaning his violent tendencies are confined to fantasy." She made a disbelieving sound as she shouldered the door open. "I've had guest psychologists on my show who might support that theory, Riker, but just as many who'd call it a crock. Anyone can commit murder given a suitably deteriorated state of mind. Was Coombes convicted on his confession alone?"

Peripherally, Jacob took in the explosion of greenery that greeted him. Plants, pottery, cushions and color. Abstract oil paintings on the walls as well. Nothing garish, just eye-catching, possibly thought-provoking under other circumstances. For the moment he was trying very hard not to think about the woman in front of him.

"There was evidence against Coombes," he said, moving deliberately away from her. "But any fool can wind up in a frame."

She shed her long crimson wool coat and tossed it over the back of a terra-cotta-colored sofa. "And having been set up, the framee immediately proceeds to confess to a crime he didn't commit? Give me a break, Riker."

"If the idea of notoriety appeals to the framee, yes. It's been done before, more often than you might think."

Doubt registered clearly in her green eyes. Deep green, like a mossy glade in the fall. Jacob focused his attention on the kitchen, visible across a cream-and-brick-tiled counter. Devon had an eye for texture and a fondness, it seemed, for the color red.

A nightmarish image of blood oozing from the side of a woman's mouth caused his stomach and fists to tighten in revulsion. He remembered with similar, sickening clarity a cold bony hand trapping his chin. Dark brown eyes set deep in their sockets had bored unsympathetically into his. *'Did you kill her?'* a gravelly voice had demanded.

The question echoed like an insidious mantra, growing louder and more insistent, until—

"Riker?"

The name penetrated, and he swivelled his head. How many times had she called him? From the expression on her face, he would guess more than once. "Sorry, I was…" He frowned. "Did you say something?"

He saw annoyance flare in her eyes, then subside swiftly as she willed it away. "I wanted to know what you—what the police—intend to do, seeing that you're apparently convinced I'm being stalked."

Good front, but the lack of color in her cheeks gave her away. He approached her from across the room, his tread measured, his face a mask of composure and competence. "The force as a whole isn't convinced. I, along with a few other officers, am. I told you, it's a gut instinct I have that Coombes isn't the killer."

She angled her chin slightly, a show of bravado that he found admirable. "Which means?"

He stopped three feet in front of her, kept his gaze steady on hers. "I've been assigned to protect you—unofficially as far as the commissioner's office is concerned."

"Undercover?"

Not able to open his locked fists, Jacob kept them jammed in his jacket pockets. "I'm listed as 'on assignment.'"

"That's nice and vague."

Jacob felt his teeth beginning to grind and knew it was time to leave. Past time if he were truthful. Guilt and a beautiful woman whose scent brought to mind woodsy Irish flowers were not mixing well in his system. There was, however, one more thing he needed to do.

"Where is it, Ms. Tremayne?" he questioned softly. "I have to see the Christmas angel pendant."

RUDY BROWN LET his twelve-year-old beagle Buddy out the back door of his comfortably messy townhouse with a growled order to get his business done fast and proper. Squinting sideways through the blowing snow, he saw that his nephew's fourth-floor condo half a block away was dark. Eleven o'clock on a Tuesday night and Jacob continued to prowl like a restless cat.

"Restless, hell," Rudy grumbled, slamming the door behind him. "The boy's obsessed."

"Who's obsessed, Rude?" Mandy Carter, Rudy's live-in lover for the past two years, yawned hugely as she plodded in fuzzy pink slippers through the kitchen door.

A faded but damned good Mae West look-alike to Rudy's mind, Mandy was privy to most of his concerns. She didn't know them all, though, and he was reluctant to tell her the gory details of this one.

He gave an irritable shrug. "Jacob's not home."

Mandy's blue eyes sparkled. "This from a retired cop who was lucky to make it home half the nights he pulled active duty." She gave his shoulder an affectionate thump, then proceeded to the cupboard. "I've heard stories about you, Rudy-boy, from more women than I care to think about. They say secrets and late nights run in your family—and not necessarily because of the cop connection. Take Jacob. He's no cop, but I know for a fact he's got a passle of secrets. Then there's that scary old bone bag you called Aunt Ida." She rolled her eyes, shuddering deeply. "She was one hell of a secretive lady. Lived in that freaky Chicago mansion of hers for—how long was it? Twenty-five years?"

"Twenty-three," Rudy warmed his chilled hands on the holly-green coffee mug Mandy handed him. "Ida was okay. A little eccentric is all. She did fine by Jacob and Laura."

"Bull. My father was a cop. He met her, Rude. She did fine by Laura, not Jacob. People talk, boyo. Laura was a spoiled bitch. And Ida was one weird old relic."

"With one of the sharpest minds I've ever known."

"I won't argue that. She was married to a gangster. She ran him, if rumors that old hold water."

"We all have our skeletons, Mandy."

Softening, she lowered her generous curves into the chair across from him. She took his gnarled right hand in hers. "I have my kids, you have me and Jacob has—something else. Live your own life, Rudy. Stop being Uncle Cop, and let Jacob handle his skeletons as he chooses."

Swallowing a mouthful of coffee, Rudy regarded her from under heavy gray brows. "I might have to do some police work for the next few days." The statement came out gruffly, unadorned. That was his way. "Probably cost me a couple long nights."

Mandy could give grief with the best of them. She could also accept an unalterable situation better than most. "You and your secrets," she said on a resigned sigh. "And here you harangue poor Jacob for working late."

Rudy sat back, more troubled than he felt he ought to be. Jacob was determined to get to the bottom of this thing. A giant crowbar wouldn't pry him away from it. Which meant that Rudy needed to be there, to watch and wait and see.

"How long will this extra work of yours take?" Breaking open a muffin, Mandy slathered it with raspberry jam. "Don't forget, my grandkids are coming this weekend. You promised them a sleigh ride in the country. Not to mention— God forbid—a spin on that monstrosity you call a motorcycle."

"It's vintage World War II." Rudy's gravelly voice roughened to granite. "Don't worry. I'll make sure I'm free."

It was a promise he intended to keep—if he had to tie Jacob up and lock him in the cellar to do it.

Chapter Two

"Hannah, you didn't. You couldn't." Devon stared at her sister, exasperated. Her fingers choked the toothbrush she held. "You agreed to let Riker move in here?"

Hannah pressed her palms together. "I had no choice, Devon. He's a police officer. Besides, it's to your benefit to have him here."

Devon relaxed her stranglehold on the toothbrush. "I'm not being stalked," she insisted.

"Detective Riker thinks you are."

"Well, Detective Riker's wrong." Returning to the bathroom, Devon gave her bangs a final critical flick, straightened the jacket of her berry-red suit and flipped off the light. She found Hannah in the living room inspecting her undecorated tree.

"This is nice. How did you get it in?"

"Riker helped me." Devon wasn't ready to let the argument die. "Has it occurred to you, Hannah, that I don't want police protection?"

"I'd be surprised if you did. Even sexy police protection. Coffee?"

"No—yes." Devon accepted a steaming mug, but refused to sit. "Sexy isn't competent." Though his dark eyes had been extremely diverting. "I don't like people hovering over me."

Hannah hid a smile. "I can't picture Detective Riker hovering. Andrew McGruder, yes, but not Joel Riker."

Devon made a face as she sipped hot Kona. "Maybe it's the curse of all dentists that they give the impression of hovering."

Hannah's gaze lowered to her lap. "He's a very—persistent man. I wish Tony hadn't let him sign a five-year-lease without speaking to me first." She shook the unkind thought away. "Be philosophical about the situation, Devon. With Riker around, Andrew McGruder won't be. He's man-shy, I've noticed."

"Except when it comes to finagling five-year-leases. Yes, okay," Devon relented at Hannah's expression, "I'll back off. Riker's here, and like it or not, he's going to protect me from the gift horse who sent me an angel pendant."

The phone on the kitchen counter rang. Closest to it, Hannah reached over to answer. "Devon? Yes, she's right here."

"Is it Alma?" Devon mouthed, with a quick glance at her mahogany grandmother clock.

"It's a man, I think," Hannah returned, covering the mouthpiece. "It's 6:45, Devon. Roscoe said we should be early for the pancake breakfast."

"Two minutes," Devon replied, then took the receiver. "Hello?"

"Devon Tremayne?"

It was a man all right, but he sounded hoarse. "Yes, can I help you?"

She wished she hadn't asked. Twenty seconds later, she removed the receiver from her ear and stared at it accusingly as a slow-burning anger warred with the fear rising in her mind.

"Devon?" Her coat half on, Hannah approached. "What is it? Who was that?"

Devon continued to stare at the phone. "I have no idea. He said…" Reaction began to settle in. Her knuckles went white on the handset. Her blank eyes met her sister's concerned ones. "He wanted to know if I liked the Christmas angel pendant he sent me."

"YOU USED the Star 69 identification service." Riker frowned. "What did you find out?"

She hadn't been expecting congratulations for her quick thinking, had she? Devon sighed. "I got the number of the phone where the call was placed from." She indicated her roll-top desk and continued to run her fingers through her hair as she paced the Persian carpet. "When I dialed the number…"

Riker's eyes came up, dark and dangerous, but beyond that he didn't interrupt.

"When I dialed," she resumed, "I wound up talking to an old woman who wondered if I knew what time the number ten bus arrived on Port Street."

"A pay phone?"

"Apparently. Inside the Port Street Billiard Hall. And, no, I can't imagine what someone's grandmother would be doing looking for a bus at seven in the morning in that part of town."

Hannah, who'd been sitting in silence since Riker arrived, offered a subdued, "I think you should go there, Detective. Someone might have seen the man who placed the call."

But Riker was already tugging on his leather jacket and pulling out his gloves. "You two stay here."

"Like hell." Devon reached for her coat. "I'm going with you."

Since she had a temper herself, she recognized that same quality in Riker. It showed mostly in his eyes, in the fierce glitter of negation that burned beneath the surface.

"It's my life. I'm going with you," she repeated before he could voice his objections.

"Devon." Hannah touched her arm.

But Riker surprised her. "No, Devon's right." He checked the gun strapped to the back of his waistband. "It's her life.

If she wants to risk it riding with me, I won't stop her.'' He sent Devon a pointed look. "This time."

Meaning, Devon presumed, that he didn't expect to find much at the billiard hall.

Since he was already heading out, she only had time for a hurried, "You might as well go to the breakfast. Bring me a doggy bag, okay?'' to Hannah.

Riker was at the bottom of the stairs by the time Devon reached the top. Last night she'd looked but hadn't absorbed much of his physical appearance. The idea of a murder threat directed at her had naturally taken precedence. Today, despite the ominous start, she realized that both she and Hannah had understated the matter by calling him simply sexy. He was six feet tall with a lithe body, dark eyes that gave new meaning to the word *seductive* and a sensual mouth which so far had frowned at her more than it had smiled.

His hair was nice, too, long, thick and wavy—the same shade of deep chocolate brown as his eyes.

All in all, he was an intriguing package. However, while Devon loved a good mystery, something about this man set off loud warning bells in her head. Best to keep her distance, she decided, taking the last few stairs at a restrained pace.

He pulled on his gloves with his teeth and motioned along the snowy curb. "It's the Blazer."

"Black, of course."

He paused by the passenger door. "You don't like black?"

"I prefer red."

"Blood's red, Devon."

"So are Valentines." She stepped up and in. "I don't upset easily, Riker. How far to Port Street?"

Did he almost smile? "A few miles," was all he said. Scanning the area, he shut her in and walked around to the driver's side.

Because she was watching him, Devon missed seeing the man who crossed the street in front of the Blazer until a tap sounded on the passenger window.

"Damn," she said under her breath. Smiling, she rolled down the glass. "'Morning Andrew. Early patient?"

"Emergency bridgework." He craned his neck as Riker's door slammed.

Devon held onto her smile. "Andrew McGruder, this is Joel Riker. He's a new tenant."

"I see." Podgy and staid, Andrew saw little of anything. He might have been attempting to preen when he casually shook his head to shift wisps of brown hair off his forehead.

Attractive, Andrew was not. From the day she'd met him, Devon had pictured an overfed chipmunk—soft and jowly, constantly sniffing the air as if on the scent of a new food source.

"I'm an oral surgeon," Andrew shouted to Riker above the revving engine. "I do fantastic bridgework."

Riker slid his gaze sideways. Devon sensed the cynical reply forming in his mind and inserted a hasty, "Riker has a fine bite already, Andrew. But thanks for the offer."

Andrew had no choice but to step back as Riker swung his vehicle into the oncoming stream of traffic.

"You might recall that it's slippery." Devon braced herself for a lane change.

"I was born and raised in New York, Devon," he said dryly. "I know all about slippery."

"I thought you were an Irish boy."

"My grandmother was Irish. I froze my butt off in Buffalo until I was thirteen."

"Not surprising then that you don't care for snow." Belatedly, she fastened her seatbelt. "Why don't you move to Los Angeles if you don't like the climate in Philadelphia?"

"There's plenty of snow in L.A., Devon."

"Cute, Riker, but you know what I mean. Besides you're homicide, not vice."

She saw his eyes narrow. "I don't remember mentioning that."

Honesty meant a great deal to Devon. She met his skeptical gaze. "You didn't. I asked a friend of mine at the station to check you out on his computer. Jimmy's wired into everything. Your precinct page, such as it is, says that you have a solid cop record and twelve years of street duty to back you up.''

''Anything else?''

Sensing curiosity as opposed to rancor, she shrugged. ''Not really. Only that you're thirty-six, widowed, come from a family of twelve, and were involved in the investigation of the first two Christmas murders.''

He fixed his gaze on the red light ahead. ''Laura West and Abigail Fountain, in that order. They were in your line of work, those two and the five who died later.''

''All radio personalities, I know. That must mean that this is an inside-industry thing.''

''Which would seem to exclude Casey Coombes,'' Riker pointed out. ''He was a salesperson for hair care products.''

Devon searched for a connection. ''Well…radio stations advertise hair care products.''

''And?'' Again that hint of a smile played on the corners of his mouth. ''Where's the rest of your tie-in? All women use hair care products, not just women in radio.''

A skiff of snow blew across the windshield. At 7:20 a.m. in mid-December, dawn had yet to break. It was dark, blustery and cold outside. Only Mellancamp's ''I Saw Mommy Kissing Santa Claus'' on the Wave and Riker's efficient car-heating system stopped the tremor in Devon's midsection from spreading. That and something about the man sitting next to her.

''Over there.'' Riker used his head to indicate the Port Street Billiard Hall.

The *D* in *Billiard* was burned out on the neon sign. But the street, except for a couple of huddled shapes near the alley and a man walking past with his head bent, seemed regular enough. The plows had been through within the last hour, Devon judged. A garbage truck rattled along the curb, and she could see movement in the bakery next door.

"Do you want to wait here?" Riker asked, scanning the building.

"I'd rather have a cup of tea."

"You won't find tea in this place." Reaching over her, he tightened her window, paused, then raised inscrutable eyes to hers. "You sure about this?"

She wanted him. The knowledge hit like a fist plunged into her solar plexus. A hard lump lodged in her throat. Desire so unexpected and fierce had never overwhelmed her like this before. She lowered her lashes and sincerely hoped the feeling would subside as swiftly as it had surfaced.

"I'm—yes, I'm sure," she answered his question even as her gloved fingers groped for the door handle.

It didn't jam the way the latch on her grandmother's Jaguar tended to. As a result she almost tumbled onto the sidewalk in her rush to get out.

If Riker noticed, he didn't mention it. But there was a hint of amusement in his gaze when he joined her on the snowy sidewalk.

Collecting herself, Devon made a point of lagging behind. She kept her eyes trained on the door rather than on Riker's lean, leather-covered spine.

It would pass, she promised herself. It had to because it had no basis in reality. Not that she wouldn't have liked to explore the feeling, but murder and romance didn't mix terribly well in her mind.

Neither did billiard halls and garland, but there it was, a long skinny string of Christmas tinsel suspended across the rear wall.

Dark shapes in mud-colored clothes circled equally muddy tables. Their manner was predatory. With one eye they watched the balls, with the other they checked out the new arrivals. Smoke hung thick and stale in the air. Behind it, she heard a swell of coarse mutters.

"Want a table?"

She continued to hang back as one of the shapes spoke.

Riker managed to fit right in. Until he opened his badge, that is. "No table, just a few questions."

Eyes bored into Devon from all directions. The place wasn't busy by any means, but there were more people here than she'd expected. A county rock station played a Garth Brooks song. She watched a black-haired woman line up a shot.

"Care for a game?"

Devon twisted her head around as wiry fingers plucked at her arm. But the wizened old man in shabby denim hadn't asked her the question. His voice came out raw and raspy—similar to that of the man who'd called her apartment, she realized uneasily.

"Got a dollar?" he asked. "For coffee."

Bloodshot eyes, defeated expression. Devon couldn't help it, she started to reach into her purse. Her wrist was grabbed and held fast before she could locate her wallet.

"Don't," Riker ordered in a barely audible undertone.

"Don't what?" a more belligerent voice demanded. "Play a game of pool? You with this guy, lady?"

The man was extremely large, a roughneck, Devon's late grandmother would have called him. He glowered at Riker, then shoved the scruffy little man aside. "Bug off, Pop. I got a bone to pick here."

"I don't think…" Devon began, only to be eased aside by Riker.

"She's with me," he told the roughneck levelly.

The little man tapped her free arm while Riker and the bully squared off. "I know your voice." He gave her a gap-toothed smile. "You're the talk lady on the radio."

"I am? I mean, yes, I am. I'm Devon. Do you—know my show?"

"Hear it sometimes," the little man told her. "Guy comes in at lunch, likes to listen."

"A guy?" She poked Riker in the ribs. "This man says a guy comes here and listens to my show."

Riker's attention shifted to Pop. "What's the guy's name? Do you know?"

"Calls himself Brando." Pop's red-rimmed eyes grew sly. "Maybe it's worth something if I tell you about him, huh?"

Riker regarded him through hooded eyes. "Ten bucks."

"Twenty," Devon put in, and felt an immediate tightening of the fingers on her wrist.

"I like the lady," Pop murmured. "Last name's Severs. Lives over on Alice Street."

"What does he sound like?" Devon asked. The question earned her a sideways glance from Riker, but no comment.

"Mumbly." Pop shrugged.

"Was he in here today?" Riker pressed.

"No," said the roughneck.

"Yes," said Pop. He took shelter behind Devon's arm. "Beat Lou here two games straight. Took two twenties off him. Got a phone call, then he split."

"Got a call or made one?" Riker asked.

"Got one. Could have made another. I don't watch that close. People here don't like to be watched close."

But they liked to watch strangers. A stray shiver feathered along Devon's spine as their eyes crawled over her. Ants at a picnic wouldn't have felt so intrusive.

Smoke rose in a thin trickle from the corner. She perceived a shape in the booth but little else.

The name Brando slid silkily through her head. Had it been so simple to find the Christmas Murderer?—assuming, of course, that Casey Coombes's confession really had been a sham.

Riker slipped Pop his twenty, then turned Devon around and pushed her toward the door.

She would have resented his method of moving her if she hadn't been so glad to escape the place. Her hair smelled like smoke, and she could still sense those invisible eyes boring into her.

"Why do I feel like I've been violated?" she wondered out loud. "I've been in pool halls before."

Riker's smile was entirely skeptical. "The hell you have. You've been in lounges with a pool table or two."

"I'm not naive, Riker. And I'm certainly not stupid. That place was awful. No one should have to spend time there. You should have given Pop a fifty."

"Devon…"

"Yes, I know. I can't save the world." She grabbed his jacket before he could open her door. "Are we going to Alice Street now?"

"We?"

"It's my life," she repeated stubbornly.

"And my mistake," he added in a vague murmur. "Okay, you can come, but no handouts."

She blew out a resigned breath. "I like to give, Riker. It isn't supposed to offend anyone. Besides, it's my money— what's that?" she cut herself off to ask.

He removed a slim, red suede wallet from his jacket pocket and held it out to her.

Her spirits sank. "Mine?"

"One of the women lifted it while we were pumping Pop for information.

Wordlessly, Devon slid it back into her purse. "I don't think I like cop work very much."

Riker's eyes hardened. "Losing a wallet's nothing compared to losing your life, Devon. Remember that."

A chill swept through her, cold and nasty. How could she not remember that when, Casey Coombes notwithstanding, the next life lost might very well be hers?

"RIKER, HUH? Detective, South Side."

Brando was probably only in his late twenties, but Jacob had seen that look in a man's eyes before. Angry, strung-out, haunted. This guy had seen a lot, and none of it good.

He resembled a skinny James Dean more than Marlon, but at least his room wasn't the pigsty Jacob had envisioned. And fortunately, he was too busy sizing up Riker to pay much attention to Devon.

His loss, Jacob reflected, though he made a point of blocking the man's view as much as possible.

"Riker." Brando said his name again, then sucked on his upper lip and nibbled. When she moved, he strained for a look at Devon. "You a cop, too, lady?"

"Special assignment," she said with just the right touch of dispassion. Jacob saw her taking in Brando's Spartan living conditions, the platter of misshapen snowman cookies and the cheap plastic Santa on the table. She was probably debating whether to label the man a killer or a junkie.

"Did you place a call to a woman from the Port Street Billiard Hall this morning?" Jacob asked.

"Place…?" The man's eyes came up sharply, then fell halfway as his defenses took over. "No."

"You sure?"

"I know what I did."

"Do you listen to the Wave?"

"Sometimes."

"Do you know Devon Tremayne?"

"Heard her once or twice. She's got a talk show."

"You like her, but you didn't call her this morning."

"No."

He was a poker player, Jacob decided. One tiny glitch in his story hadn't really meant much. He said nothing further.

"Can you make your voice sound hoarse?" Devon asked unprompted.

Brando pursed his lips. He was starting to look edgy, couldn't quite manage to stand still. "Hoarse," he repeated, then stopped fidgeting and zeroed in on her. "Wait a minute, you're her, aren't you? From the radio." His face broke out in a big grin. "Man, this is great. You're Devon. Wait'll my old lady hears this. She listens to you every day."

Devon smiled. "Thank you. But did you call me this morning?"

He opened his mouth, then closed it again, tightly. "No. I only got a call—from my old lady."

It was a pointless exercise, Jacob reflected. His impatience

mounted. Brando wasn't going to admit a damned thing—
what he knew, didn't know, had done, hadn't. Better to back
off and pay him another visit later, when Devon wasn't with
him.

"Come on," he said, curling his fingers around her arm.
"This isn't getting us anywhere."

Brando watched them leave. "Hey, you couldn't spare
a—"

"No," Jacob said forcefully, and more to Devon than to
the man behind them.

"Pretty high and mighty there, Riker," Brando scoffed
once Devon was out in the hall.

Jacob stopped on the threshold. "Something you wanted
to say?"

"Yeah." Brando managed to sound both surly and scared.
"You don't know what it's like, man, to really need."

BRANDO HATED COPS. He hated rats more, both kinds.
They'd spotted one of the breed in here last month, a big
brown sucker with a six-inch tail. His old lady had threatened
to leave him over it. But exterminators cost bucks. And he
had other needs to satisfy....

Money, that's what it boiled down to. He needed cash.
Now. Enough at least to get him through the New Year.

Heavy-footed, he dragged on his scarred leather jacket and
snakeskin boots. He'd pawned the TV last week. He had
nothing else left.

The pay phone downstairs was available, the dingy hallway cold and empty. It took time and several badly needed
quarters to find the right number, but Brando had learned that
perseverance paid off.

He licked his dry lips, rolling the worn cord between his
fingers as the phone rang. Finally, he heard the voice he
wanted.

"Yeah, hi. It's Brando. I, uh, got something might interest
you. Guy came to see me just now. A cop named Riker....
Yeah. His badge said South Side." Brando grimaced, but

plowed on. "He, uh, had a real pretty lady with him. Real pretty...."

His spit turned to glue. A person learned by watching others, and he'd done a lot of watching at the billiard hall. Too much maybe. Dollar signs popped like balloons in his brain. He swallowed the bad taste and took a deep breath.

"It was the radio lady, Devon Tremayne."

Chapter Three

Five hours of painting baseboards and wainscoting, and he still felt guilty as hell. Bone-tired, Jacob dropped his brush and stood to work out the kinks. Straddling a rickety kitchen stool, he plunked his elbows on the table and raked his fingers through his hair.

The apartment door creaked, announcing Rudy's arrival.

"You missed a spot, boy—like two-thirds of the room." A pair of grocery bags thumped on the table, crinkling as they settled. "Got us food and beer for a few days, but I don't want to stay unless I have to. Mandy's asking questions. Could be I'll have to tell her the truth."

Head slack, Jacob massaged his aching temples. "You don't have to stay at all, Rudy."

"And you don't have to paint and wallpaper the damned apartment, but you are." Another thrift-store stool scraped across the badly scratched hardwood. He'd need to rent a sander for that, Jacob mused as Rudy plunked himself down, rummaged and cracked open a beer.

"Why are you doing it, Jacob?"

It was a fair question. "Don't know. Penance maybe?"

"Is that what you told your new landlord?"

"Yeah. Who wouldn't buy a cop with a guilty conscience?" Jacob gave a cynical laugh. "Her name's Hannah Wallace. She's Devon's sister as well as a sister of mercy."

"She's a looker, too. I met her on the way up. Devon take after her?"

Jacob formed two mental pictures. The one of Hannah with her serene, cameo-sweet face and calm bearing was instantly overshadowed by a pair of shrewd green eyes, layers of golden hair and a smile more tempting than any vixen's. He warned himself not to recall her seductive scent, her long, gorgeous legs or the flash of temper he'd spied briefly in her manner.

"Devon's got more fire," he told his uncle carefully. "I haven't decided if that's good or bad."

Rudy snorted. "Trust me, it's bad. The fiery ones are too bright. Hard to keep secrets around 'em."

A perfect jab, but Jacob was too accustomed to them to react. Flexing his stiff shoulder muscles, he rose and picked up the paint brush again. He'd gotten as much coconut-cream latex on his jeans and black T-shirt as he had on the base-boards, but truthfully the manual labor felt good. Each brush stroke soothed a tiny portion of his slashed conscience.

Rudy watched him with a canny eye, the way he'd un-doubtedly watched countless suspects in his time. Jacob knew what his ex-cop uncle was thinking, that his nephew's need to find the Christmas Murderer bordered on obsession. Hell, it had probably crossed that line by a mile at this point. Posing as a cop? Was he crazy? Rudy'd gone ballistic when Jacob had approached him with the idea. He'd insisted it wouldn't work. It couldn't.

But it did, in large part because there were several simi-larities between him and Riker. Jacob had lived in Philadel-phia for twelve years now, Riker for eleven. While Jacob had been born and raised in Chicago, Riker had been brought up in New York. Close enough to pass muster, particularly since Jacob had spent three post-college years in Manhattan.

Their mothers, both of Irish descent, had died when their children were young, and neither of their fathers had been on the scene since then.

The one divergent point was that unlike his cop counterpart, Jacob had never been married. Still, that subject should be easy enough to circumvent in a pinch.

Dipping his brush, Jacob wiped off the residue paint. No sidetracks, no complications, no regrets; he would go with his plan as outlined. Not Rudy nor conscience nor Devon's stunning legs would divert him from his goal.

"She's beautiful, don't you think?"

Rudy's sage remark had Jacob's brush jerking. He swore under his breath as he fixed the mistake with solvent.

He aimed a steady gaze backward. No way to read Rudy's closed expression. "So you've seen her then?"

Rudy shrugged. "Guess I passed her when I came in. She was talking to her sister in the lobby. Thought I saw a family resemblance, but I wanted to hear your opinion." He propped up a sneakered foot. "Lying would be easier with the sister of mercy. Not as enjoyable though, I'll bet."

At Jacob's narrowed look, Rudy finished a noisy swallow and leaned forward. "I didn't say that to insult Devon. I like the fiesty ones myself. What I don't like are the lies."

Here it came. Squatting, Jacob used a rag to wipe his hands and said nothing.

At his lack of reaction, the aluminum can crushed in Rudy's strong fingers. "She deserves the truth, boy, not some cockamamie load of crap you don't even know you can pull off."

Ruthlessly, Jacob shoved away the picture that haunted him of Devon's proud and lovely face, her high cheekbones and challenging eyes that had almost—*almost*—captivated him.

Farther back in his mind, another face materialized, harsher-featured, less forgiving, harder to take on an empty stomach.

"You're a poor liar, Jacob Price." Her voice had matched her features, pointed and old. "My Ewen could lie better than a politician. You can't lie about your feelings without the truth being scribbled all over your face. That face is too pretty, boy. Scar it up some before you try lying to me again...."

Jacob squeezed his eyes closed, blotted out her flinty eyes, cut off her words. Learn to lie—it had been her dying advice to him. Damn her, it had been her motto in life. She'd passed it on to anyone who would listen. And Laura had listened well.

"Seven women are dead, Jacob," Rudy was growling. The leathery skin on his neck wagged as he shook his head. "Give this vendetta of yours a rest. Let me take care of things. Dammit, I'm the cop—"

"Ex-cop." Jacob stood, resisted an urge to stumble. He needed food quite badly. Funny, he thought distantly, that it should require more effort to block Devon's image from his mind than to hold onto his frayed composure. "You can help me or not, Rudy but I won't let it go. Coombes didn't kill those women."

The rough female voice cut in. No sympathy, only a speculative stare that had pierced him like a lance. *Maybe you did do it at that, boy. Maybe you killed Laura after all. Yes sir, maybe you really did....*

Jacob shot his uncle a black look. "It'll work, Rudy. If it's the last thing I do, I'm going to make it work."

TURKEY FAJITAS, turkey and cauliflower pizza, refried turkey, turkey surprise...

Devon's head buzzed with recipes for every conceivable leftover turkey recipe. Her poor mother would faint if she tuned into the last thirty minutes of this broadcast.

"That was great," Emmy Dahl exclaimed after the program went to commercial. "I thought I'd freeze for sure."

"I wish I had." Her cookbook writing partner mopped her round face with a tissue. "Once I got going, I couldn't stop. I hope we didn't go overboard on the turkey."

"You were wonderful," Devon assured them. Certainly the headache pulsing at the base of her skull had less to do with the middle-aged grandmothers sitting across from her

than it did with Warren Severen, who was beaming at her
through the glass pane.

Alma's younger brother was the co-owner of WWAV. A
handsome man in his mid fifties, his full cap of hair contained
more gray than black at this point. He'd thickened around
the chest with the passing years, but he remained—and he
knew it—a strapping figure. On the surface, at any rate. Beneath his Kevin McCarthy exterior lurked a lecherous drunk.
Harmless enough in Devon's opinion, but tedious to deal
with if you weren't in the mood, which she was not.

Still high from the show, the writers thanked her again,
then let the assistant producer escort them from the booth.

"Good show, Dev." Headset resting on his shoulders,
Jimmy popped his curly head in to congratulate her. "I liked
the turkey hash best. You got a copy I can borrow?"

"Get it from the web page," Devon retorted, then smiled
and leaned a hip against the control console. "Thanks for
doing that background on Detective Riker. I should have
mentioned it this morning, but I had other…concerns."

Namely Riker, who had moved into the empty apartment
one floor above her.

He'd arrived lock, stock and paint brush at 7:00 a.m. For
reasons she had yet to fathom, Devon hadn't felt quite the
same since she'd watched him muscling a large punching bag
up the stairs. Cops assigned to protective duty, should *not*,
she decided testily, be allowed to have sexy bodies, mysterious gazes or tousled hair that skimmed their shoulders. It
made women think of dark princes with troubled souls and
needs that few if any females could ever satisfy.

Jimmy grinned. "I don't mind digging dirt on people. Not
that there was much to dig on Riker. The guy's an ace."

"He didn't catch the Christmas Murderer."

"Nobody's perfect. He worked the case for the first two
years. Probably couldn't stomach any more."

Devon hated herself for prying but she couldn't resist. She
also wanted to keep Jimmy nearby in case Warren decided
to give her one of his famous aprés-broadcast pep talks.

Pushing back the sleeves of her deep rose sweater, she asked casually, "You said he'd been widowed. Do you know how long?"

Jimmy squinted, flipping through his mental files. "Ten years, I think. Yeah, she died on a flight from Philadelphia to Minneapolis, one of those flying-home-for-Thanksgiving things."

Devon's heart gave a sympathetic lurch. "A crash?"

"Nope. Heart attack. It must have been a genetic flaw. She was only twenty-five. There wasn't much on her really."

Feeling intrusive wasn't quite powerful enough to stop her from finding out more. "What was her name?"

"Delia Brightman."

That sounded familiar. Devon searched, but couldn't make the connection. "I must be thinking of Sarah Brightman," she decided finally.

"Who?"

"A singer. *Phantom of the Opera.* Never mind."

Through the tinted glass, she spotted Alma striding side by side with Roscoe Beale. The handsome publicist was smiling, using his hands, and no doubt a great deal of charm, to illustrate a point. "We could use this, Alma," he insisted. "I don't mean exploit the situation, but publicity's publicity. People eat up bad news. The gorier the better."

Devon looked at Jimmy. "Do you get the feeling he wants me to start wearing that angel pendant?"

"Probably. But don't worry. Alma's dead set against media exposure over this."

"Really? I'd have thought she'd have given it serious consideration. Setting aside my personal involvement, Roscoe has a point. Publicity of this kind is good business."

"Maybe." Jimmy seemed uncomfortable. "Anyway she's in a huff over Warren. She's probably not listening much to Roscoe. Word is Warren locked his office door this morning."

Devon slid files into her soft-sided leather case. "Not acceptable?"

"No way. Warren's a monitored man. You haven't been here long enough to know what he's like when he gets together with a bottle of Scotch. Not a pretty picture."

It wasn't one Devon cared to visualize, that's for sure. She caught sight of Warren in her peripheral vision, masked a shudder and offered a hasty, "Cover for me," to Jimmy before zipping her case closed and slipping through the rear door.

"Wait a sec, Devon. I forgot to tell you...."

Whatever Jimmy had forgotten, Devon didn't wait around to hear it. Warren, looking robust and ruddy-cheeked, had his hand on the doorknob.

"Hey, Dev." Teddi Waters, the petite brunette who owned the prime afternoon time slot, shifted her coffee to avoid spilling it. "What's the rush? Did another pendant show up? Ah—never mind, I see him." She peered at Warren over Devon's shoulder. "Looks half corked. Where's Alma?"

"With Roscoe. He's trying to talk her into doing a spot on the six o'clock news. 'Angel pendant sent to WWAV talk-show host Devon Tremayne. Details as they unfold.'"

Teddi wrinkled her pert nose. "Trust Roscoe. Oh, by the way, someone's looking for you—" Her eyes fixed on the wall clock. "Good God, I'm on in half a minute. Gotta run."

Sometimes, Devon reflected, turning down a plant- and light-filled corridor, the station had all the earmarks of a wind tunnel. People blew around helter-skelter, never quite finishing sentences or sentiments.

The dull ache in her temples reminded her that she needed to find a bottle of aspirin.

City Life's broadcast delay time was five minutes. When it ended, Teddi booted up an Aretha Franklin Christmas carol. The song drifted along the carpeted corridors. Amber lights twinkled in the leaves of Alma's potted ficus plants. With them came to mind the argument Devon had had with Hannah last night as they'd decorated her new spruce....

Riker insisted. Patiently, Hannah created an intricate pattern of red and green lights in the branches. *He wants to paint and wallpaper the apartment while he's here. He even thinks he can revitalize the hardwood floor. I think he's worried about that pendant, Devon. You should have seen how tense he was when he talked to me. And you already know how worried I am...*

Yes, she knew. She knew! Hannah's wounded-fawn expression had underscored her dreams last night. Ditto, she reflected, for her mental picture of Detective Joel Riker.

Vexed at her lack of control, Devon failed to check around the next corner. It wasn't until she came nose to chin with someone walking in the opposite direction that her head snapped up and her vision cleared.

"Riker!" She caught her shoulder bag before it slid off. "What are you doing here?"

Something flickered deep in his brown eyes. "My job."

She let out a breath that was almost reconciled. "Should I get you a studio pass, or have you talked to Alma?"

His lips twitched at the corners. "We've had words."

"Did you explain the situation to her?"

"As much as I needed to. You're lucky. She's fond of you."

Devon thought of Roscoe's publicity scheme and nodded. "I know." Curiosity crept in to override discomfort. Riker smelled good, like leather and some intriguing brand of male soap. The attraction hit again, as fiercely as it had two days ago. She would have stepped away if she hadn't spied the shadows under his eyes and the stubble on his jaw. He hadn't bothered to shave that morning. He looked troubled—not in the manner of a dark prince, but rather like a man with a host of problems surrounding him.

In an effort to lighten the mood, Devon flicked at the black cotton sweater he wore under his leather. "Try red sometime, Riker. It'll flash you up a bit."

His chuckle caught her off guard. She'd hardly seen him smile. This step was a revelation, taking his face from somberly handsome to startlingly beautiful. Her heart did a long, slow revolution before she ordered it to stop. It was too much far, far too soon.

Amusement lingered in his eyes when he replied, "Cops do better not to flash, Devon. What time do you usually leave here?"

"Five or six. I have to prepare for tomorrow's program." Because her senses were still jumping, she started walking toward her office. "We run a delay on the broadcasts, but basically the show's live. I have a holiday psychologist and a spokesperson from the ASPCA scheduled next."

"If Christmas is stressing you out, don't adopt a puppy to keep your kids occupied."

"Something like that." Her own humor sparked, Devon sneaked a look at his appealing profile. "Who was that man Hannah talked to yesterday? Rudy Something?"

"Brown. He's…an old friend. He also did some peripheral investigative work on the third and fourth Christmas Murders."

"My younger sister's boyfriend would give his right arm for a vintage motorcycle like that."

Riker shrugged. "It belonged to his brother. Rudy was too young for World War II, but the bike suits him. Scarred and cranky."

"I'm sure he'd love the comparison."

"Probably, since he's the one who made it."

"Rudy doesn't think Coombes is the killer either, I suppose?"

"He's of two minds." Riker stopped one door before her office, reaching into his jacket for his ringing cell phone. "Yeah, what?" His eyes slid to Devon's face, then away. "No…look, I'll have to call you back."

She moved on to insert her key. "If you want privacy, there's a lounge down the hall. It'll be empty. This part of the station's out of the action. I like it that way. The others don't."

"Five minutes," he said and left her to enter alone.

Not bothering with the lights, Devon let her briefcase and

purse drop from her shoulder. She closed the door by leaning against it and expelled the first unrestricted breath she'd drawn since bumping into Riker. God help her if she didn't get a fast stranglehold on this attraction she felt for him.

Her office angled toward the downtown core. A broad tinted window afforded her one of the best views in the building, especially after a snowfall. The streets and sidewalks had been muddied by traffic and snowplows, but a layer of white adorned the surrounding rooftops and, of course, the Delaware River was a picture.

Pushing off, she crossed to the window. A tiny scratch of sound behind her had her glancing back. She saw a shadow pass through the slit of light under the door, then nothing.

Devon blew out a pent-up breath, irritated with her mounting jitters. She was letting run-of-the-mill occurrences spook her now. Riker, angel pendants, Roscoe's publicity-starved attitude, not to mention her own niggling belief that Casey Coombes might not be the Christmas Murderer....

Cutting that thought short, she pushed on her right temple. Aspirin was what she craved. Half a bottle of it by now. And artificial light to soothe her frazzled nerves. The bruised light of day held a peculiar charm, but it also created a legion of dark patches, in her office and in her mind.

She almost sighed at the thought which took her back fifteen Christmases in time, to those nights when her parents had gone visiting and she and Hannah had finally bribed their younger sisters into bed. They would settle in their big flannel nightgowns, armed with quilts, tea and almond cookies, turn out the ground-floor lights and watch transfixed as Alistair Sim's Scrooge haunted the gloomy London of his childhood. Those days had been the best: days of sharing secrets and dreams—and heaping plates of Christmas cookies.

Grinning, Devon pressed the wall switch. It wasn't until her eyes lowered for an instant that she spotted the square of black construction paper, no doubt the source of the scrape she'd heard earlier. Someone had shoved it under the door.

She hesitated, straightening her fingers as reason warred with fear. How could a piece of paper harm her?

Nervous even so, she bent and picked it up, unfolding it as she stood. Her eyes caught only a blur of gold before a burst of motion erupted to her left.

Something, at first satiny smooth, yet strong as steel when stretched taut, closed about her throat. Instinctively, she clawed at the thing, twisting her neck and body and bringing her foot down hard on someone's toe. Possibly a booted toe. Her panicky mind couldn't determine anything beyond the fact that her attacker had the grip of a bionic man. And hair like silk.

Freeing an elbow, she jammed it backward into what should have been his torso. What she encountered instead was air and a sudden, startling sense of free fall.

She hit the carpet with a thump that made every thought in her head bob. The scarf hung backward over her shoulders, but there was no one wielding it, no longer anyone in the office except her.

Shooting to her feet, Devon ran for the door. Fear swelled, threatening to burst her lungs. Where had he gone? Was he waiting for her in the corridor?

By the time that question occurred to her, she'd skidded across the threshold. To her relief, the hall was empty, loaded with reindeer shapes and Santa shadows, but no human life whatsoever.

Her legs carried her unthinking and shaky to the lounge. "Riker!" She found her voice even as her frantic fingers tore the scarf from her neck. "Riker, where are...? Damn!"

She pulled up short, shoving the hair from her face. The lights were off. He'd gone.

Releasing a ragged breath, she allowed herself to sag against the wall.

"Devon?"

She whipped around like a cat, eyes flashing, fingers spread.

A frown furrowed Riker's forehead. "What is it?"

She controlled her desire to snap. "Someone," she drew a deep breath, "attacked me in my office."

He closed the gap between them so swiftly her senses scarcely registered the movement. Taking her by the arms, he pulled her close for inspection. "Are you hurt?"

"No." The heat of his body beckoned to her, an invisible magnet urging her to seek the comfort she craved in his arms. She rubbed the middle of her forehead. "I'm fine, really. He must have gotten out through the office adjoining mine. It's small, so we use it as an overflow room for old promotional material." Roscoe's turf, she recalled, wincing.

Riker's thumbs began a gentle circular rotation on her collarbone. Quite effective actually—until she remembered another pair of hands. A shiver rippled through her, causing her teeth to chatter. "Shouldn't you go after him?"

For an answer, his hands left her to remove his gun. At the door, he glanced back. "Stay right here, Devon."

He disappeared, leaving Devon to count the seconds and wonder if—no, wish that she could put the attack down to her imagination.

Of course she couldn't. She only needed to touch the bruised skin on her throat and stare at the sliver of black scarf fisted in her hand to know that. But why leave? Why not kill her and be done with it?

"Morbid, Tremayne," she chided herself. "Be grateful you're still here to ask the question."

The silence stretched on. Devon's nerves stretched taut. She'd liked it better when Riker had been, in as much as he probably could, endeavoring to console her.

Arms hugging her waist, she paced the carpeted floor. No radio speakers kept her company here. Only the hum of the corridor lights and a nasty-looking batch of black clouds beyond the window.

She halted, brow knit. "Black," she repeated, then swung her head around. "The paper..."

Riker appeared in the open doorway, his head averted as

he holstered his gun. "Whoever he was, he's long gone. That storeroom— What?" This as she grabbed his hand.

"In my office," she said, tugging firmly. "The person who attacked me slid a note under my door before he jumped out at me."

Riker's face darkened. "Did you read it?"

"I didn't have a chance." She pushed the door open, her eyes scanning the floor. "There it is. By the coat rack."

He reached the black square an instant before her, unfolded it and skimmed the words penned in gold script. Devon's voice wavered as she murmured the message over his shoulder.

"Just a taste for now, dear Devon,
to taunt you as you daily taunt me.
As you daily haunt me.
Will this torment never cease...?"

Chapter Four

"Don't brush me off, Riker." Devon matched him stride for stride as they climbed the stoop to the apartment building. "I want to know what you're going to do about that note."

Aggravated but controlled, Jacob opened the front door. "Check it out," he said flatly. More correctly, get Rudy to check it out. "Fingerprints, ink type, point of purchase."

She preceded him into the mulberry-scented warmth. "Do you think you'll discover anything?"

"No, but it's procedure. Devon…" He circled her wrist with his fingers when she would have started up the stairs.

He could see it in her eyes. She wanted to be angry and indignant but was having trouble holding those emotions. Fear had a way of sneaking through the most formidable barriers, and Jacob sensed that sustained anger was not one of Devon's best weapons.

She faced him, calmly determined. "No, I am not going to tell Hannah about the attack," she told him for the third time. "And yes, I'm still going to the charity party at the Holly Tree Restaurant tomorrow. The station's sponsoring the event. I won't wimp out because I'm terrified there'll be a madman with a scarf lurking in every dark corner."

Her skin was temptingly soft, her wrist incredibly delicate in the palm of his hand. An arrow of heat and desire speared downward into Jacob's loins. He loosened his grip in response to it, but couldn't quite let her go.

"If the party's important to you, Devon, I won't try and stop you from being there."

A wary look crept into her shuttered gaze. "I hear a 'but,' Riker. What's the catch?"

"I'm coming with you."

Her fine brows shot up. "Just like that? Has it occurred to you that I might have a date?"

"Do you?"

"No, but you could have the decency to think I might."

He ignored the stab of relief, fought a smile and indicated Hannah's apartment door. "Will your sister be there?"

She sighed. "Roscoe Beale asked her two months ago. Hannah has a hard time refusing polite invitations."

Diverted, Jacob ran the name through his mental file. "Beale's the head of your PR department."

His fingers tightened marginally as he spoke. It surprised him that she made no effort to shake him off. On the contrary, she came down a step so their eyes were level.

"Yes, he is, and yes, it's his job to promote the station. But even allowing for the fact that he's pressing for coverage of this Christmas pendant incident, I don't think he's the one who attacked me."

"Did I say he was?"

She summoned a small smile. "You didn't have to. The idea's written all over your face. Oh, come on, Riker, don't be offended." This as his arm muscles tensed. "Most of the time, I can't begin to guess what you're thinking. It's just that sometimes you let the mask drop, and there it is for anyone to see."

"That doesn't help," he muttered and kicked himself for the lapse. "What time's the party?"

"Dinner's at eight. We're due there an hour before. Dress as you choose. Roscoe and Warren will wear suits."

Suddenly, he needed very badly to be away from her. Either that, or—he didn't know what. Careful not to excite any facial expressions, Jacob removed his hand from hers and shoved it, balled, into his jacket pocket.

"Are you staying home tonight?" he asked through clenched teeth.

"Uh-huh. I'm going to finish decorating my tree." Curiosity over his abrupt withdrawal melted into a polite smile as she glanced past his shoulder. "Hello. You must be Riker's partner. I'm Devon."

Jacob turned his head in time to see Rudy's weathered cheeks mottle.

"Yes, uh—yes," he said in his gravelly tone. He stamped the excess snow from his boots, tucked his camouflage motorcycle helmet under one arm and joined them. "How do you do?"

Disbelief blended with amusement in Jacob's mind. Devon had flustered Rudy Brown. Many had tried, but he'd never seen anyone succeed before.

Devon's gaze flicked questioningly to Jacob then back to the older man. "You're...welcome to join us at the charity party tomorrow, Detective Brown."

"Rudy," Jacob supplied, enjoying the moment.

Rudy shot him a lethal glare, too quick and guarded for Devon to catch. "What charity party would that be, miss?"

"I'll let Riker explain. And it's Devon."

Eagle-eyed, Rudy spied the red marks on Devon's neck. "Are those fresh bruises?" he demanded.

A hand rose to her throat. "Riker can tell you about that, too." She fixed a smile on her lips. "You're also both welcome to join Hannah and me for a glass of eggnog later—to celebrate the lighting of my first Philadelphia Christmas tree in ten years," she added at Jacob's inquisitive look.

The mottling on Rudy's leathery cheeks deepened. Temper sparked his brown eyes. "He came after you, didn't he?"

Devon bit her lip, considered, then at Jacob's shrug, nodded. "In my office, this afternoon." Her voice wobbled only fractionally. "He could have strangled me, but he didn't. He left a note instead."

"I have it." Jacob answered his uncle's unspoken question.

Rudy's breath heaved in and out of his barrel chest. "So either we've got us a sick copycat, or it wasn't Coombes after all."

"Looks that way," Jacob agreed. He regarded the older man evenly. "Whatever we've got, it's up to you and me to figure out who's behind this threat to Devon's life—and deal with him before he makes good on it."

"MERRY CHRISTMAS, and may we all be free to enjoy many more."

Warren Severen made the slurred toast in Devon's living room at 9:00 p.m. She hadn't planned the gathering. Alma, Warren, Roscoe and Jimmy had just "happened" to drop by at eight o'clock. Evidently, the incident at the station this afternoon had flowed swiftly along the studio grapevine.

"Coming through, everybody." Hannah arrived, flushed and bearing two large trays of food that included plates of Swedish meatballs, mincemeat tarts and neatly trimmed cucumber sandwiches.

"Don't let anyone tell her," Devon hissed to Roscoe as she brushed past him to rescue her overloaded sister. He had the look of a handsome Italian gangster. Never a strand of soft black hair out of place, often a trace of amusement clinging to his lips. A pair of seductive ebony eyes completed the picture.

"What can I do?" he whispered back. "Once the small talk's exhausted, somebody's bound to work up the nerve to mention it."

Not if she could help it. Devon saved the sandwich tray from tipping onto the carpet, spied Riker and Rudy entering behind Hannah and zeroed in on them.

"I don't want her to know," was all she said. Riker sent her a look that told her plainly he thought she was wrong, but motioned Rudy over to keep Hannah occupied.

"Do you want me to threaten your guests with jail or use their outstanding parking violations against them?"

Balancing the tray, Devon poked his chest. "No sarcasm,

Riker. I'm not in the mood. Hannah's a compulsive worrier. Much as I enjoy unexpected guests, I know why these people are here. No one's come out and said it yet—they're polite enough to wait for an announcement—but they've heard something, and sooner or later one of them will ask.''

Sipping from the glass which had appeared in his hand, Riker did a dubious double take at the contents. ''Sooner, if you don't tone down the eggnog.''

''What are you—'' She glanced at the silver bowl. ''Oh, God. Warren must have brought his flask with him. Look, I'll deal with the over-spiked refreshments, if you'll just please warn everybody to keep quiet. You've met Alma. The man with the gold signet ring is Roscoe. Jimmy Flaherty's on the phone, and Warren's across the room near the Christmas tree—probably trying to keep out of Alma's way.''

She saw Riker fight a smile, and took a moment to observe him. He wore a long-sleeved cotton T-shirt tonight. Black, of course. Two of the top buttons were undone and he'd pushed the sleeves partway up. His long hair shone with bronze highlights, courtesy of the jeweled tree. All in all, he looked devastatingly handsome, which, she reflected, depositing her tray on the coffee table, was precisely the last thing she needed to notice right now.

Hannah detached herself from Rudy, ''Does your microwave work, Devon? The sausage rolls need reheating.''

With a warning glance at Riker, Devon accompanied her sister to the kitchen.

Jacob watched her go, surreptitiously, yet even as he made the required rounds, his eyes never quite left her. An uncharacteristic reaction for him, but manageable, he promised himself, as long as he didn't allow it to get out of hand.

''Ah, the ever-efficient arm of the law.'' Clearly inebriated, Warren Severen toddled over and thumped Jacob across the shoulders. He packed a wallop, but his hand was soft and fleshy. Very likely he hadn't worked at anything more difficult than a computer keypad for years. Then again, even soft hands could wield a lethal garrote.

The idea flirted with Jacob's usually reliable instincts. Coupled with Warren's effusive smile and one or two of the innuendoes he'd picked up from the Wave's female staff today, the prospect made a fair-sized impact.

"I hear you were in the vicinity when our Devon was, er, waylaid today." Warren patted his jacket pockets.

Jacob shot him a look that went right over the station owner's head. "Yes, I was. But I don't think Devon would appreciate you broadcasting the incident."

"Hannah, huh?"

Whatever his flaws, the man possessed a modicum of perception. "I hear she worries a lot."

Having apparently plunged feet first into the holiday spirit, Warren located his flask and shook the dregs into his glass. "She's a strong woman, is our Devon. Tougher-skinned than her sister, but I'll wager Hannah's got a fair bit of spunk."

Jacob raised a brow. "That's not exactly the point, Mr. Severen."

"No? Well, maybe it isn't. We learn by experience how best to deal with our siblings." His eyes darted to Alma before returning to Jacob's impassive face. He lifted his glass in a toast. "So you're protecting my little Devon, are you? You gotta love that voice, don't you?"

"Her voice?"

"Mmm." Warren's chiselled features became vaguely dream-like. "Warm cognac on velvet. Black velvet. Knew it the minute I heard her, I had to have that voice on my airwaves."

Accepting the white wine Rudy stuck in his hand, Jacob inquired, "When did you first hear her, Mr. Severen?"

"Warren. Oh, let's see. January or so, I guess. That's right. Her California station went on cable just before Christmas last year. Alma picked up on her first. Didn't mention it to me, of course." He grinned broadly, and said in a stage-whisper, "My sister's not big on sex."

Jacob's eyes held steady. "I beg your pardon?"

"That was the series that KBXA, Devon's L.A. station,

was airing at the time. A two-week series dealing with sexual problems.''

''It was marital problems, Warren,'' Alma corrected sternly from behind her brother.

Warren started visibly. He'd missed her approach. Jacob hadn't. He took note of her compressed lips, her stiff spine and her stony stare. Something here, he decided, finishing his wine in a single long swallow.

Before he could think of how best to pump Alma, she conducted her own cross-examination. ''Do you know Devon well, Detective?''

''No, but I'm working on it.'' Where the hell had that remark come from? He tossed the ball back into her court. ''Do you?''

Alma Severen had a carefully cultivated reserve that would be tricky to circumvent. She tended to look down her nose at people, especially at men, Jacob realized. On her own ground, she would not be an easy woman to dupe.

''Devon is very like my daughter, Margaret.'' Methodically, she folded her hands. ''I was grooming Margaret to take over my various business ventures. Unfortunately, that wasn't to be.''

''She lost interest?''

''She lost her life, Detective Riker.''

''Took her…ah, yes…'' A fierce glare from his sister had Warren clearing his throat. Fleshy fingers crept up to scratch his chin and tug on his shirt collar. ''More wine, Detective?''

''Thanks, I'm on duty.''

If it hadn't been for Laura, Jacob would gladly have ditched this whole scene and fled to the home his grandmother had left to him in County Clare. Better pub gossip and dark ale than this maze of secrets and lies.

''Meatball?'' Devon appeared with a green holiday platter and a bright smile that sent a fiery bolt of longing to Jacob's lower limbs. Forcing a smile, he took her arm and steered her to an unoccupied corner.

''It's quite a group of co-workers you have here, Devon.''

He regarded the telephone desk. "Your friend Flaherty hasn't stopped scowling at me since I came in."

"Jimmy?" Surprised, Devon glanced at the young man seated in one of her Louis XIV chairs. "He's harmless."

"He's jealous."

"He's still harmless."

"Yeah? Those poisoned daggers he's firing seem to have my name on them."

Amusement danced in her eyes. "Well, you do look awfully good in black. Tell me, Riker, do you have any other color in your wardrobe?"

"I like black."

"I like red, but I can occasionally be coaxed into something different."

Like the indigo silk pants suit she wore tonight. Soft and floaty, the material managed to drape itself over every curve in her body.

Annoyed with himself for noticing that, Jacob snared a meatball, ate and asked, "What happened to Alma's daughter?"

"Ah." Devon's gaze flicked to Roscoe who was hovering at Hannah's elbow, then moved along to Alma. "Hannah said she died eleven years ago."

"And?"

Devon gave her hair an impatient push. "I don't know the gory details, Riker."

He moved closer, a stupid thing to do really, but he'd been hoping to push her into a full and fast explanation. Instead, her scent created an overpowering urge inside him to kiss that challenging mouth of hers.

"How did she die, Devon? By whose hand?"

Chin up, she absorbed his penetrating stare. "She killed herself. Is that what you wanted to hear?"

"Drugs?"

"Rope."

Cop or civvy, Jacob recognized hanging as an unusual means of female suicide. "Do you know why?"

"Not really."

Her hand rose to circle her own throat, covered tonight by a solid silver choker. Jacob squashed an impulse to reach up a finger and trace the discoloration he knew lurked beneath it.

Devon sighed. "Margaret was working as a disk jockey when she died." Jacob's head came up, but she stopped him cold. "Forget it. There's no Christmas Murder connection."

"You're sure of that?"

"What are you driving at, Riker?"

"Bits of gossip mostly."

"About Warren?"

"You've heard them."

"Everyone's heard them. Not many believe."

"Sexual harassment's a serious charge, Devon."

"Thank you, I know that. I also happen to know Kira Folkstone. She worked for Warren in New York twelve years ago. Now she's in Los Angeles. She's brought charges against six men so far and dropped them all."

"Didn't think she could prove her case?"

"Knew she couldn't. She likes wine, Riker, but she shouldn't drink it. Doesn't any more actually. One night a group of us went out to a club to celebrate a friend's promotion. Kira said a few things about a few lies she'd told in the past. Warren had asked her out for dinner. Result, lawsuit. Scruples aren't high on her list of personal priorities. I'm not saying Warren isn't a pain, but he hasn't touched anyone at the Wave. Yet."

It was a telling "yet." "You're not sure about him, are you?"

She moved a shoulder. "Not entirely, no. But I don't make false accusations."

"Because he's your boss, and you like his sister?"

Her eyes came up. "Because he's a person, Riker, and without proof I tend to give people the benefit of the doubt. Not cop philosophy, but it suits me."

"Mmm. Let's backtrack to Alma's daughter, then."

"Let's not." Devon ran a hand through her silky hair, causing it to catch a multitude of light rays. "Margaret committed suicide. Maybe her method was unorthodox, but that's what she did. It had nothing to do with the Christmas Murders. She was working in Seattle when she died and had been for five years."

"You were working in Los Angeles, Devon, until Alma and Warren heard your show."

"I moved here for Hannah's sake," she reminded him. "The Severens' offer was good, but not spectacular enough on its own merit to lure me back to Philadelphia."

Jacob wasn't convinced—of anything. "They might have upped the ante if you hadn't agreed."

"Maybe. Look, what does any of this have to do with the Christmas Murders? All right, you suspect Warren. But the women killed by the Christmas Murderer were strangled. Margaret hung herself."

"It's a similar effect, Devon." Because he couldn't think of a reason not to just then, Jacob lifted his hand to the delicate column of her throat. His fingers wrapped lightly around the silver choker. The ends of his hair grazed the curve of her cheek. Her mouth, her tempting, beautiful mouth, remained tantalizing inches away.

"Is this a new police tactic?" The question emerged defiant but tremulous. "Designed to jade my idealistic mind?"

He brushed his thumb over her chin. "I'm beginning to like your idealistic mind," he murmured. His head lowered. "But I have a feeling we're both going to regret that in the end."

THE KISS LASTED five seconds, long enough for anyone watching closely to notice. More than long enough for Devon to react in a way that threw her already jumbled thoughts into a state of total chaos.

Not that she was fanatical about structure, but she preferred to think clearly when the situation warranted.

A lightning-quick touch of his lips on hers, and suddenly

all rational thought fled. She raised puzzled fingertips to her mouth. "Why did you do that?"

The question seemed to galvanize him. He dropped his hand from her throat and stepped back. His breathing was more rapid than it should have been considering the brevity of the kiss. But didn't she feel much the same way herself? Baffled, stunned—affected?

"You okay, Dev?" Jimmy stuck his curly head around the oak bookshelf.

Devon's fingers jerked away. Her eyes remained on Riker's. Why did he seem all smoke and mirrors to her? "I'm fine, Jimmy. Riker and I were...discussing security."

Jimmy looked from one to the other. "If you say so. By the way, the cake you ordered just arrived."

"Cake?" She'd managed to drag her gaze from Riker's. Now, she returned it with a frown. "I didn't order a cake."

Jimmy blinked. "No? Neither did Hannah. Must be a mix-up. I'll—"

"Where's the box?" Riker interrupted.

"Over there." Jimmy indicated a polished cherry-wood table in the foyer. "Hannah buzzed the delivery guy up." His smile had an uneasy edge to it. "What do you think it is, a bomb or something?"

"Or something." Jacob pressed a palm to Devon's stomach. "I'll check it out. You stay here."

The hell she would.

"No, Dev." Jimmy snagged her sleeve as she started out. "There could be something nasty in that box."

"Or it could be a cake delivered to the wrong address." Devon motioned to Warren sprawled in a chair, fuzzily contemplating the cross-room parlay unfolding between Rudy and Alma. "Get some coffee and quiche down his throat if you can. He has a meeting with the manager of the Holly Tree first thing tomorrow morning."

"But..."

"Do it," Devon urged. "I'll be fine."

With a last covert glance at her guests, she slipped into the front hall behind Riker.

He was on his haunches, studying the white, string-wrapped box. "The German Bakery," he murmured, reading the stamp. "Have you heard of the place?"

"It's a couple of blocks away. Trendy but good."

"Do you order from them?"

"Hannah does once in a while." She knelt beside him. "Do you think the delivery person made a mistake?"

With careful fingers, he untied the string. "No."

"Ah, should I get Rudy?"

"Might be a good idea."

It was also a tricky maneuver with Alma and Hannah both trying to catch her eye. In the end, she didn't bother being clever. She simply hooked her arm through Rudy's and drew him discreetly away. "Back in a minute, Alma. Riker needs his expertise."

Rudy snorted. "Can't be anything mechanical, then. He's better at electrical doodads than I am."

"Is he better at bombs?"

The grizzled head came up. "Bomb! Where?"

"The foyer. I received an unexpected delivery."

In the tiny hallway, Rudy hunkered down next to his contemplative partner. "What's the news? Have you weighed it yet?"

"It's not heavy."

"Could it be a cake?" Devon asked hopefully.

"Could be."

"Nitro's light enough," Rudy added, his tone sour. "Stand back, Devon. As for us," he said to Riker, "we'd do better to back off and call the experts."

Riker's stare was merciless. "We are the experts, Rudy. Do you want to do it, or should I?"

Swearing, Rudy flexed his broad fingers. "I'm not as steady as I used to be. I'll hold the box; you lift the lid. Slowly, now. No jolts or jerks."

Unable to move her feet, Devon hung over Riker's shoulder. The breath stopped in her lungs as he raised the cardboard flap.

"I'll be damned." Rudy spotted the contents before any of them. He released his grip with a snicker. "It is a cake. A bundt, isn't it?"

Devon's breath came out in a stuttered rush. She reached for the box.

Riker's hand shot out to prevent her. "Don't," he warned and drew her fingers back.

Exasperation shimmered through her. "I wasn't going to eat it. I'm not stupid. I just wanted to see."

Rudy did the honors. "Cherry frosting." His grin was oddly wistful. "My first wife canned her own cherries. Made the best pies in creation."

"It isn't a bundt cake, Rudy," Riker said quietly.

The grin vanished. "What are you talking about?"

Devon looked again. Hole in the center, cherry frosting. "It's an angel food," she said, then caught and held Riker's somber gaze. "An angel food cake," she repeated. "With cherry icing."

A trail of horror snaked slowly through her brain. She stared wordlessly. So many new angels in her life—but none more unnerving than the angel of death that seemed to have set up camp on her front doorstep.

ANGEL FOOD CAKE. A Christmas angel pendant. Of course Devon would recognize the significance. A note, a warning caress of silk around her beautiful throat—careful, dear Devon, not to damage those exquisite vocal chords. How little pressure it would take to destroy them forever.

Restless fingers crawled spider-like across the polished desktop glass to the CD player. Pop the door, insert the disk, skip to number three, and listen. Excellent version of "It Came Upon the Midnight Clear". Angels, all of them. Laura West, Abigail Fountain, Dina Gosford, and on down to— what? The restless fingers shifted upward to massage at fiery starbursts of pain. Marilyn Something. Casey Coombes would remember. He knew the story better than anyone.

"Better than I do," he whispered in an agonized voice.

Marilyn and Dina had been pretty. Laura had been a haunting beauty. Devon possessed a different brand of loveliness. Luminescence was her gift. She glowed from the inside out—and spat fire when the need arose.

Voices raised in Christmas song overrode the persistent pain, the ache of need and guilt, uncomfortably mixed.

Appearance made no difference. No death had resulted from that. The voice, that's where the problem resided. It kept returning to torment.

Anguish moved in, its heels nipped by the initial signs of rage. A tic in the jaw, a twitch of the fingers, an imperceptible jerk between the shoulder blades.

Dear God in heaven, to be rid of this consuming fury. To confess it and set it aside. Better yet, to banish it forever.

Sadly, that wasn't to be. Rigid fingers tapped the spotless glass desktop. Recollections of a conversation spewed upward like venom. Darkness pressed in, and solitude. The song played tauntingly in the background.

Hello, darling... whispered the beautiful silken voice.

The din of memories became a cacophony. Why couldn't this nightmare have ended last year? Such a perfect opportunity to make the break.

Above the song, the radio surged. Another lovely voice melded with the one in his head. Her voice in duplicate. "Hi, I'm Devon Tremayne. Please join me for City Life tomorrow at twelve noon when my guests will be..."

Enough! His fists smashed down, bouncing the disk. However she did it, she always came back. And being back, she had to die. Again. The gift had been sent, the warnings dispatched.

Satisfaction oozed through the cracks of pain. Coombes had been last year's stroke of luck. This year promised to be more rewarding still. If one could catch a fly with sugar, one could certainly catch a spider in his own web of lies.

Yes, indeed, it was a splendid setup, and possibly, just possibly, one more death would bring an end to this monstrous nightmare of betrayal and lost control. As Coombes had been the goat last year, let an impostor do the honors this Christmas. Let Detective Joel Riker kill the pretender who called herself Devon Tremayne.

Chapter Five

"I'm telling you, Brando hasn't been here since the night before last. Hasn't been at the billiard hall either. I checked."

The woman, whose name was Tanya, had red hair which currently resembled a rat's nest of tufts and tangles. Half of her make-up had rubbed off, the other half was smeared beyond repair. She'd pulled down the sleeves of her pink cardigan the moment Jacob produced his bogus police badge.

"Is he on a bender?"

She withdrew into the dregs of pride. "I couldn't say, but he's done this before so I'm not worried. Sometimes he beats it out to a friend's place in the country."

Jacob closed his eyes briefly before pressing, "Do you know where his friend lives?"

"Near Reading, I think. I'm not sure where."

He believed that. What didn't wash was her professed lack of concern.

His eyes flicked over her disheveled appearance. The smell of gingerbread reached him from inside the room. She might have a problem, but she was striving for normalcy and with that he could certainly empathize.

From his jeans' pocket he dug out a blank card. Using the door frame for support, he wrote his assumed name and Rudy's cell phone number. Blandly, he pushed the card and two twenties into her hand.

"Let me know if he shows up or calls. I'm not vice. I just want to ask him a few questions about the billiard hall."

"Questions?" Mistrust oozed from every pore, but he noticed her fingers tightened around the money.

"Just tell him, okay?"

The door clicked shut as he started down the rickety staircase. For forty dollars and the implied promise of more, she would think about his request. God knew what she would do with the money, but sometimes people surprised him. Like Laura, the night she'd stumbled, frightened and unsure, into his condo and told him she wanted to get away from their domineering great-aunt.

Jacob shuddered away from the memory, as dry as dust now in his brain. No escape for Laura; no answers yet for him.

The sky had a verge-of-snow pallor that did nothing to lift his depleted spirits. An angel food cake, cherry frosting, symbolic of the Christmas pendant that had arrived sans note at Devon's apartment last night. Add to that the attack in her office and a written threat. Gold ink on black construction paper. Symbolic of something, no doubt.

Another headache battered at the base of Jacob's skull. He was an impostor and a danger to Devon. A decent man with nothing to hide and no fear for what the truth might ultimately reveal would go to the police and tell the whole story.

Notwithstanding, his booted feet carried him through the snow to a tavern-style restaurant called Marlowe's. Fat strings of holly hung over the opaque partitions that were the British owner's trademark. There were framed pages of Dickens on the walls, Scottish carols playing in the background and waiters with white tea towels for aprons.

Rudy sat at a table for two in front of a frosted partition. He tossed a crumpled napkin inside the empty earthenware soup bowl to his left.

"'Bout time," his uncle groused as Jacob pulled off his gloves and blew on his fingers. "I've been here for over an hour. Where've you been?"

"Looking for someone." Jacob waited until the waiter had poured him a mug of coffee and moved away. "Anything on the bakery?"

Out of habit, Rudy fished out a ratty black notepad and flipped through several pages. "It's open till 10:00 p.m. weeknights. The owner was off last night. A part-time worker took the order. White angel cake, cherry frosting. She logged it at 3:00 p.m., doesn't remember if it was a man or a woman who made the call."

"What about the construction paper and ink?"

"The paper was standard issue; every place from Wal-Mart to J.C. Penney stocks the damned stuff. The gold ink is craft store material. Too much of it available at this time of year for me to narrow the field more than that. The script was nice. Calligraphy. Doesn't tell us much, except the writer's got a good hand, probably prefers a tidy environment."

Jacob recognized the brick-red color that had tinged Rudy's lined cheeks. He drank a mouthful of coffee. "What else?" When Rudy's gaze rose to the holly strands, Jacob let out a frustrated breath, propped up an elbow and pinched his temples between his thumb and middle finger. "You talked to Dugan, didn't you?"

Rudy watched as an elderly woman entered with a gray poodle tucked inside her coat. "We had a chat." His eyes moved to spear his nephew's. "Dammit, I like Devon. She's in danger. She deserves better protection than I—than we can give her. We don't know what we're dealing with here. Could be a cold-fish sociopath or screwed-up schizo."

"It could also be a split personality. Or just some kook who gets his kicks out of killing female radio personalities."

"Make your point."

"Tell me what Dugan said first."

His uncle, fearing a clash of tempers, exercised caution. "What I expected. That Coombes was tried and convicted and that we're probably dealing with a copycat."

"Son of a... That's it?"

Rudy's bottom lip jutted. "He promised to look into it." At Jacob's glare, he thumped the table. "Off the record, boy. Dugan owes me favors, besides which he's never been a stickler for procedure. Thinks his captain's a jackass. Coombes is behind bars. Case closed as far as Captain Paloma is concerned. He has his eye on state politics. He won't appreciate Dugan, or anyone else, reopening this neatly sealed can of worms."

"Nice guy." Jacob hated the feeling of relief that jittered through him. He hated the accompanying guilt pangs even more. They had no validity, couldn't have, since the police insisted on dragging their collective feet. He, on the other hand, was resolved to protect Devon from the lunatic pursuing her. Regardless, he thought, darting a look at Rudy's set face, of what the outcome might be.

Rudy caught the glance and returned it with a pointed one of his own. "I saw you talking to her last night, Jacob." He waved the waiter back with a flap of his wrist. "You're deluding yourself if you think you can keep your emotions out of this one. She's like a thoroughbred race horse. All spirit and fire." His muddy eyes gleamed. "Got a great pair of legs too."

Defensiveness swelled in Jacob, easing off only when he became aware of the tension that thrummed through his muscles. What the hell was wrong with him that he was tempted to grab his own uncle by the lapels and snarl at him to keep his mind on his work and his eyes off Devon's legs? Her fantastic legs, he amended, then rolled his eyes and heaved out a defeated breath. Might as well accept that he was halfway to hooked. Accepting and admitting, however, were two different things.

"Her legs are fine, Rudy." He didn't quite meet his uncle's astute stare. "What's not fine is the person who sent her that pendant. There's more than madness at work here. There's anger and resentment, maybe even some twisted form of jealousy dumped into the mix."

Rudy clasped and unclasped his cup. "You see all that, huh?"

"You've read the reports on the seven murder victims. Don't you see those things?"

Rudy hesitated a beat, then sat back to think. "I don't know. Maybe. Dugan's printing out copies of the computer files. We can go over them and see what crops up. Tonight, if he delivers."

"We have a charity dinner to survive tonight."

Rudy snorted. "Peace on earth, good will to men. For all our sakes, let's pray for a midnight truly clear."

IT MUST HAVE BEEN a delayed reaction that gave the day such a strange luster. Devon couldn't think of a single other reason for her skittish mood, or the tremors that chose the oddest moments to scuttle her.

"It's often forced socializing," her guest psychologist had offered disdainfully, "that causes so many of us to suffer from bouts of depression during the holiday season. That plus the expectations we put upon ourselves and others to purchase the best gifts, to be on our best behavior, to spend the most money, to outdo each other in every conceivable way. Then there are the charities…"

Devon hadn't liked the man very much, had certainly not agreed with his gloomy assessment of decaying holiday spirit.

"Surely Christmas hasn't fallen complete prey to commercialism," she'd argued gently. "I know a number of volunteers who do work for charity. They love what they do. They love the results of it even more."

The man had merely sniffed at her and mouthed the word, "Humbug."

The couple from the animal shelter had lifted her spirits considerably, so much so that she'd almost succeeded in forgetting about yesterday's attack and subsequent delivery. She wasn't quite able to obliterate the feel of Riker's mouth on hers or fully comprehend the fences he seemed determined to erect between them.

"You're emcee tonight, Devon," Alma informed her after the show. "I've given it some thought, and Warren's just too long-winded in the spotlight."

"Emcee. Right." Devon propped her chin in her cupped palm and regarded the older woman across her relatively tidy desk. "You know, don't you? About what happened here yesterday."

It was all the invitation Alma needed. She closed the door behind her and cut a brisk path to Devon's desk. One plump finger stabbed the air between them. "I told you this business with the pendant was serious. You should have been more careful."

"In my own office, in a supposedly secure building?"

"Don't use that breach-of-security bull on me, my dear. If someone can get into the Queen's Buckingham Palace bedroom, a radio station would be a piece of cake. Nothing is secure, these days. You take precautions, that's your best security."

"I have police protection."

To Devon's surprise, Alma flushed, not a pretty pink but beet red. Despite the tone of their conversation, Devon smiled. Alma had spent most of last evening trading barbs with Rudy Brown. Given Alma's attitude toward men, her current reaction was a rather revealing one.

Alma planted her hands on her ample hips. "Yes? Is there something you'd like to say?"

The smile blossomed. "I invited Riker and Rudy to the party tonight."

"Good." In total control, Alma gave a curt nod. "I like the idea of—" Her head swung around "What was that? Hello?" She raised her voice. "Who's there?"

With the door closed, Devon couldn't really speculate on the cause of the small sound in the corridor, but it had a definite aspect of stealth about it.

When no one answered, she stood. "Should we look?"

"Probably, but I've spooked myself with all this talk of precautions and Queen Elizabeth's bedroom. Who is it?" she demanded in her most authoritative tone.

Devon craned her neck. "There, I heard it again." She sighed. "This is ridiculous, Alma. It's three in the afternoon and there are two of us here." She started for the door, her tread determined if a trifle less confident than usual. "I won't jump at shadows because of a pendant."

"Be careful," the other woman instructed as she reached the door.

Sticking her head out, Devon looked right, then left, then frowned. Unsure, she continued to stare at the distant corner where one of Alma's fairy-lit potted palms twinkled.

"What is it?" Alma demanded.

"I saw someone. Part of him anyway."

"Him?" Joining her, Alma peered out. She let her round brown eyes scan the empty corridor. "I don't see anything."

"Well, he's gone now, isn't he?" Impatient, Devon ran the fingers of her right hand through her hair. "This is very weird, Alma. Too weird."

"It must have been Caleb from maintenance," Alma decided. "I told him to inspect the carpets, see if they needed shampooing."

"It wasn't Caleb," Devon told her. "He wasn't wearing coveralls."

"Well, who was it then?"

There was no mistaking the rough edge in her employer's voice. Wisely, Devon backed off. "I don't know. But he wasn't wearing navy coveralls. Let's forget it, okay? Nothing happened. I'm going to finish here then pick Hannah up at Hare and Woden."

Devon knew Alma well enough to recognize relief when she saw it. Was she worried that it had been her brother lurking in the hallway? Her brother who'd been charged not once but three times with sexual harassment during his twenty-five years in radio?

Devon hugged her arms across her chest after Alma's departure. Maybe she should have set the older woman's mind at ease. It hadn't been Warren whose curly head she'd spied ducking around the corner. She was ninety-nine percent sure it had been Jimmy Flaherty's.

"Damn." The word came out with regret. If not Jimmy with his easy grins and affable nature, then whom could she trust?

Hesitating for an instant, she picked up her cordless handset and very slowly punched in the cell-phone number that Riker had given her.

"WHAT WAS he wearing?"

"A green sweater and jeans." Devon shook flakes of snow from the burgundy scarf she'd draped over her head. Riker steered her by the arm to an unpopulated corner of the restaurant lobby. "Do you see him?"

He meant Jimmy, and she did. Black pants instead of jeans, but he was still wearing a hunter-green sweater.

"I'm not absolutely sure about this, you know." She unclasped her black wool cape and handed it to the coat check. "It was the curly hair that got my attention."

"And the green sweater."

Against logic, Devon defended Jimmy's motives. "He might have come to see me and heard Alma in my office. It isn't wise to intrude when she's around."

"So why did you call me?"

Devon paused. "I'll mull that over," she murmured. Humor bubbled up into her green eyes. She ran a finger over the lapel of his loose black jacket. "You look very handsome tonight. Matching jacket and pants, white shirt, no tie—this is almost a suit, Riker."

A veil dropped over his handsome features. "It's as close as I get." His gaze fixed on Jimmy. "Go do your host thing, Devon. I'm going to talk to your assistant newsroom coordinator."

Unthinking, Devon adjusted her drapey garnet jacket and short straight skirt. Poor Jimmy, she thought with a pang. He wasn't accustomed to lean, hungry wolves circling his doorstep.

Hannah arrived on Roscoe's arm, pink-cheeked from the cold. Devon hadn't seen that spark of contentment in her soft brown eyes since before her husband's funeral early in the year. Give Roscoe his due, he'd made Hannah smile again.

The Holly Tree was a large restaurant, beautifully appointed with an oak parquet floor polished to a rich shade of honey, round tables covered with red linen cloths and white Irish lace toppers. The chandeliers dripped with crystal; the silverware was Georgian, the place settings vintage Doulton. But it was the Christmas trees which took pride of place in the main dining room, two of them, each topping ten feet, spreading wide, tinsel-laden branches on opposite sides of the tiled hearth.

Warren offered her a crooked smile and a toast from the head of the already crowded room. Behind him lay a multitude of brightly wrapped gifts on the floor under the trees. Presents for underprivileged children. Funds from this dinner would also provide a number of people in Philadelphia with more than one hot meal during the holidays. And later, Santa Claus would arrive with bags full of extra goodies.

Devon worked her way through the chattering crowd. She liked people, on top of which, everyone in attendance had paid a high price to be here tonight.

She lost sight of Riker somewhere near the refreshment table, then reminded herself that they both had a job to do. If other couples who'd arrived together were taking the opportunity to dance to Phil Specter, that was their business— although she did love to dance and certainly could have stolen a few moments away from her duties to enjoy herself.

"You have a pleasant way about you, Devon."

Rudy's canny remark brought a smile to her lips, and had her turning from her circle of City Life sponsors to greet him.

"Actually, I'm the black sheep of my family in that regard. My parents and sisters have a lot more parlor chat in them than I do."

"You prefer getting to the point, do you?"

"It saves time." Her eyes teased. "Where's Alma?"

A gruff laugh rumbled up in his chest. "Right now? Keeping that lush brother of hers from falling face down in the punch bowl. She's a good woman, is Alma. Almost wish I were free to court her."

The word charmed. Devon covered her amusement. "That's good of you to say, Rudy."

He shrugged. "I prefer honesty myself. Figure you do, too." His gaze shifted. "And Alma. I'll head over and have a heart to heart with her. You, uh, seen Riker?"

"Not for several minutes." She hadn't seen Jimmy either, Devon realized and wondered why that should disturb her.

Leaving Rudy to bare his soul to Alma, she continued to mingle. Damn Riker, though, she wanted to dance with him at least once tonight.

"Dev?"

A hesitant tap on her shoulder made her heart stutter. She turned. "Jimmy!" She had to force back disappointment. "I thought you were—" She caught herself and substituted a hasty, "Warren."

Jimmy's grin was oddly lopsided. "Nah. He's busy playing bartender."

Devon noted the slight slur. "And you've been assisting him, huh?"

The grin faded as Jimmy's gaze dropped to his shuffling feet. "I was talking to your cop friend, actually. I don't think he likes me very much."

Devon took pity on him, laying a hand on his surprisingly wiry forearm. "He has a job to do, Jimmy. He can't afford to be…friendly."

"He's friendly to you."

A light of something she couldn't read glinted deep in Jimmy's cobalt eyes. Resentment maybe. Or jealousy. She shied away from the idea and gave him a gentle push. "Why don't you ask Teddi to dance before old Mrs. Gammon talks her into a stupor?"

Jimmy's face resumed its genial cast. "Okay, sure. Anyone can dance to the Boss."

The skin on the back of Devon's neck tingled, but she waited until the younger man reached Teddi's side before venturing a bland, "You have all the earmarks of a ghost, do you know that? Here, gone and here again, all in the blink of an eye."

Riker detached himself from the shadow of an oak pillar. "I played the ghost of Christmas Present once in high school."

"But I'll bet you really wanted to be the faceless Future."

Now it was Riker's eyes that glinted in the silvery pool of light. But where Jimmy's had puzzled her, this man's rendered her breathless, or very close to it. "It was one of many wishes, Devon. Unfortunately, as hard as I tried, I couldn't be faceless for any length of time."

An intriguing thought, Devon reflected as he reached for her hand.

Just at that moment, however, she had no desire to think. She was curious about the kind of man Riker must be. She'd already seen his reserve, and the somber, solemn aspect to his nature. But he wasn't devoid of humor by any means, nor, she suspected, was he completely unaffected by her.

That made them even, she decided, fighting a shiver as his thumb stroked the soft skin of her inner wrist.

"Oíche Chuín," he said, glancing at an open spot on the floor. "'Silent Night.' Do you like to dance?"

"I love to." She tipped her head to study him. "I didn't know you spoke Gaelic."

"I don't. I just know Enya."

"Personally?"

Amusement played on the corners of his mouth. His hands spanned her waist, drawing her forward into his body. "I don't know many people personally, Devon. It makes life easier that way."

"It makes life boring, if you ask me."

She wondered how he would react if she inched just a little

closer to him. Probably not all that well, given his philosophy of life.

On the floor, Riker's breath stirred the hair on her temple. He smelled clean, like a winter garden in the north. His hand pressed erotically into the small of her back. Whether intentional or not—likely not, knowing Riker—the contact caused Devon's breath to hitch slightly in her throat.

One thing at least. The sexual tugs she felt were far from one-sided. When "Silent Night" melted into "O Holy Night," he settled her hips against his harder ones, tucked her head into the crook of his shoulder and turned his face into her softly scented hair.

God help his senses. She smelled like spring in Ireland. Jacob had been there once at Easter, when the green of Eire had come fully into bloom. He'd been an inquisitive seven year old boy, hunting for leprechauns under tree roots and in every shoe store his mother and his unbelieving great-aunt had dragged him through.

But no bony fingers held his in an iron grip tonight.

Jacob grimaced at the lance of heat and desire that rocketed through him. He wanted Devon badly, was attracted to her on a level that came dangerously close to frightening. He hadn't had feelings of this magnitude for years, hadn't allowed himself to care for any female since Laura had died eight years ago.

The memory sobered him, but did nothing to alleviate the pain that persisted in his lower limbs and in his head. He could want Devon, but could not afford to become emotionally involved with her.

She twisted slightly in his grasp. It only took that single, small action to snap his mind swiftly back to the reality of the crowded dance floor.

She raised her head. Those moss-green eyes of hers stared into his. "Sorry," she said. "You were squeezing me."

He relaxed his hold instantly. It didn't help. Her skin was pure roses and cream, her lashes, a sinful length and thickness.

"You make me think of a Chinese puzzle." She shifted her head to a considering angle. "A mystery with a simple but tricky solution. What are you hiding in that head of yours?"

Sheer willpower kept the tension knots at bay. He moved the shoulder where her hand rested. "You tell me. I'm just a cop, doing my job."

"Is part of that job to renovate the apartment you're renting?"

"Idle hands, Devon."

She laughed. "Pretty lame answer, Riker, but I understand the feeling. I'm not much good at twiddling my thumbs either."

On the other hand, she was a master at making the blood pump hot and fast to certain of his vital body parts.

Jacob ran his fingers up her delicate spine. Skin like rose petals—God, he could feel the warmth of it through her clothes.

A hungry ball of desire lodged in his throat. How could he hope to combat that?

Music floated in the air around them, mingling with a multitude of scents: pine boughs, perfume, roast turkey from the kitchen. Voices murmured in the background. The shadows shifted with the dancers. Devon's heart beat a quick rhythm against his.

She stared at him as the song began its slow build to the finale. Need became a buzz in Jacob's brain. His right hand released hers, moving reluctantly to the gentle curve of her jaw.

She regarded him, lips parted, green eyes following every nuance of expression, every move he made.

"You're going to kiss me, aren't you?" It was half a question, half an accusation. "I don't think that's a good idea."

"Neither do I."

A sigh fluttered out of her. "You're so damned complicated, Riker. Why is that?" They slowed as the dance concluded. A smattering of applause punctuated the din in Jacob's brain. He saw her lips curve into a doubtful smile. "I'm really not sure about this, at all."

"I am." Was that his voice he heard—rough and dark, thick with conflicting emotions? Jacob's fingers moved to cup the nape of her neck. He was sure this was the worst possible idea. And he was going to do it anyway.

Tossing wisdom out the window, he brought his mouth down on hers in a kiss that was equal parts aggravation and desire. With his tongue he tasted her, the sweetness, the fire and the uncertainty.

She hesitated briefly, then responded, sighing as she hooked her arms around his neck.

A sudden bolt of panic pierced the layers of cloud that fogged his brain. What the hell was he doing! Touching, tasting, wanting her so intensely that he forgot the lies that separated them?

He started to withdraw, then frowned as Devon captured a strand of his hair.

"What?" he asked warily.

"Your hair." She stared, absorbed. "It feels like silk."

He closed his eyes, then opened them. The mask slid firmly back in place. "You find that interesting?"

She made an uncertain motion. "The man who attacked me in my office had hair like silk, too. I felt it on my neck when he bent over me."

Jacob paused. "Isn't most hair silky?"

"Not at all. My producer in L.A. had hair like steel wool." She glanced in Jimmy Flaherty's direction and cocked an eyebrow. "I could test it out easily enough."

"Forget it, Devon. We think the person who attacked you is here tonight; we can't be sure."

"It isn't hard to ruffle hair, Riker. I'll dance with Warren first."

Jacob held onto her wrist. "You can't go around sliding your fingers through the hair of every male in the room."

"I can unless you have a better suggestion."

"I do. We—Rudy and I—are going to go over the files of

the women who were killed by the Christmas Murderer. The first thing we have to do is establish whether the person who sent you that pendant is a copycat or not.''

''And poring over old records will determine that?''

''Possibly.'' Against his better judgment, Jacob cupped her cheek in his palm. ''Details, Devon. Copycats invariably overlook one or two.''

''Like covering their hair.''

He blew out a resigned breath. ''Are you always this stubborn?''

Her chin came up. ''I prefer to call it logical.''

''Call it what you want.'' He trapped her chin between his thumb and forefinger. ''Just leave the investigating to me, okay?''

She swatted him away, not bothering to leash her temper. ''You're an arrogant bastard, Riker. My life's being threatened, and you want me to sit idly by while you and Rudy try to catch the lunatic who sent me a pendant warning of imminent death.''

He strove for patience. ''You're the victim here, Devon.''

''No.'' She stopped him cold, her palm pressed iron-flat to his chest. ''The last thing I am, or ever will be is a victim. I won't do nothing.'' Her eyes shimmered with anger. ''I won't die, Riker.''

No, she wouldn't, he vowed. Not if he could stop the monster pursuing her. But could he, Jacob wondered grimly? His gaze circled the crowded room. Did he really have the power to stop any part of this nightmare?

Chapter Six

"Nothing," Devon muttered three hours later. She'd danced, eaten, socialized, emceed and danced some more. She'd discreetly fingered more lengths and styles of men's hair than most females would in a lifetime. And she knew as little now as she had before she'd started. Three-quarters of the men here had wonderful hair. It could have been any of them who'd attacked her. Any or none.

She sighed. "I should have taken Riker's advice. Let him handle things. Wherever the hell he is."

"Wherever who is?" Roscoe enquired cheerfully. He intercepted her en route to the dance floor with Hannah. "If you mean your absent cop, he's been dogging the boss for the past half hour." He snatched a glass of wine from a waiter's tray. "Here, have a drink and lighten up. That thundercloud expression of yours is starting to frighten the guests."

Hannah wrapped an arm around her sister's waist. "Are you all right?" She searched Devon's face for signs of strain. "You've been through a lot the past few days. We can leave any time you want to."

Devon saw the look of—was it dismay?—that darted across Roscoe's face, before his handsome features settled into passivity.

"I'm fine, Hannah. A little over-partied. When's Santa due to arrive?"

"Twenty minutes ago." Roscoe squinted across the tables at Alma. "I'd better check on him, make sure Warren hasn't led the old fellow astray."

"I'll see that Alma doesn't notice the time." Hannah tipped her head. "Why don't you sit down for a minute, Devon? You've been going gangbusters since dawn."

"Maybe I will." Devon agreed simply because it was easier than arguing. "Have either of you seen Jimmy since dinner?"

"Not me." Roscoe scouted the room. "I wonder, Dev, does our Santa carry a cell phone...?"

Alone, so to speak, moments later, Devon considered her options. Mingle or escape the smoky room for five minutes and possibly bump into Riker in the process. Warren liked to tip his flask in the men's room. It was a good bet he'd be there now, avoiding Alma, and possibly Riker as well, given his history.

"Ms. Tremayne?" One of the waiters beckoned to her. "Detective Riker would like to speak with you."

Oh, really? "Where is he?"

"In the utility corridor, between the service entrance and the kitchen. You go through those white doors over there, past the phone bank and straight ahead."

It took Devon several minutes to work her way through the crowd. "It's like a sea of hungry pigeons out there," she commented to Teddi, who'd just returned to the dining room through the white doors. "Are the washrooms here?"

"Turn left," Teddi told her.

"Did you see Riker?"

"No, but his pal Rudy was tap-dancing outside the men's room. If you bump into Santa, tell him to get the lead out, will you? I turn into a Christmas pumpkin at midnight." With a wave, Teddi vanished into the smoke.

Devon pushed through the door and into the softly lit corridor. Muted strains of "Jingle Bell Rock" followed her, fading as she passed the empty phone bank.

The air was fresher here. Cooler, too, she noticed as a

shiver feathered across her skin. Someone must have left the service door open.

She paused at the junction. ''Riker?''

Nothing but darkness to her left and only the kitchen wall and three empty trolleys to her right.

''Great.'' She blew at her bangs. ''Riker?''

''Here,'' said a raspy voice.

Riker's? It didn't sound like him. She turned at the whisper of movement behind. ''What are...?''

She got no farther than that, didn't even get properly turned around. Black-mittened hands appeared like talons. They circled her throat before she could react. White whiskers covered her face, tickling her skin while the hands gave her a violent shake.

Her entire body felt the pain that started with a whip-sharp crack of her head as it snapped backward.

Santa Claus, her foggy brain discerned. Squinty-eyed and intent, grunting, his facial muscles contorted beneath the white cloud of his beard.

Devon's knees turned to jelly. Shadows blurred in her head. Her mind funneled toward a black hole that had to be unconsciousness.

She kicked in the direction of the man's groin. She knew she'd hit the mark when he yelped and tossed her like a rag doll against the wall.

Her head slammed into the plaster, bringing the dizzying sound of bells to her ears and the sting of star clusters to her eyes.

''Bitch!'' Santa cursed. His mittened hands came at her again.

Devon's knees gave out. Fortunate, she thought as she slithered down the wall. She doubted she could have avoided him any other way.

His momentum carried him into the misty blue plaster and afforded her the precious seconds she needed to scuttle sideways.

Sheer force of will gave her the strength to scramble to

her feet. She headed for the cold air, partly because it felt close, but mostly because it just happened to be the direction her aching body toppled.

Her fingers caught an empty trolley and yanked it sideways. A mighty heave sent it rolling into the false Santa's stomach.

Breathing heavily, she concentrated on the door and freedom. Escape. There must be people outside. Barring that, she would run to the front entrance. He couldn't, wouldn't, dare follow her there.

Snow whipped up into her face, blinding her on the threshold. She stumbled forward.

But she hadn't counted on the agility of her attacker, or the depth of the obsession that fueled him. He caught her jacket by the hem, jerking backward so hard that her feet almost shot out from under her.

To her shock, a sob rattled from his throat as his arm wrapped around her neck. "It should have ended last year." The muscles across her windpipe tensed. His tone toughened. "This time you will stop haunting me. This time—" his hot, anguished breath howled into her ear "—it will end!"

POTENT FURY. It boiled up in his head, a miasma of noxious memories and emotions. Remember the darkness, the smell of damp wool and pine and nutmeg. The smokey scent of her perfume.

The lump of rage threatened to choke him even as he increased the pressure on Devon's throat. It would end with her death. One more task—poetic justice—and after that the Christmas Murders would be a mere ghost of seasons past.

She fought like a wildcat, kicked and clawed and squirmed so that several times he almost lost his grip. She screamed, and the sound of it caused him to flinch. That voice again. Would she never leave him alone?

A moment of wishful thinking. He must have loosened his grip. She worked her body around and planted a fist in his belly. The suit had only a modicum of built-in padding, and she packed an unexpected wallop. His body caved inward around the blow. His breath whooshed out, his eyes burned with rage and the salty bite of tears.

"Riker!" She screamed his name as she plunged into the snowy darkness. It rang in his head, a hideous, grotesque echo with a center of molten pain.

Breathing hard, he charged, caught a glimpse of her silk jacket and let out a roar. No one to hear, he assured himself. He would catch her and kill her once and for all.

The setup though, the perfect frame—he hadn't thought it through, hadn't put it in place.

No time. Kill the pretender, then construct the frame.

The old song, ever-present, swelled to a scratchy crescendo in his head. Faces popped in and out. Dead female faces, the other pretenders. One more familiar face, the first. His Christmas angel, the angel of the morning. Then, behind that, a sullen male face, wary but needful, a rat with no tail....

Had his feet slowed on the slippery ground? Devon had vanished!

He skidded to a halt far to the right of the main entrance. Snow dusted the shrubbery one way; Santa's sleigh, outlined with clear lights, marked the other. She couldn't have made the door. Shrubbery? Sleigh? Which hiding place had she chosen?

Wind tore the words from his mouth. "Come out, come out wherever you are, pretty Devon. Come and get your pretty present." He crunched toward the sleigh as he spoke. "You don't want to hide. The lies are over, don't you see? All is solemn and still. No morning angel sings." He pulled a thin red silk scarf from inside his Santa suit. "Come to Santa Nicholas, Devon, and receive the gift you most deserve for Christmas."

DEVON'S HEART thundered in her chest, so loud and hard it was a miracle he didn't hear it.

Teeth chattering, she eased around Prancer toward Rudolph's brightly lit nose. Ninety feet, maybe a hundred to the front entrance. She could make that.

Few cars passed on the street at 11:30 p.m. on a snowy night. There'd be Friday office parties, it was cold and blustery, too late for a Christmas light drive-by.

Chilled and numb, she tried not to listen as he crooned to her. First in a tune she recognized and now about cats with nine lives. Did she know the voice? Maybe. She couldn't tell through the obvious disguise.

She scrubbed at her frozen cheeks. He'd tiptoed closer, a parody of a killer in his Santa suit, his mittened hands snapping and unsnapping the silky murder weapon.

Riker's solemn face flashed in her mind. But her predicament wasn't his fault. Was it? No, of course it wasn't. She should have known better than to fall for such an old trick. She'd been invited into the spider's parlor, and she'd gone, willingly. It was up to her to find a way out of his icy web.

"Come to me, Devon," the phony Santa cajoled. He'd moved toward the sleigh. She'd never get a better chance.

Slipping on the snow, she used the lead reindeer's neck to propel herself up and away. He spotted her at once. There was no mistaking his gutteral howl of displeasure.

"Riker!" She screamed his name this time. Tiny ice pellets stung her already raw cheeks. She abandoned her high heels on a cleared patch of the parking lot and streaked for the entrance.

He followed, panting loudly, gaining with each stride. Panic bubbled up. How could a restaurant overflowing inside be so deserted out here?

Her breath rushed in and out. Blood pounded like war drums in her ears. Minus her shoes, she slipped on a patch of ice, swore and just managed to catch her balance.

He was right behind her. She could feel his fingers clutching at her.

With her hair and the blowing ice particles obscuring her vision, Devon missed seeing the hands that reached out from the side to nab her. When they held, she bared her teeth, banging her fists on the two sets of knuckles around her waist.

"Back off, lady," a deep voice objected. "You've had too much to drink if you're running around out here without your shoes."

She stopped struggling and shoved the tangled hair from her eyes. It was a stranger, huge, burly, wearing a hooded parka. No beard and only astonishment registered on his reddened face. One of the valet parking attendants?

She stole a terrified glance over her shoulder. "Is he...?"

There was no one, nothing behind them except a snowdrift and the odd flickering headlight.

"He's gone." Her head fell back in relief, then surged up again as she grasped the man's arm. "Did you see him?"

"Lady, I was lucky to see you, you were moving so fast." He peered at her pale features. "You don't sound drunk. What're you doing out here with bare feet and no coat?"

Exhausted now that the adrenaline pump had stopped, Devon considered her answer. He wouldn't believe the truth, "It doesn't matter," she said tonelessly. "Just let me go back in." Her green eyes glimmered as a small portion of her temper resurfaced. "I want to catch Santa before he flies back to the North Pole."

"I HAVE NO IDEA what hit me," the studio-hired Santa Claus confessed. "Look, I got stuck in my driveway, okay? But my son dug me out quick enough that I didn't bother to call in. When I got here, I saw the open service entrance and decided to use it. It was dark and I was hefting two bags of presents, so I guess I wasn't listening for strange noises. Next thing I knew, I woke up in the utility closet, trussed up like my wife's Christmas turkey. My suit, whiskers and boots were all gone." He gave his ample belly a weak pat. "Don't need a lot of padding, as you can see. I shouted, but no one came. If Detective Riker here hadn't heard me thumping my feet against the wall, who knows how long I would've been in there?"

Jacob shoved the bulk of his guilty feelings aside and, leaving the man to Rudy, crouched down in front of Devon. "You're pale," he noted, taking her cold hand in his. "You need to go home."

Both Devon and the untied Santa were huddled in blankets inside the manager's lavish upstairs office. The remnants of the party continued below. Although Jacob had scoured the grounds, he'd found no sign of the phony Santa. Only a red silk scarf similar to the one used on her at the radio station and a piece of white fluff from the stolen costume.

"I'm calling Dugan," Rudy muttered, hunching his shoulders. "This situation requires—" he glanced at Devon "—his particular expertise."

That being, a trained cop doing an unofficial favor. Jacob didn't need to see Devon's unnatural pallor again or Hannah's desperate expression as she knelt beside her sister. "Do it," he said. "I'll drive Devon and Hannah home."

Which would not please Roscoe Beale one bit, but right then Jacob didn't give a damn about anybody except Devon—and catching the bastard who'd tried for the second time in a week to throttle the life out of her.

"I think you should bring in a psychiatrist," Hannah said softly to Jacob. "This person, whoever he is, is crazy."

"Smart, too," Devon added. Unable to keep her agitation at bay, she stood, wobbly-legged, and paced the lovely Aubusson carpet. She ticked off items on her fingers. "He rambled about cats and nine lives, compared me to that. He also talked about the lies being over. He was sort of singing. He used words that didn't fit the song "It Came Upon a Midnight Clear". He said that this time, I would stop haunting him. It must be that I—that the women he's killed—remind him of someone, maybe of the first woman who died. What was her name?"

"Laura West," Jacob replied with absolutely no inflection. "I don't think so, Devon. Every man in Laura's life was grilled and regrilled. There was no indication that any of her male acquaintances could have been the killer."

"Are you saying that this guy's obsessing over a woman who's still alive?"

"It's one possibility."

"Could another be a fatal attraction?" Hannah wondered. Renewed fear clouded her brown eyes. "I've heard people can get very violent in those cases."

"Many situations become violent," Alma put in, her tone as uncompromising as the line of her mouth. "But jumping to unsubstantiated conclusions is a waste of time and energy, Hannah. Devon was attacked right under our noses, to say nothing of our sixty-five-year-old Santa Claus. Something must be done to insure that this incident and the one in Devon's office are not repeated."

Hannah's eyebrows speared upward. "There was an incident in Devon's office?"

"A minor one," Devon said. She shot Alma a warning glare and turned back to Jacob.

Restless fingers combed through the damp, tousled layers of her hair. Jacob caught a hint of peach blossom blending with her woodsy scent, and consciously resisted the impulse to haul her into his arms. A wiser man would turn tail and run back to the healthy niche he'd carved for himself here in Philadelphia, to that neat, career-driven, emotionally unencumbered lifestyle which, although solitary at times, had suited his needs equally enough in the past. The past before the Christmas Murders, that is.

The past before Devon.

He knew she was studying the play of expressions on his face. "What are you thinking, Riker?" she asked when he closed them down.

Unable to resist, Jacob slid his fingers through her hair capturing her warm nape. "It's my fault, Devon. I should have expected something like this to happen. I should have been prepared for it." Pointless recriminations, but he felt better getting them out, better still fixing the blame where it deserved to be fixed. "Did he say anything else?"

His heightened senses picked up on the tremor she struggled to conceal. "Not that I can remember. I saw his eyes, but he was squinting. They looked dark."

"Brown?"

"Or black. Maybe dark blue. The Santa beard was too big for him. It covered most of the rest of his face. And I only got a quick glimpse while he was—well, let's just say, I didn't have time to form a clear picture in my mind."

On the sidelines, Hannah appeared infinitely more distressed than her sister. Hell, Jacob thought, he probably looked worse than any of them.

The constant movement of Devon's fingers gave her away to him. That and the restless nerves she displayed when she swept those fingers through her hair. She was shaken down to her bones, yet for Hannah's sake, she was determined not to show it.

A song teased his conscious mind. A song and a memory. A connection he couldn't pinpoint.

"Dugan's tied up," Rudy announced, coming back in. He scanned the room, then did a double take at Jacob. "What? Have I got something on me?"

Jacob shook his head but couldn't shake the stare—or the words that filtered through his mind. "Peace on Earth," Rudy had said to him today at lunch. "Pray for a midnight truly clear."

"'It Came Upon a Midnight Clear,'" Jacob murmured.

"That was the tune he sang. Well, sort of sang. It was creepy, Riker, really creepy."

Jacob helped her into her coat. As he did, his gaze slid sideways to Rudy. Coincidence that he'd alluded to the same song sung to Devon by her attacker? Or was it just possible…?

Jacob blocked the thought, ruthlessly, completely. Not possible, not in a million years. And yet…

"You look positively grim, Riker," Devon observed, bracing one hand on the wall as they descended the broadloomed staircase. "You are glad, aren't you, that no one was seriously hurt tonight?"

He caught a small rustle and glanced upward into the shadows. "Of course I'm glad." He kept his tone and expression carefully banked. "I'm also mad as hell over what might have happened." Seeing no one, he steeled himself to meet her gaze. "Are you sure you didn't get a good look at any part of him?"

She pressed her lips together. "I'd love to say I did, but it all happened in a flash. And then I hit my head..."

Hannah's gasp cut her off. Jacob's teeth gnashed. He halted her on the landing to probe the back of her skull. "Hit it where?" he demanded.

"Right—ouch—there."

"We should take her to the hospital," Hannah said instantly.

"No hospital. It's not that—"

"I agree." Jacob's brows came together in a frown. "Who's your doctor?"

"I don't—"

"Lennon," Hannah told him. "She's my doctor actually; Devon only goes for a checkup when forced."

Terrified by the discussion taking place over her head, Devon held up both hands. "Stop it, right now, both of you. Look, I appreciate your concern, but I'm fine. Really fine. No double vision, no slurring of words, nothing but a headache which will only get worse if I have to sit in an emergency room for what's left of the night." She tried not to look desperate as she appealed to Riker. "I want to go home. I promise I won't stir out of my room until tomorrow afternoon."

"Devon," Hannah objected.

"Deal," Riker agreed.

His expression was shrewd, his manner only slightly hesitant. He looked troubled and very, very tired.

Rubbing her throbbing temples, she willed away all thoughts of Joel Riker and concentrated instead on reaching his car. Too many doubts and questions rattled around in her brain. A hot bath, a warm terry robe, a pot of tea and a fire—

that's what she needed first. Then, just maybe, she'd allow herself to entertain one or two of the thoughts nagging at her about this complicated man beside her.

The ride home took forever. Hannah's fingers linked with hers and squeezed, but whether in reassurance or fear Devon couldn't be sure. Riker lapsed into a meditative silence, punctuated by numerous unreadable glances stolen whenever he thought she might be diverted.

"Like I could be diverted when he's hip-deep in his Heathcliff impression," she muttered fifteen minutes later as Riker opened the car door for her.

She took the hand he offered, shaking her head at his skeptical, "Excuse me?"

Hannah ran ahead to open the apartment. Left alone with a man whose character she couldn't begin to unravel let alone anticipate, Devon let one of the less pleasant questions slip in. Where had Riker gone while the phony Santa had been attacking her? He'd materialized from some obscure place while the valet she'd run into had gone off in search of a towel and someone to relate his weird story to. The valet had found Warren Severen. Riker had located Devon.

"You should have pulled his beard off," he'd snapped at her. Yet, oddly, the hands removing his jacket and wrapping it around her chilled shoulders had been infinitely gentle, verging on tender. "I never send messages, Devon."

She'd been too cold to respond. Not that she could have been bothered with a thousand jackhammers clattering away inside her skull....

Riker followed her into the apartment, as determined now as he had been at the restaurant. Devon located the sofa and sank onto the overstuffed cushion, grateful at least that it was Riker and not Hannah who crouched down to trap her chin and stare into her blurry eyes.

"I'm fine," she lied. "Don't alarm Hannah, okay?"

His gaze narrowed. "You need someone with you tonight, Devon. If not your sister, then it'll have to be me."

Panic speared through her. "No!"

"For God's sake, I'm a cop, Devon. I'll sleep on the sofa, but I'm staying here tonight."

This was ridiculous. A waste of time, too, she suspected. She pushed back the unreasonable panic. Let him do his macho cop thing. She wanted to sleep, needed to, without nightmares. Everything else could wait until tomorrow: hot bath, Christmas carols and all thoughts of Detective Riker included.

Relenting, she leaned her head against the cushioned rest. "All right, you can stay. But don't worry Hannah about it."

His silence had her cracking open her eyes. She saw speculation on his face, but he made a motion of acceptance and stood when Hannah returned with a tray of steaming tea.

He didn't understand. How could he? Maybe she'd explain it to him in the morning. She wanted him to understand a great many things. At least she thought she did. Funny, she'd never cared if a man understood her before. What made Riker different?

She drew an outline of him in her head. Large, dark eyes. A haunted, vaguely hunted, look. Exhaustion pulling at him; world-weary it seemed. And hiding something. Yes, definitely that. Something that troubled her as much as it intrigued. What was it? Why did her instincts tell her it mattered? Who had attacked her tonight in the service corridor of the Holly Tree Restaurant? Where had Riker been? Not kissing her, that much was certain....

Her mind tilted. She imagined that Riker was watching her, a solemn, steady regard.

Then the eyes seemed to alter. White whiskers sprouted below them. The wind swirled around her. She heard Santa Claus calling her name, sobbing, swearing. "Never again, damn you. This is the last time you'll come back to haunt me." The scarf snapped sharply in his mittened hands. "I'm going to kill you, Devon, remove your voice from the airwaves once and for all. If a cat has nine lives, then yours are about to expire."

If a cat had nine lives…

Devon shied away from the angry, crooning voice, from the questions that lurked even deeper in her mind. In her dream, she ran. His voice followed her, echoing through the snowy air.

"Your ninth life is about to expire, Devon Tremayne! Upon a midnight clear!"

Chapter Seven

If there was a hell, Jacob had been dropped into the heart of it. Nightmarish figures nipped at him, their sharp teeth sinking into the fleshy part of his brain.

He spent half a sleepless night fighting a desire to kiss Devon's tempting mouth, the other half wrestling with dreams that pinched and prodded in the guise of an old woman's bony hands. She poked her wrinkled face into his mind's eye. "Get tough," she ordered finally. "You'll die a young man if you don't. Worse, you won't amount to a damned thing. You'll fail in everything you do, Jacob Price. You'll fail, and who will you have to blame but your own idealistic self…?"

He shuddered free of the dream—then almost shot from the chair when a hand clamped down hard on his shoulder.

"Rudy!" Jacob's heart slammed into his ribcage twice before it steadied. "What are you doing here? How did you get in?"

In the weird half light, Rudy's leathery face looked infinitely older than his sixty-nine years. "I came to check on Devon."

"Only Devon?"

The grip on Jacob's shoulder tightened momentarily, before Rudy released him. He confined his response to a low growl. "You're too wrapped up, boy. I don't like it. This isn't your style, all these lies and half-baked schemes to catch a killer. It's police business. Official police business.''

Devon shifted restlessly on the large bed.

Jacob glanced at her in sleep, at the sprigged quilt which didn't quite succeed in hiding her long limbs and graceful curves. With a brutal mental wrench, he motioned toward the living room.

"You talked to Dugan." It wasn't a question.

"I did."

"And?"

Rudy tossed his beat-up helmet onto a chair. "They're up to their butts in paper right now. He'll do what he can about the attack tonight."

Jacob sensed more. "But?"

Rudy thinned his lips. "He doesn't believe it's the work of the Christmas Murderer."

"Just a random act of violence, huh?" Anger seared the blood in Jacob's veins. "Your friend Dugan's as big a jack-ass as his captain, Rudy, if he buys that load of bull. Did he check out the Holly Tree?"

Rudy ran a tired hand over his face. "Where do you think we've been till four o'clock in the morning?" He straddled the sofa arm, palms flat on his thighs. "We went over it like ants at a picnic. Fingerprints are out, for obvious reasons. Bootprints, same thing. I asked earlier; there were no witnesses, and the Santa who got conked didn't know what hit him. All we have is Devon, and I can't see that he said anything to her that'll help us make the guy." He gave his head a slow shake, lower lip jutting. "We're spinning our wheels here, Jacob. Now maybe if Devon were to go to the police herself.... Ah, hell," he finished in disgust, "I don't know what to tell you. They'll investigate the incident the best they can."

Shoving a hand through his long hair, Jacob tuned out the testy last part of Rudy's speech and circled a cluster of potted plants on the floor. Memories of bad dreams, of bony fingers yanking on his arm, taunted him from the corners of his mind. He hadn't thought of the old woman for over seven years. Why lately? he wondered, then set the question aside and continued his pacing.

"Do you have the files here?" he asked.

Rudy grunted. "In your new apartment. I dropped them off before I came here."

Jacob regarded him, half-lidded. "How *did* you get in, Rudy?"

His uncle shrugged. "I knocked. You didn't answer. So I picked the lock."

Jacob's humor kindled at the idea. "One of those useful talents you acquired on the force?"

"As I recall," Rudy retorted gruffly, "I acquired that particular talent from you. Caught you, cool as a cucumber, when you were ten years old, picking your way through the old woman's mansion, and her sitting downstairs, insisting you wouldn't know an impure act if it came up and bit you on the butt."

The amusement dimmed but didn't quite die. "The old woman didn't know me as well as she thought."

"Yeah, well, she was a funny old duck, I'll admit. Every blessed bit of her estate would've gone to Laura if—well, you know. You only got the bulk by default...." Rudy's comments trailed away to a cough. Difficult, Jacob supposed, for an uncle to miss the deadly calm expression on his nephew's face. Dammit, if only he could shed the Christmas carol echoing in his head.

"Listen, boy," Rudy began.

But Jacob cut him off with a firm, "I've done nothing but listen, Rudy, ever since this nightmare of murders began eight years ago. I listened to Riker, then I listened to you. I listened to Casey Coombes's confession and to the life sentence he received for it. It's crap, all of it. Devon's been attacked twice. She's been threatened, subtly and openly. Dammit, she hit her head on a wall tonight trying to escape a lunatic Santa with a scarf in his hands. She wound up running barefoot in the snow. She's planned victim number eight, Rudy." The muscles in his body vibrated like an over-wound spring. When he pictured Devon's pale cheeks, pictured a "midnight clear," they wound even tighter. "Forget the book. Devon's life is worth more than your precious police procedure. He had no right to touch her, let alone attack her. I'm going to nail this guy, Rudy." Jacob's eyes glittered with a light just fierce and foreign enough that he knew the old woman would have been shocked by it. "I'm going to nail him, and then I'm going to kill him."

"IT WAS A GERMAN IDEA originally to decorate fir trees." Devon flipped from book to file to paper at her table. "The custom traveled to England courtesy of Queen Victoria's husband, Prince Albert. Father Christmas metamorphosed from St. Nicholas. And then came Santa Claus."

"Who made the Santa we know?" Hannah asked from the counter. She was supervising Roscoe who was tearing lettuce leaves for a Caesar salad.

"Coca Cola. Before that, though, back in Victorian times, Christmas carols gained popularity and beef and goose lost out to turkey as the dinner of choice." Devon thumbed to the index. "Mom should read this before she tries to fob her veggie turkey off on us again this year."

Riker, who'd been testing his spicy lasagna sauce, arched dubious brows at her. "Veggie turkey?"

Devon grinned. "It's an acquired taste."

"One which requires the participation of an adventurous soul," Roscoe added, giving Hannah a squeeze around the waist.

Raising wary eyes, Devon regarded first her sister, then Riker who made a small motion with his head at the door.

Fair was fair, she decided, pushing away from the over-flowing table. Riker, and everyone really, had done their best all weekend, to take her mind off Friday night's attack. Alma had dropped by Saturday afternoon armed with mincemeat tarts and a Scrabble board. Jimmy had sent her a floppy reindeer with gold lamé antlers and plaid hooves. Warren had wired a huge bouquet of lilacs, orchids and roses. "For a woman who looks and sounds like a Christmas angel," was printed on the attached card.

Andrew McGruder had even gotten into the act, although how he'd heard about the incident, Devon couldn't imagine. There'd been no mention of it in any of the newspapers she'd read, and she knew Hannah hadn't spoken of the matter.

"A female alone," he'd said, his pudgy cheeks wobbling as he shook his head in disapproval. "You should learn self-defense, Devon." His flat brown eyes had brightened. "I could show you a few moves if you'd like." His chest had puffed. "I took karate in college."

Devon had smiled. "Yes, I can see how dentistry and karate might mix."

Amusement aside, however, all she'd wanted was for him to disappear into the corridor shadows like the Cheshire cat he'd resembled right then. Instead, he'd continued to grin hugely at her. He'd even gone so far as to skate one large foot across the threshold.

"It isn't really late," he started to say. Thankfully, he'd stopped and snatched his foot away when Riker had come bounding down the stairs.

"Problem?" he'd asked at Andrew's flustered appearance.

"Not anymore." Too kind by nature to be deliberately cruel, Devon had smiled at the blotchy-faced dentist. "Thanks for caring, Andrew, but I'm completely recovered, as you see."

She wasn't sure what to make of the poisonous look Andrew darted at Riker, but she didn't suppose it really mattered. She'd rather know how he'd learned of her situation in the first place.

Riker had wondered the same thing, had pondered it out loud while he'd prowled her apartment, checking locks, deadbolts and windows.

"There's something about that guy, Devon. He makes me think of Dr. Jekyll."

Devon had agreed. "But I don't think he's experimenting

with the dark side of human nature, or whatever the good-bad doctor did. My guess is he's lonely.''

"A lonely eavesdropper.''

"Possibly.'' And preferable to the alternative that had popped into her head when she'd answered her door tonight. Andrew's eyes were naturally squinty, his voice, if not precisely raspy, was certainly gritty enough to descend into such a sound.

Devon hadn't dwelled on those thoughts. She'd been tired and jittery, too much so to do more than thank Riker for coming down. Too bad, too, because he'd looked unutterably attractive in his faded jeans and cream denim shirt. His hair had been damp from a recent shower, his scent clean and masculine, disturbing to every one of her functioning senses. But he'd kept his distance just as studiously as she'd kept hers, giving her the time she'd needed to put things back in some sort of semi-rational perspective.

She'd been immersed in the last bits of research for her series of Christmas shows when Riker had arrived late this afternoon, loaded down with grocery bags and wine, with Hannah behind him and Roscoe close on her heels. He made, he'd claimed, a killer lasagna. All she had to do was lend him her kitchen for a few hours, relax and enjoy.

"Your sauce will burn,'' Hannah warned now as Devon and Riker exited the kitchen.

Roscoe sent them a get-lost smile and reached for the spoon. "I'll stir it. Carry on.''

"He's pushing,'' Devon remarked, crossing to the CD player.

Pretty as it was, maybe the Christmas tree didn't provide quite enough light with only two of them in the room. She had to grope for the disks in the slots.

Riker came to stand behind her while she slid the "Nutcracker Suite'' into the machine. His shirt was red cotton today. The color made her think of a bullfighter. "Why do you protect her so vigorously?'' he asked quietly.

Devon hit Play. "Because she's my sister.''

"Hannah isn't being threatened, Devon."

She sighed but didn't turn. Not with him standing so close and her feelings in such an uncharacteristic turmoil. "I'm the structured one, Riker, the perfectionist who sees more imperfections in other people than she really wants to. I don't love the world the way Hannah does. I like it. I hope for things and people, but I don't make excuses for their flaws."

She forced herself to face him then, but she did so carefully, curling her fingers around the marble table behind her. "Hannah's a very sweet person. I'd hate to see her become jaded."

"That's up to her, isn't it?"

"Don't be ridiculous. Haven't you ever loved someone, seen qualities in them that you would hate to see destroyed? You came from a family of twelve, Riker. You must have felt protective about one of your brothers or sisters."

"Adopted brothers and sisters."

"Is there a difference?"

He shrugged. "No, but we weren't talking about me. I've done my homework, too, Devon. I know Hannah had a nervous breakdown."

Damn him, she thought, but couldn't quite decide for what. She expelled a resigned breath. "I wasn't crazy about Tony myself, but Hannah was very upset when he died."

"Which is why you moved to Philadelphia."

"Yes."

"And why… Ahh…" Comprehension dawned. She saw the subtle shift of his facial muscles. "You feel guilty. That's it, isn't it?"

She frowned, "About Tony's death?"

"Maybe that, too. You said you didn't like him."

Her temper flared. "I said I didn't care for him, not that I wished him—what do you mean, 'that, too?'" She forgot to be insulted and straightened to face him at dangerously close range.

He widened his eyes. "The attacks, Devon."

She stared back, trying to assimilate his meaning while at

the same time battling an urge to pull his mouth onto hers. ''I think you've lost it, Riker,'' she said finally. ''I'm threatened, and that gives me a guilt complex?''

''You moved here for Hannah's sake, right?''

''So?''

''So, now someone's trying to kill you. Whether consciously or not, Hannah probably feels responsible for that. You don't want her to feel responsible, because it's your job to protect her. Therefore, you downplay the attacks, keep them a secret if you can.'' To Devon's disconcertion, he took her face between his hands. ''It's a nice gesture,'' he said, holding firm when she would have jerked free. ''It *is* nice,'' he repeated, ''but you're selling Hannah short. She loves you. She can deal with this. She wants to deal with it. People choose what they become, Devon.'' An odd look passed over his face, but he shed it to continue. ''We're influenced by others but ultimately we create ourselves.''

''Hannah didn't create a nervous breakdown.''

''No, she recovered from it. With your help, undoubtedly, but also with her own strength.''

Why did she think he knew what he was talking about?

Consternation fogged Devon's mind. He was too close, jumbling her thoughts. Was she wrong to shield Hannah where the attacks were concerned? Unfair to shield her? God help her, unkind?

She shook her head to clear the muddle. What she saw when her gaze fastened on Riker's was a man who looked as torn apart as she felt. And every bit as stubborn.

''How do you know so much about Hannah and me?'' she asked ignoring the breathless hitch in her voice. ''Whatever else, you certainly seem to understand a thing or two about guilt.''

''We learn through experience,'' he murmured. ''I knew two women once.'' His knuckles grazed Devon's cheekbones. She stopped breathing completely for a moment. ''One was younger than me, the other decades older. The older one liked to control people, needed to, I think. The younger one didn't have enough other influences to understand that there were alternatives. She let herself be controlled. Baron Munchausen had nothing on the pair of them.''

''They liked to tell stories?''

His smile held more harshness than humor. ''They preferred to lie. The tendency led to other unpleasant things.''

What was he saying? ''I'm not a liar, Riker.''

A muscle in his jaw twitched, but the shadows playing across his narrow features gave nothing away. ''I never said you were.''

''I hate liars.'' She bit the side of her lip. ''But I love Hannah.'' She wasn't sure yet how she felt about Riker, about where attraction and trust might ultimately meet. Or collide head-on. ''I'll think about what you said. I don't want to lie to myself about my motives.''

It could have been pain that rippled through his eyes. Or maybe it was some subtle change in the colorful fairy lights.

His fingers shifted, sliding through the layers of silky hair, while his dark gaze made him a prisoner to hers. Devon didn't bother to conceal her unsteady breathing, or her erratic heartbeat. She might not understand this man. That didn't mean she couldn't want him.

One touch, one exploratory kiss for the benefit of her curiosity, and in all likelihood, she'd be satisfied. Their relationship could resume its professional course. Assuming it had been professional in the first place.

Questions buzzed like agitated bees in the back of her mind, about the women Riker had mentioned, about the upheaval she could sense in him but not begin to comprehend, about a man who sent her gifts prophesying her death, about guilt and control, attraction and trust, about doubt and fear and feelings much finer than that.

She gave in to the finer feelings, stepping deliberately closer, her eyes unwavering on his. Her heart thudded in her chest.

''Devon...''

Say no, his instincts warned even as he spoke her name. *Back away. Don't let this happen.*

But another set of instincts took over as the scent of her skin and hair washed over him. Lavender mingled with lemons and spice. His loins tightened painfully; his lashes lowered against the fiery rush of blood that coursed through him.

"Oh, to hell with it," he muttered when he couldn't force himself to move.

He touched her cheek, her chin, her lips with his thumb, then slowly lowered his head and used his mouth.

Devon's tiny moan excited him, spurred him on. His tongue circled her lips, then dipped boldly inside to explore. She tasted of wild Irish nights, moonlit and cool, with a fire burning hot and fast in the center. The heat drew him forward, spun him into the heart of the flames, deeper than he'd intended, or had ever expected to go in his lifetime.

Her hands followed the line of his waistband to the base of his spine. Shivers racked her as her fingers feathered upward to his shoulders. She made another sound in her throat, a small sound like a sigh of pleasure.

Heat pooled in the lower portion of his body. Jacob's mind shrouded itself in a haze of desire. But the guilt lingered. He felt it gnawing at his wants and needs, prodding him like a sore tooth.

Though not immediately aware of what caused him to ease his mouth free, he resented the tendril of conscience which must have been at the root of it. He also knew better than to repeat the kiss.

Touching the back of his wrist to his hungry mouth, he took a step away from her both physically and mentally. He doubted he could have done much more than that at this point. Every part of him longed to crush her against him, to feel her silky limbs tangled with his.

Devon made no attempt to disguise her uneven breathing. Her green eyes were large, dark and confused when she stared at him.

"It didn't go away," she said. Her confusion seemed to

mount as she glanced briefly sideways. "I thought it would, but it didn't."

Jacob had no idea what she meant, decided he'd be better off not knowing. Closing his own eyes, he ordered his thoughts to settle. Sex was the last reason he'd come to Devon under false pretenses. He had a purpose—to catch and expose the person responsible for the Christmas Murders. To keep Devon from becoming the next victim.

Classic holiday music poured through the stereo speakers and Jacob's overheated system. When he opened his eyes, Devon was studying his face, no doubt searching for a reaction. Curiosity, wariness, wonder—all those emotions were visible. But he saw no hint of accusation, no regret or disappointment, no sign of the mistrust he knew lurked deep in her mind.

She fingered her still-damp lower lip. "You didn't want that to happen did you?"

Wrong, he thought, a ghost of a smile playing on his mouth. "What I want isn't always what's best, Devon. I enjoy kissing you. That doesn't make it a smart thing to do."

Clinically put, and he kicked himself for it. But he'd underestimated her reaction. Apparently, the kiss hadn't affected her the same way as it had him, and even knocking the remnants of his ego aside, he had trouble buying that one.

Grinning, she released a philosophical breath. "You certainly know how to put a woman in her place, Riker. But," her eyes sparkled, "I think you enjoyed that more than you're letting on. I may not know you, but I know a knee-jerk response when I hear one."

The remark was largely bravado. She knew knee-jerk responses; he recognized pride. He admired it. He admired her.

He did not, however, admire himself at this moment. Self-deprecation would eat him alive at this rate. Blanking his features, he left her to stand in front of the window.

A wonderland of snow and lights and stars reflected in the frosted panes of glass. "I can't let this happen again,

Devon," he said, credibly calm. "And you can't want it to."
He faced her, steely-eyed. Lucky that the room remained in shadow around them. "I'm not what you think."

She folded her arms. "You're a man, I assume?"

"Men make mistakes."

"So do women. What are we really talking about, Riker?"

Because he couldn't answer that with anything approaching the truth, he opted for the low blow of a scare tactic— careful to keep his gaze off her softly tempting mouth as he advanced on her. "We're talking murder here, Devon. Strangulation to be precise. We're talking madness, cleverly hidden beneath a mask of civility. We're talking anyone around you, known or unknown. We could be talking dentist," his gaze flicked to the kitchen, "P.R. man, letter carrier or delivery boy."

She swallowed and he felt just low enough to stop. His breath ruffled the silky hair that swung alongside her cheek.

Her lower lip trembled only slightly when she spoke. "Could we also be talking cop, Riker?"

A slap would have hurt less. "Anyone, Devon," he repeated evenly.

"Including Rudy?"

Using a single knuckle, Jacob brushed her cheekbone. Peaches and cream, he thought with a pang. "Including Rudy." His hand dropped. His eyes didn't. "And me."

TWO O'CLOCK Monday morning. One hour until he had to leave.

Newspaper clippings rustled as he sifted through them again, and then again. Why wouldn't she die? Why was there no mention of his gift or of him in the newspapers?

Because the police didn't believe, he answered his own question. He propped his chin in his hands and tried to absorb the absurdity of this charade, the uncanny twist of fate. And he'd thought Casey Coombes was a godsend.

Skittish inside, he stood to pace, turned up the radio, sorted his well-read files, tucked the clippings back in their locked box and stared at the snow-crusted darkness beyond his window. Forty-five minutes to go.

Must stay on top of the details, he reminded himself. No one knew better than he did how badly the smallest oversight could trip a person up.

Had he tripped up? He paused and thought. Possibly. He got the numbers wrong sometimes. His blood chilled. Would anyone notice if he had?

No, surely not. Too many lies simmered and stewed in this blackened pot of his. Too many fears. Take Devon's Detective Riker, for example. So many truths for one man to conceal, while at the same time he sought to expose a killer.

He steepled his index fingers, tapped them nervously together. Must consider the setup to come. His eyes gleamed in anticipation. His fingers wiggled. First things first, however.

Thirty-five minutes to rendezvous.

Stupid junkie rat. Had his habit eroded all of his good sense?

A headache brewed behind his eyes, snaked downward into his neck. Devon couldn't be got at this night, so other things must be accomplished instead. Squash a rat and envision the fall of Detective Joel Riker.

Thirty minutes.

With rock-steady hands, he uncorked a bottle of California chardonnay and poured himself half a glass. He raised it for inspection. Good bouquet. Excellent color. The perfect indulgence.

Swirling it slowly, he settled in his favorite chair, her chair before…

The satisfied line of his lips deteriorated into a grimace of pain. He jumped up, spilling the wine. He wouldn't think of her as she'd been, an angel appearing at dawn. She was Devon now, afternoon talk-show host. Think only of that. And of dead rats. And exposure.

Steadying himself, he regarded the box of news clippings. He saluted it with the dregs in his glass. "To an end," he whispered in his normal voice. "From one pretender to another."

Chapter Eight

"Fantastic again, Dev. The audience loved your idea."
Jimmy burst into the broadcast booth, his youthful face
flushed with excitement. "One woman called the segment,
'the spirit of Christmas revived.' Another man's taping the
series to play for his kids when they come home from college
for the holidays."

Devon stood, stretching the cramped muscles in her lower
back. "You couldn't have said a nicer thing to me, Jimmy."
She mustered her first relaxed smile of the day. "I love Dr.
Forester, but he's impossible to keep on topic."

Teddi stuck out her tongue as she wandered in, faxes in
hand. "Dr. Forester *is* a topic, Devon. He filled your listeners
in on all sorts of interesting tidbits about Christmas past.
What you neatly kept him from delving into, but I got an
earful of as he was toddling out, is that he thinks the whole
Nativity thing was orchestrated by aliens. You know, that
freaky, the-star-was-really-a-spaceship theory."

Jimmy blinked. "He thinks God's an…? Oh, man, he must
be whacked out on something."

Teddi patted his arm. "You're a good Catholic boy,
Jimmy. I'm a good Baptist girl. Dr. Forester might look like
Albert Einstein, but we both know he's a nut. What's on tap
for tomorrow, Devon?"

"St. Nick to Santa Claus. The mutation." Pushing up the
sleeves of her oversized fuchsia sweater, Devon inspected the

control panel. "Phil Collins, Hootie and Alanis, then into commercial. You've got about ten minutes, Teddi."

The smaller woman sent her an impish smile. "Can I use it to seduce your cop friend?"

Not by the flicker of an eyelash did Devon react, though her stomach did a quick backflip. "Riker's here?"

"He arrived right after your show started. Devon?" Jimmy blocked her path when she would have slipped out the door. "I, um, did some more checking on him. I thought you'd want me to be thorough," he added when her brows rose.

"I asked you to check out his status at the department, not pry into his personal life."

Jimmy lowered his eyes. "I didn't pry, exactly. It's just that I can see he likes you. You have a right to learn all you can about him."

Devon understood now why she'd always maintained her distance from computers. "Thanks for the thought, Jimmy," she said firmly, "but I'm not interested in meeting the skeletons in Riker's closet."

"No skeletons, really. Well...except that his mother was an addict."

She managed not to sigh. "My Uncle Samuel drank himself into an early grave. Families have histories, Jimmy. Leave Riker's alone, okay?"

"She could have been addicted when he was born."

"Jimmy!"

Hanging his head, he rubbed the side of his nose. "I'm only trying to help."

"I know." Devon gave an affectionate tug on his shirt sleeve. "I appreciate it. I'm just not interested in dirt. If I were, I'd have gone into tabloid journalism."

"She died, alone and using, when he was thirteen."

Rolling her eyes, Devon gave Teddi a quick thumbs up and removed herself from the booth.

"Warren!"

Alma's bull-horn shout funneled into Devon's right ear. "Sorry, my dear." The older woman gave her arm an apologetic pat. "I seem to have lost my brother. You haven't seen him, have you?"

Devon ignored the ringing sensation. "Not since this morning."

"What about you, detective?"

Devon swung her head and spotted Riker walking toward them. He had his hands stuffed in the pockets of his leather bomber jacket and a vexed look on his handsome face.

"What about me?" he echoed, clearly distracted.

"I was asking about my—" Alma puffed her cheeks. "Never mind."

Riker's eyes narrowed on Devon. "Can you leave? Can she leave?" he repeated without pause to Alma.

"I suppose so." Bewildered, Alma regarded Devon. "Is there a problem?"

Devon glanced at Riker. "Is there?"

His mouth moved into a succinct smile. His eyes did not. "Nothing earth-shattering. A call from a sick friend." Taking her by the arm, he steered her in the direction of her office.

Devon's brow knitted. "Do I have a sick friend?"

"Say a friend of a friend, then. A woman just finished identifying her boyfriend's body. A pair of longshoremen fished him out of the Delaware early this morning. We know him, Devon. It's Brando."

THE LAST THING Jacob expected was for Brando's friend Tanya to stagger out of her run-down apartment, tumble into Devon's arms and start weeping.

"He didn't fall in," she sobbed, wadding the handerchief Jacob gave her. "I don't care how wired he was. He always knew what was what."

Jacob crouched while Tanya cried on Devon's shoulder. "Maybe he got into some bad stuff."

Tanya sniffled and raised her head. "No, he didn't. He called me on Saturday and said he'd gone to see a buddy in Scranton. He..." Her red-rimmed eyes toughened. "You're not gonna use this, are you, Riker?"

He made a negative motion with his head, caught Devon's eye and murmured the required, "Promise. What was he doing in Scranton?"

"What you figure."

"And his buddy?"

"They went to school together."

Jacob bit back the obvious retort. "What else did Brando say?"

Tanya drew a stuttering breath and looked to Devon for support. "He promised last month that he'd get off the stuff—for a New Year's resolution. We were going to quit smoking and everything. Then, suddenly, he took off. When he called, he told me he fell into a premium supply. I know his buddy. He's hard-core. Brando knows we need money. He said he only sold the guy enough so we could pay our rent and maybe go to one of those glitzy clubs on New Year's Eve."

When she hesitated, Devon smoothed her tangled hair. "Is there more?"

"Yeah, but I didn't understand it." Tanya wiped her eyes. "Before he hung up, Brando said I'd get a kick out of his 'source.'" She made quotation marks with her fingers. "He said the thin blue line was getting thinner by the day, and that I shouldn't be so gung-ho to turn into one of them, when a lot of the so-called best of them are ten times worse than any of us. He was babbling, I think. He said something about squeezing blood from a stone, figured he might just take a shot at it when he got back." She choked on a sob. "He sort of laughed, then he hung up. That's the last I heard from him. Okay, maybe he slipped in Scranton and again last night. He's human, right? But he didn't fall into the river. If he was in the water, it's because he was pushed in."

Jacob considered the notion. It sounded to him as if Brando had put the squeeze on the wrong stone. The question was, had it been the same stone that attacked Devon? Certainly, the possibility existed, though proof might be difficult to come by. He'd need Rudy for this one. And Dugan.

At a look of urging from Devon, he separated himself from the women, gravitating to the tinseled window with its grimy glass panes and peeling brown frame. The apartment smelled like nutmeg and Lysol with an undercurrent of stale beer. For all his past's major flaws, he hadn't known a life like this. As a child, he'd only felt true despair the day his mother had driven her car over a cliff and left her children in the custody of her weird but wealthy Aunt Ida.

Riker had been lucky to come from a large if adopted family. Lots of kids, two parents. Jacob suspected that his own father, whom he hadn't laid eyes on for more than thirty years, was still alive somewhere. He no longer cared where. Laura had died next and finally Ida a year later. That left only Rudy for family. And Devon for—God help him—he didn't know what yet.

Not a lover, he promised himself, fighting a twist of discomfort in his torso. He couldn't love her and lie to her at the same time; therefore, his feelings had nothing to do with love. Or was that simply another lie?

"Riker?"

His bicep tensed where she touched it. Behind her, a wispy old woman minus several of her top teeth sat with her arm around Tanya's thin shoulders. "Who's that?"

"A neighbor. She'll take Tanya to her place for a few days. She doesn't think Brando fell into the river either."

Jacob used his thumb and middle finger to erase the dull ache behind his eyelids. He couldn't recall suffering from headaches before undertaking this charade. "I'll check it out," he promised, then slanted her a direct look. "Right after I drive you home."

"Back to the station," she corrected. "My car's there. First, though—" she hitched her shoulder bag higher, a sure sign of stubborn intent "—we're going shopping."

Jacob stared, narrow-eyed. "Now?"

She ground her teeth. "For groceries, Riker."

He opened his mouth, prepared to argue the point, glanced into the kitchen with its cockeyed cupboard doors and pitiful fridge, and immediately closed it again. Groceries it was. Then he'd move on to Rudy and Dugan and endeavor to salve his wounded conscience—assuming that was possible at this stage.

On impulse, he went to his haunches in front of Tanya. She was huddled now on a moth-eaten sofa bed. "If there's a way," he promised, "I'll find out what happened to Brando."

"Check out the billiard hall." Her tone bitter, Tanya throttled his soggy handkerchief. "Cops and junkies aren't the only ones who hang out at the tables. Dock rats and lawyers go there, too. Brando got hold of some top stuff, he said. He didn't score it from his regular street sources. It was someone with clout or money who got it for him. Now he's dead. That's all whoever killed him cares about. Brando's dead, and who in this city except for me cares about that?"

Devon squeezed her hands. "I care, Tanya."

"So do I," Jacob told her. And for the first time was forced to accept the fact that he really did, an admission only fractionally as frightening—he darted a look at Devon's delicately sculpted profile—as acknowledging the reason why.

"DEVON?" From his messy art deco desk, Warren flapped a loose wrist. "Would you mind stepping into my office for a moment?"

"Not my day," Devon murmured to Teddi beside her. "Have fun tonight."

"Yeah, sure, fun." Teddi pulled an exaggerated face. "Practice reading 'Christmas in Connecticut,' the condensed version. Kick Warren in the shins for me, will you, Dev? I heard this book-a-night thing was his last-minute harebrained scheme."

Devon had time for a quick grin before Warren's beaming countenance turned amusement to a beleaguered smile.

Lopsided in his chair, he wagged a finger at her. "Shame on you, Devon. It's almost ten o'clock. You should have been out of here hours ago. You know what they say about all work and no play."

Could a ridiculous encounter like this be deemed sexual harassment? She couldn't see how, not with Warren practically splatted in his chair, his jacket off, his tie askew and his shirt sleeves crookedly rolled up on his hairy forearms. Devon settled for crossing to his desk and demanding, "What is it, Warren? I'm busy."

"My point exactly." He took a stab at rising but teetered back into the cushions. "Damn. Could you—" He extended a hopeful hand.

He reminded her of a beached whale. Masking a bubble of sudden laughter behind a cough, Devon shook her head. "Sorry, no, Warren. But I'll call someone to help you."

"Don't bother." He flopped back limply. "I just wanted to give you a message."

A chill of undetermined origin rippled over her skin. She'd heard that line recently, from the waiter at the Holly Tree Restaurant.

"A message?" she asked cautiously.

"Doctor something-or-other. He dropped by after your show today, but you'd already left. I found him outside your office. Flabby fellow. Two chins. Mid-thirties, I'd guess. Kept staring at my teeth."

Devon's bangs fluttered as she blew out an impatient breath. "Andrew McGruder. What's the message?"

The silly grin returned to Warren's classically handsome features. "By God, you've got a voice, Devon. Better tonic for the nerves than my best Napoleon brandy. The radio loves you." He lumbered to his feet, swayed and wound up banging his hip against the desk when he tried to circle it.

Devon measured the distance between desk and door. "You said you had a message, Warren."

"I'm getting to it." He nodded at the coat rack which stood just inside the threshold. "It's in my jacket." He staggered, then tipped toward her across the corner of the desk.

"Er, would you care to partake of a late-night cocktail with me, pretty Devon?"

She could handle a drunk in his late fifties, Devon reflected. On the down side, Warren was a rather large, powerful-looking drunk, with a light in his dun-brown eyes that spoke plainly of the lewd thoughts behind them.

Wisdom prevailed and she turned. "Forget it, Warren. I don't play sexual games." She glanced over her shoulder. "If you have a message, give it to me. If not, I have things to do."

Did his lips thin a fraction, the light in his eyes intensify for a split second of time? His intercom buzzed before she could decide.

He stiffened, as if stuck by a knife in the small of his back. "What?" he snapped, then located the red button and offered a more sheepish. "What?"

"Ms. Severen on two-six, sir," the receptionist informed him.

The last of the air rushed out of his chest, leaving him deflated and obviously discouraged. "Right-hand pocket, Devon. Er, hello, Alma?" he said hollowly into the speaker.

Devon snagged the envelope and escaped swiftly to the corridor. What a roller coaster of a day. First news of Brando's death, then the empathetic depression of talking to Tanya and now, coupled with that almost-ugly scene in Warren's office, a note from Andrew. She should have listened to Riker and gone home to Hannah's wild rice and mushroom casserole and a good video.

"Night, Dev." Jimmy waved to her from the distant elevator bank. "Don't work too late."

"I won't," she called back.

Uninterested, she thumbed open Andrew's note. In his customary spidery script, he'd written, "Dinner? Tomorrow? My place?" Then in brackets below it, "I have a present for you...."

One by one, the overhead lights dimmed. No air moved to

speak of, yet the paper in her hand trembled. She saw it but couldn't prevent it.

Andrew's words rolled through her head, a scratchy old record played at slow speed. She heard the slow pulse of blood in her ears and felt it in the hollow of her throat.

More lights winked out. Devon crumpled the notepaper, realized her knuckles had gone white and swore under her breath. For heaven's sake, think. Would the murderer be stupid enough to advertise his name side by side with his intent? Good Lord, she pressed cold fingers to her forehead, she was in worse shape than she'd thought.

The hallway, broad as it was, stood now in eerie shadow. People swarmed out like locusts once the skeleton night crew came on-shift at 10:00 p.m. She wasn't alone by any means, but a phone call and a familiar voice certainly wouldn't hurt.

She hastened to the elevator bank and the wall phone beside it. Hannah's line was busy, as it had been since before nine o'clock, and Riker didn't answer on his cell phone or at his apartment. She waited a beat, released a shaky breath and dialed the police station.

The desk sergeant sounded harassed but not unkind. "Riker's on assignment, ma'am. Do you want someone else?"

She considered the alternative. "Rudy Brown?"

He chuckled. "The old sarge. Sorry again, ma'am, but he retired two years ago."

Devon froze. "Are you…?" Yes, of course he was sure. "Thank you, sergeant. I'll—try him at home."

She hung up, her hand strangling the receiver column. Had Riker mentioned that his partner was retired? Could cops be reactivated for special duty?

Shivering slightly, she found Rudy's number.

A groggy female voice answered on the fifth ring. "Hello?"

Devon twined the cord around her fingers. "Yes, I'm trying to reach Rudy Brown. Or Detective Riker," she added as an afterthought.

"Detective who?" The woman yawned.

"Joel Riker."

"Know the name, not the…uh…right. Joel. Sorry." She cleared her throat. "Rudy's not here right now. Can I take a message?"

Torn, Devon gave in to her nerves. "Look, I'm awfully sorry to bother you, but I need to find him. Is he…" how to put this. "Do you know if he's involved in a police investigation at the moment?"

The pause was drawn out. "I couldn't really say," the woman told her. "He's a cop down to his toes, if that means anything. Hey, your voice sounds familiar. Do I know you?"

"I'm Devon Tremayne."

"Really? Fancy that." The woman gave a delighted laugh. "Rudy said he'd met you."

"Did he?" A click like a pencil sharply snapped had her whipping her head around. Devon's eyes combed the fluttering shadows. "Has Rudy spoken to you about my—me?"

Another laugh. "He said you knocked his socks off when he saw you up close. 'She's as beautiful as she sounds on her show,' he told me. Which is a helluva compliment coming from Rude. I think he might be with Ja—uh, somebody else tonight." She rushed on as Devon made another uneasy sweep of the area, "I'll tell him to call you, if you want. My name's Mandy, by the way. I listen to your show every day. It makes me feel good."

"Thanks." Devon wished she felt good right then. "Have him call my apartment, okay? I'm at the radio station right now, but I'll be out of here in less than ten minutes."

"I'll pass that on," Mandy promised. She sounded almost as jumpy as Devon felt. Unless her nerves were impeding her judgment.

Devon hung up and turned, running clammy palms down the legs of her black pants. She hated feeling scared like this, but so many things had happened to her lately. And the clock was ticking inexorably toward midnight. If that meant anything to the murderer. No one really seemed to know. He'd killed his first four victims at midnight and the last three at any hour that apparently struck his fancy.

Certain her heart was going to knock out a rib, Devon sought the nearest sanctuary; the broadcast booth and Tim Woodrow who worked the 10:00 p.m. to 2:00 a.m. shift.

She smelled hot coffee when she poked her head inside, but there was no Tim. He often lined up anywhere from thirty minutes to an hour of uninterrupted music when he went on-air. Whatever the time frame, his microphone was dead, his chair cool and empty. So much for companionship.

The tension knots in Devon's stomach cinched the longer she prowled the booth. This was ridiculous. Who knew when Tim would return? She needed to get out of here and go home.

Muscles taut, she started for her office. She should try Riker's cell phone again. It would calm her jitters to hear his voice. Forget questions and vague mistrust. She would tackle the Rudy question later, when every pulse in her body wasn't clamoring to drown out its nearest neighbor.

Visions of Andrew's sickly smile flashed like a neon sign in her head. She heard his whirring dentist's drill and shuddered deeply.

Then Warren's face appeared to leer at her. Overlapping that, she saw Jimmy's whipped-puppy expression after she'd reproached him this afternoon. Even a picture of Brando crawled in, his face gray and bloated, followed by Tanya sobbing brokenly on her shoulder.

Finally, over all those things, another image emerged, a shadowy figure, indefinite but sinister. It was…

Devon halted, her breathing suspended. The darkness seemed to close in, a tangible force, suffocating in its stillness. Had she seen that last thing or imagined it?

She grappled with the lump in her throat. Imagined it, surely. Shadows could form shapes at will, and heaven knew her nerves were zinging at this moment.

Even so, Devon's heart continued to race. Her eyes darted about, scouring the most obscure corners. It was darker here than in the central corridors, the price she paid for being out of the heavy traffic zone. Tiny lights twinkled ahead, but only a limited number. Fireflies would have been as effective in the late-night murk.

She still had Andrew's note balled in her fist, Devon realized. Add to that a host of images too gruesome to dwell on and she'd be running in a minute; back the way she'd come.

She was alone; she needed to believe that. If the shadows shifted, it was because open doors led to unshaded windows, and the city moved beyond the studio walls, especially at Christmas time.

Her office lay directly ahead. A pool of golden light spilled into the hallway. "Thank heaven," Devon whispered. Her pent-up breath rushed out. She pressed a palm to her fluttering stomach, and actually managed a shaky laugh. Ghosts and goblins. She'd listened to too many fairy tales as a child.

Her footsteps steadied as she neared the comforting light of her office. At least here she could recover for a few minutes, close the door, lock it, and make a quick...

The thought vanished with an icy tink, like broken crystal. She stopped dead, as terror formed a hard, black fist in her stomach.

Her office door was open. She always extinguished the lights when she left, then closed the door behind her. Always!

Backing up a pace, she spun and prepared to bolt.

"Devon..."

She whirled again, breathing in frightened spurts. She knew at once that it was a mistake, but she tended to respond on instinct, even, apparently, in a desperate state of mind.

He stood for a split second, illuminated, a prophetic figure wearing a ski mask and a bulky black coat that skimmed the muted honey carpet. In that brief instant, Devon received a fleeting impression of height—taller than her by a few inches—followed by a menace greater than anything she'd previously envisioned.

He moved with lightning speed, snatching a knife from his

pocket and holding it in such a way that the blade gleamed brilliant gold.

"A different present this time, Devon," he promised, raspy-voiced. "Like the very first time. One thrust of gold through the heart. A merciful death for you. A nightmare just begun for the other pretender. Rebirth and hope for me. Goodbye again, Angela."

The knife flashed. His muscles twitched as he raised both his arms. "Let this be the last time I must kill you!"

Chapter Nine

"Yeah, I killed her. Did all seven of 'em. Voices on the radio's what they were, talking to me, calling to me, telling me they wanted me. But they didn't really want me. They made fun of me behind my back. Women always do that. Said I was nothing and they were the angels of the airwaves."

Blue cigar smoke spiraled around the two-dimensional face of Casey Coombes, confessed Christmas Murderer. Jacob straddled a hard-backed chair in his apartment, elbows on the table, half a bottle of beer positioned between his cupped palms. Rudy's cop friend, Dugan, noticed his disgusted expression and removed the cigar from his mouth.

"Don't sweat it, Jacob. Life's full of Casey Coombes's. Little minds twisted like pretzels. Brains no bigger than baby peas."

"He didn't do it, Dugan."

The big cop let out a gusty sigh. As far as he was concerned, Jacob was Rudy's nephew, period. He might not follow the book to the letter, but impersonating a fellow officer would be too big a stretch even for him. "Yeah, right. Coombes didn't do it." His tone was ripe with sarcasm. "He only confessed, was only cognizant of every damned detail in the case."

From the sofa, Rudy gave a quiet snort. "People have hacked into police files before, Dugan. And Coombes had a truckload of computer equipment in that trashy basement apartment of his."

His uncle's remarks both surprised and oddly disturbed Jacob. In a strange sort of way, it had been a balm to think that Rudy believed in Dugan's copycat theory, though it didn't make Devon's situation any less deadly. Controlling a shudder, he finished off the lukewarm beer and returned his attention to the TV screen.

"Laura. Oh, yeah," Coombes slathered his tongue over her name. "What a babe she was. Abigail, Dina, Jennifer, Bonnie, Susan, Marilyn—all babes." His face contorted. "They said they loved me. But they didn't."

For an almost convincing actor, the man was a pathetic specimen of humanity. Skinny, gangly, with wire-rimmed spectacles positioned in front of bulgy blue eyes, hardly a strand of hair on his head, and what remained of it on the sides was the color of dirty dishwater. Even Coombes's teeth were crooked; they gave him the look of a shocked ferret.

Dugan rapped the stack of photocopied case files for attention. "It's all right here, boys. In these folders and on that video tape. The victims were broadcast personalities, whether they did the news, had talk shows or spun disks. You heard the guy. They talked to him. Talked but didn't care, didn't love. No love, no life. We've had kinkier M.O.'s."

Jacob cocked a dark brow and shifted his eyes to the screen. "What made him start killing?"

"What makes any serial killer start? The guy snapped. Could be he knew Laura West..." Sucking on his upper lip, Dugan cast both men a rueful glance. "Okay, fine. He didn't know Laura. At least we never connected him to her, but she was the first. We went through every strangulation case in the country prior to her death and came up empty."

Rudy made a sound like an irritable snort. "Facts are facts, Dugan. Devon was attacked."

"A crime you want me to investigate on the sly without her or the department knowing about it. Fine," he held up a hand in surrender. "I agreed to do old Rudy a favor. But if you want official action, you'll have to call it in. Officially.

Hell, at least you could call Helmsford or Boyd or Riker. They worked on the damned case. Rude, you and I were just background players, barely got a sniff of it over our way.''

Jacob considered cracking another of Rudy's beers but decided against it. He was having enough trouble keeping his mind off Devon. A few more swigs and he'd wind up sleepless and hungry, fighting the kind of sexual urges he hadn't experienced since college. Maybe not even then.

Dugan planted a meaty fist in Jacob's punching bag. ''You know Riker, Jacob. Why not pick his brains? He's on leave in New York, probably tearing out his hair by now.''

Jacob refocused on Coombes. ''Family problems?'' he asked absently.

''Don't see how he could avoid it, coming from a family of ten.''

''Twelve,'' Jacob corrected automatically. One thing he knew was the real Riker's background. Joel had been adopted into a brood of siblings at the age of thirteen, mere months before his mother had overdosed on barbiturates. All of them had been adopted by a well-meaning couple who, currently in their sixties, couldn't always cope with the antics of the teenagers still in their care.

Dugan slanted him a contemplative look through a veil of smoke rings. ''What's your take on this Devon Tremayne thing, Jacob? You can't be in this deep because of Laura. Are you involved with her?''

Jacob's eyes came up, dark and unreadable. ''And if I were?''

The other man shrugged. ''Then I'd say you're treading in dangerous water. Whoever's behind these attacks isn't likely to look favorably on you.''

Curious by nature, Jacob tipped his head. ''You think I'd be a target?''

''It's almost a sure bet you've got a crazed fan out there, man. You know the type. They sit in some stuffy little room, hear a voice that turns them on and start to fantasize. Only this particular guy's not like you and me. He doesn't stop at fantasy. He wants, he needs, but he knows he won't get. So he sends gifts and notes.''

"And angel food cakes," Rudy muttered.

Dugan curled his lip. "He's unoriginal in this case. He goes for something that's been done before. It's Christmas, why not use one of Philly's most notorious crimes to punish the object of his desire?''

There was a certain logic in that idea, but Jacob's gut instincts still resisted the pat answer.

A soft knock on the door had him cutting the video and leaving a sitcom to blare through the VCR.

"Have a beer, Dugan," he suggested, nudging a drop cloth aside so the cop could sit. "And try not to scowl."

He opened the door to Hannah, who was wearing an antique lace robe and dainty nightgown. Too Victorian for Devon, perfect for her gentle-natured sister.

She glanced past him, saw he had company and twisted her fingers. "I didn't mean to interrupt."

Her stance indicated that she wanted him to join her in the hall. Jacob obliged, pulling the door shut behind him as a claw of fear scratched at his stomach. "Is it about Devon?" he asked carefully. "Has anything happened?"

She fidgeted with her braid. "I hope not. It's just—I can't reach her. She isn't downstairs, and she's not answering her office telephone. It's a direct line at night. The operator leaves at ten o'clock." Hannah worried her bottom lip. "I've been talking with my mother for most of the night. Devon and I have two younger sisters. I gather Daria wants to dye her hair green.''

A voice from the past ricocheted through Jacob's head. Laura's petulant voice challenging, "What's wrong with blue streaks? They were free and they're guaranteed to wash out."

But a missing twenty-dollar bill from Jacob's dresser, added to the fact that five washings later the streaks were as blue as ever, had exposed those lies. Jacob shoved the unwelcome memory aside. "When was the last time you tried calling, Hannah?''

"Right before I came up here.''

"Could she be in another part of the building?"

"Possibly." Hannah rubbed chilled hands over her fore-arms. "But I don't think so. I have…a feeling, I guess you'd call it." Her large eyes launched a more than credible appeal. "I think something's wrong. Devon knows I worry about her. She'd have called you if she couldn't get through to me."

Jacob's brows drew together. His cell phone was in his car and— "Damn!" He scrunched his eyes closed. "I unplugged it."

"Excuse me?"

"My apartment phone. I was painting yesterday. I un-plugged it." With an urgency that felt suspiciously close to desperation, he turned Hannah around. "Go downstairs and call her again. Keep calling. I'll drive to the station. If you reach her, contact me on my cell. You have the number, right?"

He felt her tremble. "You're worried, too, aren't you?"

What could he say? "I won't take chances where Devon's life is concerned." He ushered her to the staircase, nudged her forward. "I'll be on my way in less than sixty seconds."

"Riker…" Hannah's fingers gripped his wrist with equal amounts of fright and love.

To Jacob's amazement, he understood the silent message. Threads of panic twined around the knowledge that he'd do anything to ensure Devon's safety.

"She'll be fine," he said, grim-faced. "That bastard won't get her. Not if I have to kill him to stop him."

"You've been listening to a double shot of Sting. Before that, it was Elton John, 'Can You Feel the Love.' You're surfing the Wave with Tim Woodrow. It's a chilly seventeen degrees outside our studio.…"

Devon heard the promo through a stilted layer of terror. She'd give anything she possessed to be outside the studio right now, seventeen chilly degrees notwithstanding.

The man before her kept his knife poised. She didn't know why or for how long. The seconds dragged on interminably. She couldn't think, forgot to breathe. Then a beam of light sliced along the sharp edge of the blade, and miraculously, her paralysis shattered.

Swallowing a scream, Devon plunged backward and sideways, a diagonal move her attacker had apparently not anticipated.

The knife slashed downward with a whoosh that brought a spurt of blood to her mind's eye. Her blood unless she could think of a way to escape.

He'd hesitated, she was sure of it. Maybe he didn't like blood. He'd strangled his first seven victims, would have strangled her at the restaurant if she hadn't gotten lucky and collided with the valet.

Shoving off from the wall, she ran for the nearest stairwell. She heard his long stride on the carpet behind her, the angry breath that rushed in and out of his lungs.

He sounded out of shape. Warren, she wondered muzzily? Or was agitation affecting his ability to breathe properly? Whatever the case, he charged with the ferocity of an enraged bull.

"Angela...!"

His tormented wail jangled across her nerve ends. Be calm, think, she ordered herself. She had to outwit him. It was her only chance.

Unable to calculate distances properly, Devon caught the lobby desk with her fingertips and used it to take the ninety-degree corner without skidding. Her eyes scoured the gloomy corridor, but registered little except imaginary impressions of the person chasing her.

Knife with a golden blade. Gold Christmas angel pendant. A single stab wound through her heart. And someone called Angela....

Devon raced along the corridor, panting. A red Exit sign caught her eye to her right. She dove into the niche, kicked the door open, hesitated, then continued on her original straight path. The door clanged shut as she ducked into an ancillary corridor.

Please use the exit, she prayed, too terrified to check. If

he took the bait, he'd be barreling down the stairs in a moment. If not—she gave a shudder of pure dread.

Another door loomed on the far end wall. She'd have to use this one. Heaven help her if it was stuck, or locked, or whatever other glitches happened to emergency exits.

She shot forward, depressing the bar as silently as possible. It clicked at the last second, and with a single terrified glance behind her, she plunged into the dusky stairwell.

Fourteen steps down, then fourteen more and another fourteen. Catching the rail at the bottom, she pivoted and plunged, again and again and again. How many floors remained? Fifteen? Ten? The station was located on twenty-seven. Her legs had turn to rubber, her lungs were on the verge of bursting. Surely she'd gone down more than a dozen flights by now.

The metal treads echoed under her feet, clanging loud enough to wake the dead. Devon shut that thought out and continued running. Was it Andrew? Warren? Who else might have lingered tonight? Roscoe? Jimmy?

Her calves ached. A cramp shot through her side. A frightened sob climbed into her throat. She needed to slow down, couldn't slow down. How many flights left to ground?

Fragments of light cast stark shadows on the walls. Her vision blurred.

Out of nowhere, a pair of hands emerged to clamp around her waist. Devon yelped and began to buck as they hauled her back onto the landing and hard up against a lean male body.

"Devon, it's me. Ja—Riker."

Unbelieving, she spun, muscles rigid, eyes wide with residual panic. "Riker?" She croaked his name, stared, then touched his shadowed face to be sure.

He gave her only that split second to reassure herself before his arms came around her in a crushing grip. He pressed his face into her scented hair, knew his heart was racing twice as fast as hers right then.

"I saw you flying down the corridor upstairs." His voice was low and rough, muffled by her hair and emotions too complex to analyze. "I shouted, but you didn't answer." His grip tightened. "I thought he had hurt you."

She made no attempt to free herself. "Did he—did you see him?"

"No. I only saw you and only for a second."

A panicky tremor she didn't bother to hide zinged through her. "He was going to stab me. One quick thrust through the heart, he said. He had—oh, Riker. He had a knife with a long golden blade and a design on the hilt."

"A what?" Jacob stopped his rhythmic stroking of her hair.

"A knife with some kind of pearl handle with a gold figure stamped on it. I thought—" she paused, aware of a change in him. Her head came up. "What?"

"Nothing." Easing her cheek back onto his shoulder, Jacob kissed her temple. "You're safe. That's all that matters."

But in his heart he knew that wasn't all, and it most certainly wasn't nothing.

Visions wafted up unbidden. Bony fingers lovingly caressing first a golden blade, then an elegant pearl handle. *This came all the way from Ireland, boy. See the harp. That's their symbol. Belonged to my Ewen's Great-Great-Uncle Ewen. Old Ewen stole it from what's-his-name, that underling of Lord Pirrie's, after the little twirp fired him from Pirrie's ship-building company. The twirp had called old Ewen a thief, threatened to tell Pirrie himself, but sent him packing instead two weeks after work started on the* Titanic. *Old Ewen hated that man, decided to get even. He broke into the guy's home, stole his money, his wife's jewels, this knife and a bottle of champagne for good measure."* Her cackle rang out, rich with malice. *"I always said that's what sank the poor* Titanic. *Old Ewen swiped the champagne that should have been used to christen her. Then, to add insult to injury, old Ewen posed as an Irish privy councillor and sailed to the States on the* Lusitania. *The knife's all that's left, boy, but what a trophy it is. It'll be Laura's in the end, of course....*

"Riker?"

Jacob heard the puzzlement in Devon's voice, laced with the remnants of fear that had yet to abate.

"It's okay." He focused on her rather than on the anger, resentment and uncertainty that rolled greasily in his stomach. His dark eyes rose to the upper landing. His lips thinned. "I'm going to find that piece of slime and make him pay for what he's done to you."

JACOB DID NOT find him. Nor did he harbor any illusions about how the next scene would play out. He'd inform Dugan of the attack. When the cops arrived, either Devon would call him Riker, and Dugan would expose him as a fraud, or Dugan would call him Jacob, and Devon would discover the deception. Any way he looked at it, she'd be furious and rightly so.

On the other hand, she'd also be alive, which was the most important point. He'd try to remember that while she was scratching his eyes out.

After giving security Dugan's number, Jacob took Devon up to her office to wait. He wanted desperately to hold her. But if he allowed himself that luxury, she'd only wind up angrier in the end, and he would be that much more torn apart inside.

"Okay, people, search the building." Dugan made his entrance fifteen minutes later, notepad in hand, wool coat flapping. A harassed Rudy had slipped in five minutes earlier.

One glimpse of the cop's broad Irish face and Jacob knew he'd been made. No doubt he could thank Rudy for delivering the early bombshell.

Devon sat on the sofa, clutching a steaming coffee mug in her icy hands. Jacob paced silently behind her. Damn, he wished he could touch. Instead, he jammed his fists into his pockets and waited with a fatalistic air for Dugan to make his move.

"Ms. Tremayne?" The cop shot Jacob a cutting glare, then perched on the parquet table in front of her. "I'm Detective Dugan from homicide. Riker and I—" another deadly glare "—work together on occasion."

Rudy's bushy brows went up a mile. Jacob narrowed his gaze and wisely held his tongue.

"You were attacked tonight, Ms. Tremayne. Can you tell me anything about the perpetrator?"

She drew a deep breath. "He was wearing a long black coat, wool, I think, a ski mask and thin leather gloves. He threatened me with a knife. I ran."

Jacob saw her head drop forward and went to his haunches behind her. With the knuckles of his right hand he massaged the tight muscles at the nape of her neck.

She summoned a ghost of a smile before she continued. "I went through the east-end fire door; I'm not sure how far down I got before Riker grabbed me." Her breath blew tiredly out. Her head dropped back this time. "I thought it was the man who attacked me at first, but I gather he went down another staircase."

"We're checking the building now," Dugan told her. His gaze curled upward. So did his lip. "What about you, Riker? Did you see anything?"

"Only Devon streaking past."

"We've got something, sir." One of the uniformed officers entered, carrying a long black coat and a bag containing other articles of black clothing and a gold-bladed knife with a pearl handle. Rudy frowned. Jacob didn't bother; he simply sighed at the inevitability of fate and shifted his knuckles higher on Devon's neck. At least her tension was ebbing.

Dugan examined the bag, then held the items for Devon's inspection. "Is this the knife, Ms. Tremayne?"

"It looks like it."

"And the coat?"

"Yes."

Dugan glanced at the officer. "Take them downstairs and label them. Anything else?"

"Colby saw a man near the garbage chute five minutes before we found these things in the basement dumpster. We have him outside."

"Bring him in."

Devon leaned back. "It's probably Tim." She sounded exhausted. "He's on-air until 2:00 a.m."

Momentarily distracted by the texture of her hair and skin and the lovely, soft curve of her cheek beneath the bright office lights, Jacob let his fingers linger unmoving. Exquisite, he thought, then snapped out of it and tilted a surprised brow as Roscoe Beale was escorted in.

"Knock it off, will you?" Roscoe snatched his arm free and scowled at the trio before him. "What's going on, Devon? I pitch a McDonald's wrapper, and suddenly I'm a criminal?"

"There were a dozen McDonald's cups and wrappers in the dumpster," Colby confirmed. "One of them could have been his."

"Was his," Roscoe stated sullenly.

Jacob caught his attention with a faint movement of his head. "What are you doing here so late, Beale?"

"Working. Is that a problem?"

"Where are your shoes and tie?" Dugan inquired, making notes.

"I—"

Jacob ran a considering finger under his bottom lip. "Your hair's out of place. It's not your usual style."

"Look, I don't—"

"How tall are you?"

"Six feet. Does it matter?"

"The height's right," Jacob said to Dugan. "But I don't think he'd be stupid enough to ditch his paraphernalia in a garbage chute in plain sight of a uniformed cop." At Dugan's thinned lips, he shrugged. "Just an opinion. Why is your hair messed up, Roscoe?"

The man's shoulders slumped. "I was—exercising."

"While chowing down on a Big Mac?" Dugan sounded skeptical, but he let the question ride as he jotted another quick note in his book.

Twenty tedious minutes later, he wrapped up with a slap of the leather cover. "That'll do for now, folks. We'll leave a few men here tonight to finish checking things out. You can go, Mr. Beale, just not too far at present, hmm?'' His voice gruffed up. "You taking Ms. Tremayne home... Riker?''

Jacob matched his level stare. ''Unless you need her at the station.''

''No, but you and I need to have a nice long chat.'' Dugan's smile had all the earmarks of a shark preparing to chow down. ''Say, first thing tomorrow morning?''

''Your office.'' Jacob climbed to his feet. He was so knotted up at this point that even the smallest movement hurt. Taking Devon by the hand, he drew her off the sofa. ''Come on. You look all in.''

Dugan made an unintelligible sound in his throat and strode over to where Rudy had been standing silently the entire time. ''Tomorrow—Riker,'' he barked over his shoulder.

Devon offered Jacob a tired smile. ''If we're lucky, the sun'll come out.''

He removed her coat from its peg and helped her into it. ''Did I miss something?''

''It's a song concept from Annie.'' A shiver enveloped her. She glanced at the muddied blackness beyond the window. ''Something tells me it's more likely to snow tomorrow.''

It would for him, Jacob thought, recalling the knife that had been found downstairs. But not for Devon, not if he could help it.

A bleak sense of doom slithered into his mind. It had bony fingers and a jackal's bitter smile. It wore black and wielded a weapon it had no business possessing. No business and with only one possible purpose. Whoever the hell he was, the Christmas Murderer wanted him to take the fall for Devon's death.

Chapter Ten

Devon dreamed that Riker not only put her to bed, but actually slid between the rose-colored sheets with her. Then, by red-and-white candlelight, he made slow, erotic love to her until the first shadowy threads of dawn crept over the windowsill.

He drove her home, that was no dream. He reassured Hannah, brewed a perfect pot of chamomile tea and only looked dangerous when she emerged from the bathroom clad in a voluminous white flannel nightgown. It should have been virginal and utterly unprovocative. She'd chosen it strictly for comfort. But from the glint that appeared in his dark eyes, she might have been clad in a black lace bra with sheer stockings and her skimpiest pair of bikini briefs.

Instead, folds of flannel enshrouded her in a cocoon which did little to combat the dreadful flashes of memory pummeling her. However, while the gleam in Jacob's eyes didn't steady her nerves, better a gleam of desire than one of torment and madness.

She shuddered free of the macabre recollections, sipped her tea under Riker's watchful gaze, and in the end didn't possess sufficient energy to offer even a token resistance when he ordered her to snuggle into the overstuffed feather pillows.

She wanted to stay awake. She felt Riker brush the hair from her forehead, thought—hoped—that he really did feather a light kiss across her brow. But that could have been her imagination....

She tumbled like a child exhausted from a day of hard play, into a fluffy cloud of dreams. Soothing at first, the fall took a last-second detour into a nightmare. Luckily, she wrenched free of those sleeping images. Awake and perspiring, she spotted Riker sprawled in an armchair, looking rumpled and sexy in a fitful drowse. Pleased and strangely comforted, she took a second tumble into a much more intriguing dreamscape....

Riker's body was slick in her night fantasy. Lithely muscled in the manner of a jungle cat. Predator as opposed to prey. He closed the door on Detective Dugan's scowl of displeasure, took her by the hands and led her away from the obvious horror.

"Ave Maria" played harp-sweet and poignant in the wood-smoked air. He hadn't shaved, but his hair felt damp. The ends of it skimmed over the heated flesh of her shoulders as he lowered his mouth to hers.

He tasted of sex and sin and risk. Blood throbbed in her veins. The vibrations that started deep in her stomach spread slowly to the rest of her body. Desire brought a shiver of anticipation to her skin. And yet...

Devon sensed a stone wall between them. Invisible, perhaps beginning to crumble, but tangible enough to her mind that she was reluctant to stray too close.

Questions lurked as they always did, below the level of consciousness for the most part, but every once in a while they bobbed to the surface.

Where had Riker come from tonight? Where had her attacker gone? What about those two earlier occasions, in her office and at the Holly Tree. Where had he been then?

Ah, but where had anybody been?

She soothed her rising fear with that question. She avoided the unpleasant possibilities of the others—or tried to.

The dream resumed its assault on her battered senses.

Devon's heart swelled as she absorbed Riker's hungry

kisses. Could she be in love with him? No. Almost, but love couldn't happen until the wall broke down and she caught at least a glimpse of his other side.

Was that asking too much? Was it a cop thing to erect walls? A survival technique? If so, was it fair for her to tear it down? Did love require learning every secret?

The dream began to dissolve. Nothing to do but let it go. Clouds seeped in, black and threatening. Edged with purple, as if by a winter storm.

Something flashed gold in her mind. The angel pendant. Except the angel held a knife aimed directly at her heart.

Blood spilled onto her white gown. "So ends your ninth life, cat," a man's horribly familiar voice rasped. But he didn't say "cat," he said, "Devon". Then he held the knife up and called her Angela, shouted the name Angela at her as he gave chase.

One scene bled into another, primary colors melting in the rain.

Detective Dugan strode in, a brawny Irishman with frizzy red hair and broad features. She thought he liked Riker deep down, but he'd sniped at him in the aftermath of the attack. Riker had reacted with smoldering silence. He was good at that, Devon decided. Rudy had simply stared at the floor. Very peculiar all around.

Dream voices droned in her head, but always it was Riker's face she saw, troubled and brooding, staring at her, through her, resolved, he swore, to stop a madman. Oh, yes, she did almost love him.

So why, she wondered, as black storm clouds bubbled and boiled on the fringes of her sleeping thoughts, did his face continue to superimpose itself over a wall of fractured stone…?

RUDY STRODE into his old precinct the same way he had in the past, eyes down, ears alert, twitchy fingers jingling the loose change in his pants' pockets. The usual babble surrounded him, talk of boozers and junkies, pimps and porno kings. Three people murdered on a South Side street corner. Big robbery in Germantown. None of their concern here, but nice to know the snobs had problems, too. Internal affairs had been nosing around lately. Two guns had gone missing, along with a mink coat, a box of Cuban cigars and a quantity of designer drug.

Rudy snorted to himself. Designer drug be damned. Call it heroin and be done with it. As for the Cuban cigars, empty a few pockets and sock tops on the way out, boys. Cuban puffs were hard to come by and the best money could buy, law permitting.

"Right turn, Rude."

Dugan stood like General Patton at the top of a dingy corridor, feet straddled, beefy fists planted on his hips. His suit was shiny in spots, a dreary dark gray with two cigar-shaped bulges in the jacket pockets. Rudy smothered a snicker and turned.

"No excuses," Dugan warned. "Interrogation room one. No interruptions," he added to the desk sergeant.

The door had barely clicked shut before Dugan blasted forward to slap his palms on the tabletop. "Is he crazy, impersonating one of mine?"

"Ours."

"Don't get smart—or technical. You're not part of us, anymore, and Jacob never was."

"He made a few rounds with Riker."

"Years ago; limited rounds, and only because the old captain admired his grit. I hate grit, and I hate reporters even more."

"Jacob's more than a reporter."

"Yeah, right. He bought the *Beat*. But deep down he's still a reporter on the scent of a hot story." He straightened, fingers splayed. "Okay, I don't have a problem with that. But steal Riker's name, rank and badge number? Damned straight there's a problem. Bottom line, Rudy: he backs off now, or I bust him for fraud."

"He's doing it for Laura, Dugan."

"Like hell." He stalked to the far wall, pivoted. "Maybe that's how it started, but Laura's long gone. He's doing it for Devon Tremayne, whether he—or you—realize that."

Rudy's mouth opened, then slowly closed. How could a man argue what was so obviously true. "I'll pass the message on," he promised. "But tell me the scuttlebutt. Is anyone talking Christmas Murderer, yet?"

Dugan's lips clamped.

"Figured as much. Coombes is still the man."

"We'll investigate, Rudy. Devon Tremayne was attacked, no one doubts that. But I've got a question for you." His stare burned into Rudy's. "Why did you agree to help Jacob with this idiotic scheme? You weren't so fond of Laura that you'd be hellbent on turning over every clue searching for flaws."

Rudy looked away. "I'm fond of Jacob, Dugan."

"Fond of, or worried about?" Sensing he'd struck a nerve, Dugan prodded further. "Maybe you think he's a little too obsessed about this guy, huh? Maybe you wonder why he's so insistent that we're wrong and he's right. Say Coombes didn't do it. Maybe Jacob knows something the rest of us don't." Insinuating red brows lanced upward. "Like who the Christmas Murderer really is."

"I DON'T LOVE HER," Jacob muttered as he tore into yet another cardboard box. "This is for Laura. It has to be."

But it wasn't, and both his heart and his intellect knew it.

He swore volubly as he yanked the last item from the box. No knife. No surprise either, and no damned way he could do a thing about it.

"What's all this?" A world-weary Rudy stepped over several lids and a wad of packing material. "You said you needed to go through the stuff in storage; you didn't tell me you were going to use a vandal's tactics. Why the mess?"

Jacob blew out an exasperated breath and, from his knees, shook the long hair from his eyes. "The knife's gone, Rudy."

"Which knife?" Rudy's hand froze halfway to his face as comprehension dawned. "Ewen's? Jesus, Jacob."

Feeling surly, Jacob climbed to his feet and tossed down a burlap wrapper. "It was here when Laura died. I packed everything Ida'd already given her. He stole the knife deliberately, Rudy. Whoever he is, he's done his homework on me; which is to say, he knows I'm not Riker."

"Dugan warned you, Jacob. So did I. You're in a fine mess now, kid. Dugan's hopping. He'll keep mum, but only if you back off. Now, today, this minute."

Jacob slid his uncle a lethal stare, "Back off and let Devon die? Wind up in prison on a frame?"

"You don't know..."

"Dammit, Rudy, he wants her dead. The knife's gone. I admit, it probably can't be linked to me since it was stolen to begin with—unless my prints happen to be on it—but that doesn't alter the attempted frame. I can't back off. I won't."

"I figured as much." Rudy kicked at a patch of straw on the plank floor. "So, how's Devon?"

"She's fine. She's strong. A team of mules couldn't have kept her from working today."

"You being that team, I suppose."

Jacob cursed and picked up a slatted lid. "He'd have killed her, Rudy. Stabbed her through the heart with my knife." He paused, sidetracked. "That's out of character."

"She's lucky. A cat with nine lives," Rudy remarked sagely. "Isn't that what he called her?"

"Something like that. Cats have nine lives. Seven women are dead. And—" he frowned. What had Devon told him? Someone called Angela. "Do you remember an Angela, Rudy?"

His uncle patted his plaid shirt in search of a cigarette. "Doesn't ring a bell. Could bear out Dugan's copycat theory, though."

Jacob's lashes lowered in thought. "It could also mean that he murdered someone before Laura."

"Not as part of the Christmas Murders. That angle was pushed, poked and prodded until dead."

Jacob sighed. "Four of them killed at midnight. You made reference to that last week."

"Did I?" No particular emotion registered on Rudy's face. "Don't remember it."

"You said we should pray for a midnight clear. When Devon was attacked at the Holly Tree, the murderer used the tune 'It Came Upon a Midnight Clear.'"

"Yeah, I know. He's used it from the start."

"I went through my clippings, Rudy. That song wasn't mentioned in any of the articles."

His uncle inspected a figurine. "Police have to hold back a few secrets, kid."

Jacob digested that, let none of his niggling doubts show in his expression. "Riker never mentioned it to me."

"But then you're not a cop, are you?"

"No." A portion of Jacob's tension eased. "No. Why that song, Rudy? Did anyone ever ask Coombes?"

"Yeah. He took the question in stride, like all the others. Angels in the song; angels on the airwaves. Said it just came to him, the connection."

"Bull."

"Judge didn't think so. Prosecutors should've tried to trick him. They should have asked him about 'Hark the Herald Angels Sing.' If he didn't do it, and he'd answered the same way, they'd have had him. I don't think anyone was looking too hard to break his story. Confessions are a bugger."

Satisfied, Jacob stared unseeingly at the floor. His mind wheeled and dove like a hungry seagull. When it dove to a picture of Devon in her white nightgown, however, he yanked it back. He did *not* love her, dammit. It was only his conscience that compelled him to check on her before she left the studio.

"You got a smoke?" Rudy demanded grumpily, turning out his pants' pockets.

Jacob regarded the mess of bric-a-brac, household goods,

books and clothing as he tugged on his leather jacket. "You quit, Rudy. If you need to keep your hands busy, you can repack these boxes. If not, I'll get Ben and Sadie to do it tomorrow."

Rudy's canny eyes gleamed. "Slow days at the *Beat*."

"I'm overstaffed, but—" he shrugged "—it's Christmas."

The gleam dulled. "You're right, boy. He's setting you up. Like it or not, we have to deal with that. But the impersonation's got to stop. You've been walking in a minefield for too long. It was bound to blow sooner or later."

Zipping up, Jacob waded through the chaos to his uncle's side. He hesitated only slightly before replying. "I might—" His jaw tensed. "I'll tell her the truth."

Was that relief in the older man's eyes? Hell, after a chat with Dugan, Rudy probably considered his own nephew a suspect in the case. And why not? Hadn't he, somewhere in his gut, suspected Rudy?

"Truth's always best, Jacob," his uncle grunted. "She called the police station last night, you know. Dugan told me. Asked for Riker first, then me."

"Terrific," Jacob pulled on his gloves. "I'll give her my gun. She can shoot both of us at the same time."

But guns and bullets were the very last things on his mind as he jogged across the snowy city parking lot five minutes later. He had a name in his head and a question that had been nagging at him almost as persistently as his feelings for Devon. If not a Christmas murder victim, then who the hell was Angela?

"I HAD THE information sent, my dear. These are police facts, not national secrets." Armed with a file of faxes, Alma plunked her ample backside next to Devon's on the older woman's office sofa. "Here's a summary of all seven Christmas Murder cases. The victims worked in radio broadcasting as you know. All were under thirty and quite pretty." She made a huffy sound. "Trust a man to look for youth and beauty in a female he intends to kill."

On a late lunch break from Hare and Woden, Hannah glanced at her sister. Devon responded with a small shrug of acceptance. Best to let Alma blow off her excess steam, then they could all get back to work.

Closing an eye, Alma jabbed a finger at Hannah who was biting into her egg salad sandwich. "I had words with Roscoe this morning. That young man has a great deal to answer for. I should be told when he plans to work late."

"Maybe he told Warren," Devon suggested, while Hannah, suspended mid-munch, looked from her to Alma and back again. "Warren was home all evening, I assume."

Alma bristled. She did that, Devon noticed, whenever she defended her brother. Defended as in lied for?

"He came straight home," Alma said shortly. "I don't remember the time, but he left here right after I phoned him at ten o'clock. I soak in the tub from ten until eleven o'clock. I'm quite nit-picky about that."

"Did you see him come in?" Hannah's tentative question brought a smile to Devon's lips. She bit it back at her employer's aggravated expression.

Alma slapped the summary sheet onto Devon's lap. "I didn't ask you here to discuss my brother. He admires your sister's radio voice, nothing more sinister than that."

"I wasn't implying…"

"Oh, yes you were, Hannah dear, and with reason." She breathed to steady her voice. "But Warren is no more a killer than I am."

"Or Rudy," Devon added. "I gather he was with Detective Dugan when Hannah spoke to Jacob." Assuming, of course that that meant anything in a world of approximate times, fast transportation, and shortcuts.

Alma pursed her lips. "People occasionally hire other people to do their dirty work." She waved a dismissing hand before Devon could protest. "Ignore me. I'm feeling crotchety today. I care about you, dear, that's all. As men go, Rudy's a diamond in the rough, Roscoe's a question mark and Riker's a sexpot. Don't splutter, Devon. He is. But back to business.'' She tapped the summary. ''As you see, the victims worked for four different stations in the Philadelphia area. Before it was the Wave, this station was WPAX, a—'' she shuddered ''—country station. The second victim did the weekend news and weather for them. Thankfully, Warren and I came down from New York a year later.'' She emphasized the time frame. ''We made an offer to the cowboys, were accepted and ventured into light rock.''

''Mmm.'' Devon caught her meaning, despite only half-listening. She ran her finger over the first victim's name. ''It says here that Laura West was an heiress.''

''A twice-married heiress,'' Alma supplemented. ''Rich, spoiled, the niece of some disreputable old dowager with gangland ties. Probably finagled her way into the broadcasting business. Many do, you know.'' She looked up as the door opened. ''Yes, Brian?''

''Message for Devon, ma'am.''

His words jarred, but Devon covered with a smile. ''From?''

''Jimmy. He's in your office. Says he has to see you, pronto. His words, not mine.''

''Well, really!'' Alma exclaimed. ''That young man's becoming entirely too high-handed.''

Devon grinned. ''I have to get back to work anyway.''

''Me, too.'' Hannah wiped her mouth and stood. ''Thank you for the lunch, Alma.''

''My pleasure. Devon, mind you study those faxes. I didn't have them transmitted for nothing.''

No, much as Devon liked her, she knew Alma seldom did anything without a very good reason. To give herself a chance to point out that Warren had been in New York at the time of the first two murders, perhaps? Well, wouldn't she do the same for her sisters? Devon reflected. Defend them to the bitter end? One thing she knew, Alma wouldn't want to see her die.

Jimmy was pacing her office like a caged tiger when she

arrived, a tubed piece of paper slapping against his palm. His youthful face brightened the second he spied her.

"Devon, here, look at this." He exploded without preamble, grabbing her arm and hauling her to the window.

"Look at the snow?" she inquired dubiously when he stopped to gape at her.

"What? Oh, no. I mean—" Reaching out, he touched the sleeve of her clingy moss-green dress. "You look really pretty today. Really—"

"Green?" Devon smiled. "Hannah says I wear too much red." Riker had mentioned it, too, as she recalled. "I thought a change might be in order."

Jimmy smiled back. "Maybe you should wear green more often." Shyness took over. "It's my birthday on the twenty-eighth, you know."

Actually she hadn't known. "We'll have to have a party, then, won't we? A real post-Christmas, pre-New Year's bash."

"I'll be thirty-five."

She stopped the surprise before it showed. Or thought she did.

"I don't look it, do I?" he asked rather forlornly. "I had a girlfriend once a long time ago. She used to tease me about my adolescent appearance."

Devon quirked a brow. "She'll be envious soon enough, Jimmy."

"No, she won't. She's not—" His fingers tightened on the rolled paper. "She's dead, Devon. We talked about getting married, but well… Anyway, that's pretty much why I don't date. No, don't feel sorry for me. I didn't tell you to make you sorry. I'm not sure why I told you really, but it wasn't for that." He shook his head as if to clear it. "What was I saying before?"

Devon tried a light, "You wanted me to see the snow?"

"No. No!" His initial excitement returned in a rush. Unrolling the tubed sheet, he thrust it under her nose. "Do you know this—'' A sound at the door interrupted him, and he finished with a squawked, ''—man?''

At Jimmy's round-eyed stare, Riker glanced over his shoulder. ''What?''

''Afternoon, Detective.'' Preoccupied, Devon studied the solemn photo of a man. ''He's nice looking, whoever he is. Norwegian or Irish ancestry, I'd guess. Does he do something, Jimmy?''

''Do—? Uh, no. That is— I thought I'd see if you recognized him.''

''Sorry. He looks a bit like Fabio. Grittier, though. Tougher. Jimmy, what are you staring at?''

The young man paled as Riker advanced. ''I have to go. I'll take that.'' He snatched the photo away.

Confused, Devon appealed to Riker, but he shrugged, as perplexed as her.

''Jimmy?''

He waved her off, skirting her coffee table en route to the door. ''I have work to do. Good show today, by the way. I didn't know St. Nicholas was a real person. Ouch!'' This as he almost blinded himself on one of the coat rack's pegs.

Riker caught his arm, frowning when Jimmy backpedaled into the sofa.

There was little Devon could do except remind herself that it wasn't amusing to watch a full-grown male deteriorate into a complete klutz. ''Mr. Bean,'' she murmured, then rushed forward just in time to catch the photo Jimmy dropped.

''Must be a bad coordination day,'' she teased. She'd hoped to lighten his mood. Instead, he grabbed the picture, cast Riker a look of fearful resentment and bolted into the corridor.

''Well.'' Palms pressed together, Devon let several seconds expire before she raised her brows in greeting. ''Very weird display. Did you come all this way to check on me?''

Riker removed his gaze from the closed door. ''Actually, I did. But you seemed to be surviving just fine on your own.''

Removing a hand from his pocket, he hesitated, then stroked her cheek.

The contact still had the power to jolt, though he'd done this same thing a dozen times or more by now.

"I am." She held his unfathomable gaze, then, curling her fingers around his wrist, moved his hand to her mouth and pressed a kiss to his palm.

She'd expected him to tense. What she didn't know was whether he would pull away or pull her close in response.

For a moment he did neither, simply stared at her while delicate flute music filled the air with subtly erotic strains. "Devon…" He seemed to want to say something specific, but settled for a weary, "This just isn't the right thing for us. I need to… I want…" His eyes rolled. "Oh, to hell with it."

He drew her forward effortlessly, sliding his strong fingers around the nape of her neck and tipping her head back. His eyes detailed every porcelain-fine feature on her face, the slender line of her throat, the silky hollow where her pulse fluttered and danced in time to her heart. A frantic drumbeat. Hot, wild. Seductive.

He should run, he knew that. But the invitation of her lips, hands and body made flight impossible. Moth to a flame, he thought with a distant stab of irony. He wasn't being fair to her. But, God help him, he wanted her more than he'd ever wanted anyone.

Problems and protests filtered in. A knife, a photo, a lie told that must be untold. A killer. A woman he refused to believe he loved…

Head lowered, he explored her mouth with care and fascination. He dipped and tasted as if savoring the finest French wine. He wanted this woman, badly. His heart wanted her. His head wanted her and so did the fiery hot region of his lower body.

No telephone sounded to distract him, but something shrilled deep in his brain. The clang of his conscience again?

His guilt? His fear? Maybe it was all of those things. Or maybe none.

A low groan emerged from his throat as she placed her hands on either side of his face to deepen the kiss. Desire hammered at him, powerful fists beating down his resistance.

She melted into him, molded her long, silky-limbed body to his. He felt hard as iron, knew he couldn't take much more of this torture. Couldn't take even a second more.

He broke off with a curse, trapped between soft regret and self-censure. The best thing in the end for her; a nightmare of deprivation for him.

Devon appeared as shaken as he felt. Just as well. Forcing his arms to drop, he stepped deliberately away.

She stared, bemused. "That was…incredible." She touched her mouth. "It's always so different."

An implosion would have been Jacob's description. "We have chemistry," he agreed, wincing at the inanity of the remark.

She pressed her fingers to her flushed cheeks. "You could call it that, I suppose. Maybe that's what sent Jimmy out of here in such a rush."

Jimmy! Reality rushed in, black and ominous. The photograph. That was the source of the mental clang. He'd glimpsed it, had heard the description of the subject, but he'd been preoccupied with fantasies of Devon and more distantly, of Ewen's missing knife.

In a single, swift motion, he caught Devon by the upper arms, brought her up to meet him and planted a brief, fervent kiss on her beautifully damp lips. "I'll be back," he promised. "Quick errand to run."

She recovered admirably. "Cop business, Riker?"

"My business." He halted, considered. "I'll cook us dinner tonight, okay? My apartment for a change."

Assuming all hell didn't break loose between now and then. An ugly image took shape as he made the required left turn that would carry him to the production offices: a picture of Joel Riker's somber face—in Jimmy Flaherty's jealous hands.

Chapter Eleven

"Phil, our head of newscasting said he was acting very strangely." Cross-legged on Riker's apartment floor, Devon arranged the wire limbs of a crooked five-foot pine tree. Boxes of leftover decorations were strewn across the table and carpet. A piece of red and gold garland hung around her neck. More hung on his punching bag. Her hair was mussed, her faded jeans and white T-shirt were covered with glitter, and she'd just polished off her second glass of California red.

She stopped fiddling to muse, "Maybe he wasn't feeling well. Why else would he have run out of the station so quickly? Are you listening to me, Riker?"

His voice drifted ghostlike from the kitchen. "No one knows why Jimmy left the station in the middle of the afternoon. How much is a pinch?"

Devon laughed and set the star on the top branch. "Ask Hannah. She's a better cook then me. Riker?" She paused in the process of securing the lights. "Why did you go to production to see him, today?"

"To find out where he was last night." Riker appeared in the kitchen doorway, a towel tossed over one shoulder and flour on his cheeks and the longest tips of his hair. "Stroganoff's not as easy as I thought."

"Tell me about it." Scooting back, Devon regarded her handiwork. "What do you think? Eclectic?"

He grinned and came to join her, squatting down so that

his knee brushed her arm. "I'd call it more of a hodgepodge, myself. What's that brown thing?"

"Where? Oh." Devon removed the stuffed cloth ornament. "My aunt took a craft course with my mother several years ago. She never got the hang of it. I think this is Dancer. I put the other seven reindeer on the sides and back." She struggled to conceal the fear that had been slinking around inside her for days now. "He's not going to give up, is he? I've done some reading. They never do. Serial killers, I mean."

"Devon…" He'd have reassured her if he could; she saw it in his eyes. Going to one knee, he took her hand, and, turning it over, studied the delicate skin of her palm. "It's a complicated problem."

"To be a serial killer?"

He almost smiled. "Probably that, too. I meant all of it, this whole Christmas Murderer thing. All those women before you who died. And now you." A ridge formed between his brows. "I couldn't live with myself if anything happened to you. You have to believe that, Devon. The last thing I want is for you to get hurt."

Did he mean hurt by the killer—or by someone else? Devon wished that the doubts would vanish once and for all.

Because they refused to, and because her pulses were beating like birds' wings, she brought his hand to her face and pressed her cheek against it. "I believe you're doing your best to protect me."

A light leapt into his eyes, but vanished before she could decipher it.

"We need to talk." His mouth was dangerously close to hers when he spoke. "Not everything is the way it seems."

The words fuzzed in Devon's brain as she inhaled the soapy scent of his skin. Christmas lights sparkled around them. Lute, harp and violin played softly on the stereo. The rooms smelled deliciously of beef stroganoff, red wine and strawberries. Cinnamon as well, from the apple pie Hannah had dropped off. "White Christmas," muted, flickered on the television screen, Bing crooning persuasively to Rosemary at a Vermont ski lodge. Devon loved the movie. She thought she might, just might, love Riker more.

"Nothing's ever the way it seems," she told him. "I try not to be disappointed."

Riker's stare was solemn, intent. "Does it work?"

"Not always. But things usually work out in the end."

He kissed each of her fingers. "So you believe in fate, do you?"

"If it's fate not to worry about the uncontrollable future, then I guess I do. I won't take stupid chances with the Christmas Murderer, Riker, but I won't crawl into a hole over it, either. We all do what we have to do in our lives."

"I didn't need to hear that," he murmured. Eyes unwavering, he resumed his crouch. "I should check on dinner."

And she should leave, Devon thought as he rose. Go straight to her apartment, lock the door and sift through her feelings for Riker layer by complex layer until she understood them all.

Loved him? Very likely. Trusted him? Yes, with her safety at any rate. With her heart, though? She brought a frustrated fist onto the top of her leg. What demons secreted themselves behind that emotional barrier of his?

Feeling shredded inside, Devon dropped her forehead onto her upraised knees. She listened with half an ear as Riker clattered and banged in the kitchen. Questions continued to badger her. Why had Jimmy charged out of her office this afternoon just as Riker had entered? Who was the man in the photo? Why was Riker so determined to keep his distance from her?

Because she'd been brought up not to dwell on the unanswerable, she raised her head, stood and crossed to the kitchen door. Riker's movements between oven and counter were economically fluid. He'd have made a good chef, certainly a watchable one.

"Riker?" Devon dug her fingernails into the painted wood

door frame. "Why were you really looking for Jimmy after you left my office this afternoon?"

He bent to squint at the flame under the rice pot. "I told you. It was just routine."

"You think Jimmy could be the murderer?"

He gestured her closer, dipped a wooden spoon in the sauce, blew on it, and held it to her lips. "Taste this. He's a suspect, Devon. Everyone is."

"I understand suspecting Warren and Roscoe." She savored the subtly spiced sauce. "It's good. But Jimmy's like—well, like a brother to me."

"That's not what he thinks."

"Yes, it is. It just isn't what he wants."

He slanted her a wry glance. "I've done some background on him. You don't think sexual frustration's a viable motive?"

"Not for Jimmy."

"Staunch defense, Devon, but unsound. You want him to be innocent; that doesn't mean he is."

"All right, I have another question then." She bit into the pasta shell he forked up for her. "Needs another minute. Why were you and Detective Dugan glowering at each other last night?"

Riker poured more wine and handed her a fresh glass. "I didn't know we were."

"That's not an answer." It also wasn't easy to stay on topic with him leaning negligently against the sink, sipping wine and looking like a lazy cheetah.

He moved a shoulder. "Dugan and I don't agree on this case, Devon. We never have. I'm told the Irish are a stubborn breed."

Easing a hip onto the table, she raised the wineglass to her lips. "Stubborn, full of blarney and as evasive as leprechauns most of the time. What is it you're not telling me? Share something, Riker."

He looked sideways, of two minds it seemed to her. Running a hand through his hair, he let his head drop forward.

"All right. Fair's fair." He brought his gaze up. "The knife he threatened you with was mine. More specifically, belongs in my family. My great great Uncle Ewen was notorious for—well, let's say he 'acquired' things. I doubt if the knife can be traced, but I think it's safe to assume that the Christmas Murderer is trying to frame me."

Devon nearly choked on the wine in her mouth. "Your knife," she gasped. "He—" She set her glass on the counter, forcing calm. "How did a murderer get hold of your knife?"

"Rudy…"

"Was with Detective Dugan when I was attacked." She paused, bit her lip and thought back. "But so were you, weren't you? At least you were with them until after ten o'clock when Hannah came to find you."

For the umpteenth time her mind scrambled backward through the time frame. No way to be sure, unless Hannah could manage to remember the exact moment when she'd knocked on Riker's door.

"Devon." Riker stared at her. "I'm not a murderer."

"A mur—" She blew at her bangs, impatient. "It's Rudy I'm wondering about, not you." Not right then at any rate. "You said I should suspect everyone. Did Rudy stay with Detective Dugan after you left?"

A light of strain glimmered in Riker's dark eyes. "I thought he did, but apparently they both left right after me."

"The desk sergeant told me Rudy was retired. Why is he helping you?"

Riker waved that question aside. "It's done sometimes, when the police are short-handed, or a certain officer has had experience with an ongoing case."

"So Rudy knows all about this particular case?" Her brow furrowed. "What about you? I know you've worked on it before, too."

A muscle in his jaw twitched. "I covered the first two victims. Ron Helmsford headed the next two investigations, Frank Boyd the last three."

"Who caught Coombes?"

"He was arrested by a beat cop after the seventh murder. A witness saw him kneeling next to a woman's body. He took a scarf from around her neck and stuck it in his pocket. He ran when he spotted the uniform, but not far."

Whether from wine or the jumble in her head, Devon's temples began to throb. She massaged them with the index and middle fingers of both hands. "Is that one of the reasons you think Coombes didn't do it? Because he took the scarf and all the others had been left at the scene?"

"You knew that." An admiring light sparked briefly in his eyes. Before she could react, he closed the gap between them and, moving so that he was behind her, replaced her fingers with his own. "I won't let him kill you, Devon." He turned her, tipping her head back until she stared straight into those compelling black-brown eyes. "I swear to you, I'll stop the bastard."

Why on earth should she believe such a promise? Yet despite that damnable guard of his, contrary to reason and logic and a legion of uncertainties, Devon did. Unfortunately, Rudy might not feel the same way. Unlikely though it seemed to her, he could conceivably have used his beat-up motorcycle to shortcut his way to the radio station.

Riker's fingers continued to work their magic on her headache. In a few short moments, a lovely drowse embraced her. She hesitated, then allowed herself to lean into Riker's warm, lithe body. "Did you talk to Andrew at all?"

His breath stirred strands of silky hair near her cheek. "He says he stayed home all night, waiting for you to call."

"And Warren?"

"Alma insists he came in twenty minutes after she called him."

"But she didn't actually see him arrive."

"She claims she heard the front door."

"From her en suite bathroom?" Devon asked doubtfully. "Well, but Warren was working in New York during the time of the first two murders. That is a fact."

"It's a short enough commute, Devon."

"For what purpose, though? Why would he come all the way to Philadelphia to find victims? New York's bigger, easier to disappear in. Unless he killed seven to cover up one. But then, why come after me?"

"No reason except insanity." Removing his fingers from her temples, Riker slid them with exquisite slowness through the golden layers of her hair. Lifting them off her neck, he lowered his mouth to the tender nape.

Devon melted as his lips brushed over her skin. A shiver of anticipation feathered along her spine. So many more questions to ask, dinner on the verge of burning, a clash of reason and desire in her head—and a fire building in the center of her that threatened to blot out every other sane thought.

With her fingers, she caught long strands of his hair where they tumbled across her shoulder. Beautiful, dark hair, thick and healthy with just the right amount of curl.

His mouth shifted to the delicate curve of her neck. Sensation rocked her, creating sharp pains of need deep in her belly.

"I want you, Devon," he said fiercely against her heated flesh. He fisted her hair, holding it back while his mouth traveled along the smooth line of her jaw. "I want you, but I have—I need to tell you something."

And she wanted to hear it. But not right then.

Twisting in his embrace, she wrapped her arms around his neck and tugged. "Tell me later, okay?" She said it softly, but didn't feel soft inside at all. She felt hot and needful, greedy to touch every part of him. She wanted to taste him, to feel him inside her, to experience the exquisite moment of climax. She wanted to understand him, to smash through the stone wall he'd erected around his heart. But for now she did not want to think about explanations.

Freeing one hand, she groped for the controls to the stove. Let dinner wait all night. Let more insidious problems wait forever. This was a time for more beautiful things. For candles and Christmas and making love. And as Riker's mouth came down hard and urgent on hers, Devon knew she would take the greatest pleasure in every sinfully wonderful moment....

THE WORLD had gone black, cold. Empty. He no longer felt the tiniest prick of warmth on his skin. His heart might have been made of lead, so heavy had it grown in his chest.

She would not be killed. God knew, he'd tried to end it. But he'd made all the wrong choices, it seemed, employed the worst possible tactics.

The knife had been a mistake. His fist pounded the windowsill in a gesture of stupidity. Never rummage through items in storage. Not overly bright either to inject an overdose of drugs into a rat's blackmailing body. All that had achieved was to create another corpse. Confusion came with it, true, but with confusion came questions, and he'd heard so many of those in the past ten years.

Ah, but he was skilled, a seasoned professional whether people realized it or not. He'd survived the onslaught and then some.

He stared blindly at the winking lights of the city. A junkie rat, gone. Bad move. Another gone missing. He sighed a little at that one. A better move, he decided. Where the knife had probably failed, this ploy might very well succeed. Still, one never really knew how a frame would bend. The best laid plans of mice and...

His forehead hit the sill with a dull thump. He heard the moan that rolled out of his throat. So many dead, and all because she refused to stay in hell where she belonged. No absolution before death. Oh, yes, hell was her domain. Hadn't he caught her red-handed in the middle of committing a sin?

Keeping his head down, he groped for his rosary beads. Didn't use them much these days, but old habits died painfully hard, especially ones so deeply rooted.

Devon's face took shape in his overtaxed mind, but it was *her* voice that brought the old anger billowing upward. Angela's voice, unheard for a short but happy few years, only to return and taunt him again during his bleak period of mourning.

No surprise in that. His mourning usurped by the Angel of the Morning. Angela had brimmed with gall, and an appallingly warped sense of fair play. Given her way, she'd punish him from now till Doomsday, past it if she thought she could.

Unable to locate his beads, he raised his head six inches and blinked owlishly into the twinkling darkness. Must focus on goals. No more wallowing in the past. Work the frame; kill the woman; pray the cat's ninth life truly would be its last.

The rage sneaked up on him. Before it choked him, he wondered vaguely how many others had suffered because of the Angel's traitorous nature. More, he imagined, than he could count in his head.

The years blurred. There'd been a brief period of clarity, of thinking the past no longer mattered. And of course the career he'd chosen had been helpful. Handy, too, at times like this.

Forcing himself to his feet, he regarded the telephone. His fingers twitched. He needed to deepen the frame and at the same time unnerve Devon. A spooked cat was always easier prey.

He dialled with care and offered a cheerful, "Hi, there, Gina. You wouldn't be alone, would you? What? Really? A judge! Moving up in the world, huh? Sure, I'll call back." His smile took on an aspect of malicious cunning. "You'll like the job I have for you."

Her reply sent a bolt of annoyance through his brain. "What are you talking about—you've gone straight? Does your judge know that?" The annoyance turned to white-hot fury. "Don't hand me that crap, Gina. It's a small favor, hardly worth risking your newly acquired reputation on. One little performance, that's all. I want you to help me tear the mask off one pretender and wipe out the other one at the same time. Never mind what I'm talking about. Don't call me that!" He inhaled deeply, forced a pretence of calm, but the rage continued to gravel his voice. "Help me, Gina, and this'll be the last time." Picking up a pencil he sketched a gallows, complete with hangman's noose. His lips curved as he sketched a shapely female body. "I promise you, it'll be the very last time I ask for anything."

IT WAS WRONG and every instinct, every scrap of decency Jacob possessed hurled that very basic truth at him.

"Devon, wait." He didn't entirely break the contact of their lips, couldn't quite summon the will to capture her hands and drag them from his body. The reason being—and he'd be damned for this, he was sure—he didn't really want to do either of those things. He wanted her, with an urgency that stunned him, or would have if he hadn't already been so involved with her.

Her nails dug into the small of his back. Stifling a groan, he splayed his fingers around her neck, drawing her up tight against him. He felt the heat in her body, the mounting edge of excitement. His teeth nipped at her lips, her earlobes and her brow before returning to her mouth. Thought was impossible. He could no more tear himself away from her than he could sprout wings and fly. Mesmerized, he explored the dips and hollows of her mouth. The taste of her intoxicated him, left him giddy and bemused, craving more of her and slightly panicky because of it.

The silky layers of her hair belonged on an angel. He breathed in her scent, woodspice and winter roses, then, on a flicker of humor, marvelled that he could breathe at all considering how tightly wound up he was.

She rubbed his tense shoulders with the heels of her hands. "You're like a coiled spring, Riker." Her sea-green eyes teased. "I promise not to bite or take unfair advantage of you."

"That isn't quite the problem," he muttered through gritted teeth.

In the mellow light, one delicate brow arched. "Oh, is there a problem?"

His answer stuck fast. It was there, but it got tangled up in the lump of desire lodged smack in the middle of his throat.

"No," was the best he could manage, and at that it was a rough sound. "No problem at all."

And no longer an ounce of resistance left with which to fight this uncontrolled attraction.

Eyes wide but steady, Devon disentangled herself from his arms and, taking him by the hand, led him wordlessly out of the kitchen.

Acoustic guitars and soft brass trailed them into the bedroom. The walls here were half-papered. Dropsheets still adorned the dresser, nightstand and window chair. Only the bed stood undraped, a four-poster queen-size covered with silver-blue sheets and an intricate patchwork quilt he'd picked up from an Amish roadside stand two summers ago.

"It's beautiful," Devon exclaimed when she spied it. Her eyes sparkled as she ran her palms over the stitched surface. "It reminds me of water. An ocean or one of the Great Lakes. Mysterious and unfathomable." Her gaze came up. "Like you."

He'd never have believed he would have difficulty swallowing, but there it was. His throat had seized. It remained to be seen if his vocal cords would function.

He tried again, one last, almost desperate attempt to purge his guilty conscience. "Devon, I want to talk...." She met his eyes, and his voice faded into the oblivion where voices run when emotion floods in and washes away all trace of rational thought.

Her head assumed that prideful tilt he'd seen before. She straightened, a true Christmas angel complete with halo courtesy of the Christmas-tree lights reflecting in the picture glass behind her. "I don't want to talk, Riker. I want to know you. I want you to know me. I want us to make love."

Jacob's eyes closed in defeat. No monk could endure this

torture. He was no monk, and Devon was the only woman he wanted. The only woman he'd ever wanted this badly.

He advanced on her, a lean and dangerous cat. Her scent filled his head with thoughts of lust and love, of clothes torn off in a frenzy of unleashed desire.

But she deserved better than that. If he gave her nothing else tonight, he would at least give her tenderness. A night to remember when the truth finally came out.

Because it would. Truth was inevitable in the end, no matter what his great-aunt claimed to the contrary. Jacob only hoped his end wouldn't turn out to be of the fire and brimstone variety.

On the other hand, he reflected, reaching out to stroke Devon's cheek with his fingers, this woman just might be worth an eternity of fire.

Letting a tinge of fatal amusement play on his lips, Jacob bent his head and delved into the flames of her enticing mouth.

Chapter Twelve

She felt as if she were tumbling through the clouds, through snowflakes—white-hot ones—and the silvery stars of night. In actual fact, a distant part of her realized that he was lowering her onto his bed, into the folds of his heavenly midnight-blue quilt.

The pattern formed a series of illusive ripples and waves that immediately brought to mind the Atlantic crossing she'd made once with Hannah and her grandmother. But those were hazy recollections, a pleasant backdrop to the feel of Riker's hands and mouth on her body.

Desire…she'd never dreamed it could be so intense. It was like wanting a thing so badly that it hurt.

He drew the wanting out, as much for his benefit, she sensed, as for hers. His eyes glittered in the colored wash of light. His facial muscles were strained, his body strung as tightly as a bow.

With a patience born of innate gentleness, he brought her from her back to her knees. Then, keeping his eyes steady on hers, he loosened her T-shirt and pulled it slowly over her head.

A smile as wistful as it was hungry lit his normally somber features when he stared at her. "You're incredible, Devon. Your mind and your body."

It should have sounded trite, but oddly it didn't. Shaking the hair from her eyes, Devon framed his face with her hands, hesitated for one brief moment, then pushed all traces of doubt aside and pulled his mouth onto hers. She loved to kiss him. Every kiss brought with it a new and wonderfully different rush of sensation, none of it tinged with doubt.

Her hands skimmed downward. When they reached his waistband, she tugged at his black jersey shirt, eager to touch. The heat inside her would reduce her to a pile of ashes in a minute. Did he realize that, understand it?

He dispensed with her jeans and his in the same manner that branded all of his actions. Swift, silent and without fuss.

Beneath the ultra-thin barrier of white silk, Devon's nipples hardened. Then, that barrier gone, and she gasped in shock as his mouth closed over one rosy peak.

At the same time, his hand slid between her legs to cup her. Her head arched back, her hips forward. Her fingernails dug into the sleek flesh and bone of his shoulders.

Beautiful, she thought, and for an instant felt as if she were soaring upward through a very warm mist.

She heard a harp, a Celtic carol, something to do with the sea and time. Her head spun as sensation rocked her. His mouth was doing the most exquisite things to her breast. And his hand...

A shudder, born of deep longing, swept up and outward from the center of her. Her own hands slid over the smooth skin of his ribcage and around to where he throbbed hard and needful against her.

So magnificent. So sleek and powerful. Her breath hitched as desire poured through her in fiery waves, an ocean tide complete with dark undercurrents and whispers from the depths of emotions barely realized that suddenly begged for release.

The harp drew her out. Riker drew her in. Or rather his clever lovemaking drew from her a response she hadn't known she could give. Her heart expanded, blocking her lungs until she was afraid she might suffocate.

She squeezed her eyes closed as the first wave rolled over her. Disjointed sounds swam in her head. Quiet words murmured to her, a bird singing above the harp, water surging in to shore, crashing, then finishing with a teasing lap that beckoned her to follow it out.

"Open your eyes, Devon." Riker slid a hand over her stomach. "I want to look at you. I want you to look at me."

She could try, Devon supposed, her mind colored with too many emotions to count.

Easing her lashes up, she beheld him in front of her. His body was all golden sinews and clean fluid lines. The ends of his hair skimmed his shoulders. His chest rose and fell with each labored breath. The fact that he hadn't shaved that day only added to the air of danger that surrounded him. Black Irish with some darker ancestral blood mixed in. Something older and marginally less civilized.

He stared for the longest time, and with that penetrating stare excited feelings in Devon that made her ache for him. He swayed, caught himself, then, as if galvanized by her expression, captured her mouth again in a kiss so deep and wrenching that it sent shock waves through her entire system.

More gently than her feverish mind craved, he pressed her onto the quilt. "Slowly, Devon," he murmured. But slow was not her style—or her preference at this moment. She wanted the heat to scorch; she wanted to fly straight into the heart of it and not come out until every last bit of her energy was spent.

She kissed him that way, knew he felt the same by the trembling muscles in his arms as he supported himself above her.

Her eyes opened to his. "Not slow," she said. And with a groan edged by the faintest hint of a growl, he took possession of her mouth again.

Devon's thoughts didn't scatter so much as disintegrate, a flame held to a wisp of fine cotton. Her hands closed around him, urging him on. In answer, he flicked his tongue over her nipple, suckling her until her head thrashed on the pillow.

Devon gasped to breathe, but neither of them were finished yet. She was still spiraling upward through the clouds. He kissed her long and deep and then, pressing his palms onto the mattress, levered himself up so that he could enter her.

Not for a moment did she hesitate. If there was a flicker of doubt, she ignored it. Only the pleasure broke through to engulf her.

Desire rocketed her to the summit, and over, until, in free fall, she careened out of control and with no idea of how hard she might land.

One climax, two. Sensations overlapped. He was inside her, and she loved him. For now, it was all that mattered.

She lay still for a long time afterward, limp with exhaustion, drained of every thought she'd previously possessed.

A near dead weight on top of her, Riker made an unintelligible sound and started to roll away. Then his eyes fastened on hers, and he stopped.

"That was incredible, Devon." His breathing still ragged, he toyed with a strand of her hair. His lashes lowered to shield his eyes. "I didn't mean for this—I should have told you something first."

Devon ran her fingertips experimentally along his spine. "There was nothing I needed to know." She'd convinced herself of that. A stray thought hit her, and her gaze steadied. "Nothing medical, right?"

"No." He squashed that concern cold. "It was…" She felt his gaze where it lingered on her slightly swollen lips, heard the quiet sigh that issued from him. "Unimportant." As carefully as he might handle a piece of Doulton china, he pressed a kiss to her mouth. "Nothing we can't hash out tomorrow."

BUT IT WAS a tremedous relief to him that they had no time to hash out anything the next morning. In truth, talking was the last thing on Jacob's mind when he cracked his eyes to a pale gray dawn and felt Devon nestled as trustingly as a child next to him.

As if cued, she rolled onto her back, stretched like a cream-fed cat and smiled a blissful smile. "You're better than beef stroganoff any day, Riker.'' Then her eyes flew open and she sat sharply upright. "What time is it?"

Jacob focused. "Eight—damn—forty-five."

Devon made a strangled sound and jumped from the bed. She paused briefly in her hands-and-knees scramble to locate her clothes to grin at him over her bare shoulder. "Helluva night, though. What was it you kept insisting we talk about?"

Jacob called himself a gutless coward as he countered with a casual, "It'll keep." Pulling on his jeans, he zipped up and crossed to the door. "Toast? Coffee? Cold stroganoff?"

Rocking back, Devon sighed. "Coffee, please."

"Instant?"

"Whatever's fast. We have a staff meeting scheduled for ten o'clock. Even allowing for Warren's opening bluster, I'm going to be late. He'll probably insist on escorting me to the Kat tonight as punishment."

"The Kat?" Already in the kitchen doorway, Jacob frowned. "Do I know about this?"

She skidded in, combing her hair with her fingers. "Christmas cocktail party. Us, our AM sister station, local VIP's and anyone else who wants to pay the two-hundred-dollar entrance fee to crash. All proceeds to charity. Dinner and wine complimentary; drinks not. Alma rented the top floor of the club and hired a local jazz band. Is that mine?" She pointed to a steaming mug.

"Mmm." One dark brow arched. "Black tie or casual?"

Sipping, she made a see-saw motion. "In between. I picture a nineties style Thin Man crowd. Boisterous but not wild. Word has it that our new deputy mayor enjoys a good Christmas tipple." A glance at her watch as she swallowed and her cup hit the counter.

In a move that appeared as natural to her as it was foreign to him, she set her hands on his shoulders and kissed him hard on the mouth. "Have a nice day, Riker."

Jacob's first inclination was simply to gape. But he shook himself and managed a rough, "You too, angel."

Where had that come from? Baffled, he blinked, glanced

away. He of all people never used pet names. Or had this been more along the lines of a Freudian slip…?

Devon hesitated, but fortunately had no time to stop and ponder. Staff meeting in sixty minutes, and she still needed to shower, make up and dress. Most of all, though, she needed to get out of Riker's apartment before she thought too deeply about the endearment. Men had been known to call women 'angel' without it meaning anything sinister.

But what on earth was Riker feeling? They'd made love three times last night, yet despite the intimacy, that guard wall of his had scarcely cracked. She, on the other hand, had bared a great deal of her soul to him. No skeletons lurked in her closets, at least none of significance. Was it so difficult for him to set aside his own barriers for one short night?

She disregarded the apprehension that challenged her current tunnel vision and raced down the stairs. Barefoot, with her hair tumbling into her sleepy eyes, she glimpsed the shadow beside the newel post at the last second and barely missed crashing into its owner.

"Good morning, Devon." Mouth downturned, Andrew surveyed her disheveled state. "You seem in a hurry."

Devon forced a smile and more patience than his disapproving expression warranted. "I am. Excuse me, Andrew."

He caught her upper arm before she could skirt him. "Did you spend the night with a friend, I wonder?"

This time, her smile was as succinct as her response. "That's none of your business. Let go."

Instead, he gave her arm a shake. "You didn't answer my note," he said in a tone just short of a snarl. "I thought you had better manners than that."

"And I thought you'd have the good sense to check your answering machine. I left a message. Let go of my arm, Andrew. Now."

Either her words or the level glare that accompanied them worked, because his fingers loosened their grip.

Devon jerked free the rest of the way. "Go to work," she said flatly. "And next time don't accuse until you're sure."

"I thought the messages were all complaints and appointment changes." Now he sounded whiny. "I'm sorry, Devon. What about—"

"No. Thank you." She cut him off, moving around him to her door. "You might mean well, but I don't respond nicely to manhandling. Goodbye, Andrew."

The door closed on his raised finger of protest. Devon clicked the deadbolt, spied the wall clock and promptly forgot all about Dr. Andrew McGruder. She had less than fifty minutes to reach the station.

Within thirty, she was showered and dressed in a purple skirt suit with a plain black silk tank top beneath the V-necked jacket, a pair of black suede pumps on her feet and subtle amethyst studs adorning her earlobes. Snatching up her purse, she made a quick final check in the mirror and reached for her black cape. She'd just gotten her ring nicely tangled in the wool when her sharp eyes spotted the folded red paper on the carpet near the door.

Panic leapt into her throat and lodged tightly. Had the paper been here when she came in? She hadn't noticed it. But then, she'd been distracted, hadn't she?

Devon stared for a full minute before she summoned sufficient courage to bend over and grab it from the floor. It was, after all, only paper.

Nevertheless, her heart stuttered as her trembling fingers unfolded it.

Gold lettering…

Devon's eyes closed then slowly opened on the neatly scripted words.

You cannot win, Devon Tremayne.
Who "morns" an angel such as you.
I know who you really are,
who you always have been.
You will not be either of you much longer.

As a rule, Jacob enjoyed the bustle of a newsroom, or any other room where affable chaos reigned. Today, for some reason, he simply couldn't face it. Rudy had a computer at his place. He'd use that, breakfast on Mandy's over-spiced Christmas cake and do his utmost not to dwell on the more phenomenal aspects of the night he'd just spent with Devon.

He drove too fast along the snowy Philadelphia streets. He brooded, remembered and brooded some more. He actually stooped to snarling at the toothy adolescent whose snowball smacked wetly against his rear windshield.

Not that the kid cared, or that doing it improved Jacob's mood, but he had to exorcise his guilt pangs somehow before they chewed him up and spit him into the gutter.

He whipped into a parking space beside a four-foot snow-drift outside Rudy's modest townhouse. A layer of white clung to the trim and low eaves like sugar frosting.

Mandy had gotten Rudy to set up a rosy-cheeked Santa and his workshop elves. For her grandchildren, Jacob supposed, feeling suspiciously like Scrooge. Lucky kids to have someone who encouraged them to believe in magic. The world was comprised of lies—that had been his dreary knowledge since the age of eight. God, what an old prune his great-aunt had been. And she'd done her level best to mold Laura into her likeness, would undoubtedly have succeeded in spite of the cancer that had finally sunk its deadly fangs into her aging liver, if Laura hadn't committed the unpardonable sin of preceding her to the grave twelve months earlier.

Twelve months. Strangled at twelve midnight. A Christmas angel pendant. Jacob fought to combat the chill that prickled his skin.

"Well, hello there, stranger." Mandy greeted him from the doorway, arms folded, her chewing gum and blue eyes both snapping nastily. "Too long a time, no see. How goes the fakery?"

He winced but didn't show it. "Not great. Is Rudy around?"

Her lip curled. "Gone to the store for smokes. You wouldn't know anything about the relapse, I suppose."

Halting at eye level with her, Jacob shook his head. "I don't need more guilt, Mandy."

"What do you need?"

"Rudy's computer."

"Something wrong with yours?"

"I don't have access to police files."

Her irritation broke and she chortled. "Since when has that ever stopped you?"

His shoulders hunched. "I'm running out of time, Mandy." To say nothing of enthusiasm for this charade. "I need to get in and out fast."

"Well—I guess it'd be okay." She nudged the door open wider with a fluffy pink foot. "But you mark my words, Jacob Price, she'll find you out, and then you'll be in hot water."

"I already am," he muttered.

Five minutes later, he was settled in Rudy's den, surrounded by child art that he realized with a pang belonged to him. Home-framed drawings hung lovingly alongside Rudy's two awards for Officer of the Month.

Riker'd won seven of those awards already, and he was only thirty-six. Dugan had eight, but then he was well into his fifties.

Knuckling a tired eye, Jacob punched up the file on Devon. Assault with a deadly weapon, namely a gold-bladed knife. Prints too smudged to identify. Origin of knife, unknown. German made, circa the early 1900s. Investigation continuing.

A tiny portion of the weight on Jacob's chest lifted. He hadn't left any clear prints when he'd packed the knife away. So far the frame fell flat.

"Who's Ralph 'Brando' Severs?"

Mandy's voice startled him. He fixed on the screen and reached absently for the nut cake and coffee she offered on her antique Coca Cola tray.

"Just a guy I met. He died of a drug overdose."

"I can see that. Found him in the water, huh? Rolled in himself or was dumped, do you think?"

"The water's secondary." Jacob ran the file. "It was the heroin that killed him."

"Too bad." Mandy sounded genuinely sorry. "So many junkies; so few cops to police the dealers." Jacob hit a series of keys. An image appeared, prompting her to let out an approving, "Ooh. Very nice. Is that Brando?"

"No." Sitting back, Jacob studied the man who had, until recent years, sported a short blond haircut. Brown-green eyes stared solemnly back at him. "He shouldn't have been able to get this."

"You're mumbling, Jacob." Mandy tapped the top of his head. "Who shouldn't have been able to get what? Who is this guy?"

"It's Joel Riker's official departmental photo. One of Devon's co-workers hacked in and snatched a copy of it. He shouldn't have been able to."

"Why not? Cops are allowed within ID range of the media. Why not a visual on computer?"

"Because Riker does a lot of undercover work in homicide."

"Says vice here." She used a glossy red fingernail to point.

"He started in vice, Mandy, then transferred to homicide. If Jimmy Flaherty can access his photo, what's to stop any other halfway good hacker from doing the same thing? Even with long hair and stubble, Riker could be made from his picture."

Mandy cracked a canny eye. "He could be made...or you could?"

Jacob conceded the point with a shrug, reached for another piece of cake and slouched back to think. Ten seconds later, Rudy's grumbling entrance shot a hole in that prospect.

"Dugan's crawling up one side of me and down the other,

kid. Wants to know have you eighty-sixed the impersonation or not?''

"Tell him yes." On a hunch, Jacob used two fingers to punch in the name *Angela*. "Nothing," he said when the computer came up blank. "I wonder if she was out of state."

Bewildered, Rudy demanded, "Who?"

"Whoever Angela is."

"Forget her." If the chair had swiveled he would have jerked it around. Instead, he grasped a handful of Jacob's black sweater and gave it a vigorous shake. "Dugan's not gonna buy a half-baked 'yes,' then obligingly scuttle off to a dark corner."

"Fine. Let him arrest me." Jacob directed his gaze at the monitor. "Until he does, I'm going to keep trying to nail the creep who attacked Devon."

Rudy's mouth opened, ripe for an argument. Only Mandy's well-aimed tap in the shin silenced him.

Jacob saw it, together with the look which passed between them, a look that spoke of promised explanations and smoldering indignation. Ignoring both, he returned to his musings.

Jimmy Flaherty should not have been able to access Riker's photo. At the very least it should have taken him a month or more of worming to do so. Had he gotten lucky? Did he know someone on the force? Disregarding the hows, why hadn't he exposed the fraud to Devon? Where had he gone yesterday afternoon? He'd already ducked out by the time Jacob reached the newsroom.

"Hell, if not yesterday, he'll spill the truth today, won't he?" Vexed, Jacob cursed the corner he'd painted himself into, then abruptly shoved back and located his jacket.

Rudy, forestalled by Mandy's hand on his arm, settled for shouting, "Where are you going?"

Jacob's gaze landed on a happy, bright-eyed helicopter he'd finger-painted at age five. A wry smile tugged on his lips when he recalled that he'd wound up more brightly painted than the 'copter. "To cut a deal, if I can." At the doorway, he glanced back. "For what it's worth, the old woman would be proud of me."

Rudy made a scornful sound. "Are you proud of you, kid?"

The smile returned faintly to Jacob's lips. "I don't know what I am anymore, Rudy. And that's the problem in all of this. I don't know what the hell I am. Or who."

Chapter Thirteen

"Roger from production's been calling Jimmy's apartment every hour. No one's seen or heard from him since yesterday afternoon."

Devon had to shout to make herself heard above the jazz music of Philadelphia's trendy new Kat Club. Black-and-white etchings of jazz musicians blowing saxophones and trombones adorned three of the four walls. The tables were laid with black toppers over white cloth; the floor was a polished swirl of black, gray and white granite; the band might have come straight out of the late thirties.

Riker, in a black suit, leaned closer to shout back. "Has he ever pulled a disappearing act before?"

"No." The shrill first bars of the song mellowed to a more acceptable level. Devon blew at her bangs and repeated, "No, never. It isn't like him, Riker. Maybe we should, uh…"

"Break into his apartment and check it out?"

"I'd have phrased it differently myself." She followed his restless eyes around the crowded room. "What are you looking for?"

"Anything that strikes me as wrong."

She accepted a glass of punch from a passing waiter. After the note she'd received, she preferred not to think what "wrong" might entail. "As crowds go, this is a fairly normal one. Where politicians rub elbows with the media, nothing's likely to get too weird."

A man's arm suddenly weighted down Devon's shoulders from behind. With it came a gusty breath from Warren Severen's throat.

"Here she is, the woman of my dreams." He puckered, aimed for her cheek and wound up stumbling as Devon maneuvered herself neatly out of range.

"Forget it," she murmured when Riker's eyes flashed. "He's easily avoided and seldom tries twice in one night."

"Jerk," Riker muttered into his glass.

"If that's all he is, I'll be happy." She shivered despite the cloying warmth of the club. "I wish I could remember whether or not that note was on the floor when I got home this morning. If not, then Andrew…"

"Then Andrew what?"

Devon spun. The man standing there looked peevish despite his splotchy cheeks and over-bright eyes. "Andrew! What are you doing here?"

He peered through his lenses at Riker, then shuffled conspiratorially closer. "I wanted to talk to you. I play your station in my office. I heard about this party tonight so I wangled a ticket. I paid the price," he added with a defensive lift of his head. "Can we talk? Er, privately?"

"I don't think…"

"No." Riker shot him down more rudely than Devon would have, but since the end result was the same, she made no comment. Before Andrew could grow indignant, Riker slipped a hand under his pudgy arm. "But you and I are going to have a little chat."

"Oh dear." Mandy, resplendent in a lime green silk sheath that feathered daintily around her still shapely ankles, joined Devon. "He looks irked."

Devon watched the two men leave. "Is that bad?"

"Usually, although he's quite even-tempered as a rule. Humorous, too, when you get to know him. I don't suppose you've seen much of that side yet."

"Not much," Devon agreed. Though she'd glimpsed a

sweetness and patience that she'd found both confounding and endearing.

Mandy fluffed her sprayed blond hair. "He needs a good woman is all. Never quite had one—" a shrewd brow went up. "Until now?"

Devon refused to blush, or to meet Mandy's inquisitive gaze. "He must have thought he found the right woman when he got married. Delia, wasn't it?"

"Who? Oh—right. Yes. I forgot." Mandy fidgeted with her puffed sleeve. "I wasn't with Rudy then." Her brow knit. "Was I? No, I don't think so."

Something churned in Devon's stomach. She banked it to ask, "How long have you been with Rudy?"

"Two years."

"Riker's wife died ten years ago, Mandy." Her fingers tightened on the glass. "Why are you so nervous all of a sudden? Is there something about Riker that I should know?"

"Good Lord, no." Mandy's laugh almost rang true. "He's a puzzle, I'll admit. But if you've got any evil thoughts running through your head, you can just shoo them out right now."

Could she? Devon never felt entirely sure. Riker concealed something behind that emotional barricade of his. Did that something involve his dead wife? Or was it, God forbid, a more malevolent problem than that?

No, she wouldn't think that way. Riker had no evil tendencies. She loved him. He couldn't be bad.

But why did Mandy suddenly seem so flustered? There must be a reason....

"Ah, there you are, my dear." The crowd parted to let Alma stroll through. Her tidy black dress stopped just short of prim. "And you must be Rudy's better half." A firm hand came out. "He's told me a great deal about you. Mandy, isn't it?"

"Yes." Mandy's eyes flicked to Devon then away. "Rudy's spoken of you as well. Unfortunately, I lost track of him over near the bar. Then, I got turned around, and, well…''

Alma laughed. Devon noticed that her punch glass was heavily lipsticked and empty. ''In that case, we'll have to unturn ourselves and find him.'' Winking, she hooked arms with the other woman. ''We'll follow my brother, shall we? In a galactic labyrinth, he'd select the most direct route to the bar.'' She perused the swarm of elegant bodies around her. ''On the other hand, he seems to have disappeared as well. And here I am out of punch. Roscoe?'' Her voice rose several decibels. ''Where are you, man? My glass is empty, and my brother's missing.''

Certain they'd reach their destination eventually, Devon left the women and scanned the doorway through which Riker had ushered Andrew. Cop Riker she reminded herself, into whose life she had no right to pry. Maybe that's what had flummoxed Mandy. Riker didn't strike her as a man who would appreciate intrusion, especially when it pertained to him.

She spied him finally and, with a smile, headed towards him. Rudy, scowling fiercely, walked alongside him, his leathery face all creases and worry lines.

Devon raised her glass as they approached. ''I trust you left Andrew in one piece. I haven't mentioned it, but his father's a corporate lawyer.''

Riker's lips twitched. ''He mentioned it quite loudly as I was backing him into the washroom wall.''

''A verbal backing, I hope. Andrew's not above crying police brutality.

Rudy sniggered. ''Told you he was the type, kid. They just talked, Devon. Riker here favors the good cop role.''

Funny, it didn't strike Devon that he'd favor that role at all. The churning in her stomach returned, albeit at a manageable level. She opted for a teasing tone to combat it. ''I thought only the bad cops wore black, Riker.''

His eyes danced, surprising her. ''I'm wearing red underwear. Besides, you're wearing black.''

"Ah, but my outfit shimmers. And it has a slit up the back."

"I noticed that."

Reddening, Rudy tugged at his striped tie. "Hot in here, isn't it? Think I'll go grab some fresh air. You two carry on and—"

"Jacob?" A woman's lilting voice cut through the din of music and chatter. "It *is* you, isn't it? I thought I recognized that gorgeous face." A striking brunette jostled Rudy's arm causing him to slop his drink. Laughing, she planted a kiss on Riker's mouth, stood back and beamed. "You look wonderful, darling."

Devon didn't say a word. Rudy spluttered. Riker stared, narrow-eyed.

"Jacob?" The woman batted her lashes. "Don't you remember me? The Blue Fox? Last year? You were following up on that story about gigolos and how they—well, I won't go into detail. Good Lord," she exclaimed in the same breath. "You're Devon Tremayne, aren't you? Of course you are. I saw you on a television commercial. "City Life" on the Wave. Is Jacob—" She glanced over. "Are you interviewing Ms. Tremayne?"

The mask slipped into place as it invariably did. "Something like that, Ms…?"

She huffed. "White, darling. Eden. For heaven's sake, we had dinner, took in a show. You remember!"

Riker studied her, half-lidded. "Actually, I don't."

"Well, then I'm insulted." She gave a little wave over his head. "Yes, I'm coming, dear. Must run." Her fingers curled briefly around Riker's arm and squeezed. "You do remember, I'm sure you do. Call me sometime and we'll…talk." Another wag of her fingers and she was gone.

Confusion temporarily blanked Devon's mind, except for the green tinge now coloring the room.

"Well," she said. "That was…interesting." Only her lips registered a smile. "Jacob?"

Riker held her gaze. "It's a long story, Devon. One thing I can promise you is that I've never met that woman before."

"Ah-ah." Rudy tapped his forearm. "Wait a minute, now. You could have done."

"For Christ's sake, Rudy, I'd know if I'd met her."

"Not necessarily. There was that case last year, remember? Two men dead. Suspected smuggling operation. You posed as a reporter, checked out the Blue Fox one night. Turned as green as a Christmas tree next morning," Rudy confided to Devon. "Undercover cops have to play the part all the way sometimes. A few glasses of 150-proof whiskey, and you could meet a chorus line of Eden Whites and not remember them. On the other hand," he took Devon's cold fingers in his and raised them to his lips, "no man could ever forget Devon Tremayne."

A charming remark, but Devon wasn't prepared to buy charm.

Riker sighed. "I've never met the woman, Rudy, drunk, undercover or otherwise."

Devon eyed him levelly. "She seemed to know you well enough."

"It can only be the Fox stint," Rudy insisted. "This sort of thing happens from time to time, kid. You know it does. It's the price we pay for hitting the streets."

Devon believed that. What she didn't trust was the frown that invaded Riker's lean features. No, there was more to this than either man was telling, something that involved Riker's guard-wall defense system and her inability to see through it.

Capturing her jaw in his long fingers, Riker locked his gaze on hers. "Trust me, Devon. I'll explain everything to you as soon as I can. I need to find that woman before she leaves here. Just believe me when I tell you that I have no idea who she is."

"I—" Devon drew a deep breath, released it. "—maybe." She half believed him. But people had died in the past for believing falsely. She wondered with a twinge of discomfort what the seven victims of the Christmas Murderer had believed. And more importantly—her eyes slid to Riker—in whom.

JACOB'S PALM HIT the frosty cornerstone with force. His head dropped back; his breath steamed up toward the cloudy night sky. He'd lost her. How the hell had he lost her?

Out of breath, he leaned against the wall of the all-night bar and grill and attempted to regain his bearings. He was somewhere near the downtown core. Nightclubs, a flock of them, stretched out in a zig-zag pattern to his left. Not the glitziest clubs in the city, but you could spend time in them and still have your wallet in your pocket when you left. He should know. She'd led him a merry chase through several of them.

Eden White... Grunting, Jacob pushed off from the stonework and cut across the street to an empty phone booth. He'd never heard of the woman. Which was undoubtedly why she'd taken off like a jack rabbit the minute she'd left him at the Kat.

Nudging up his coat sleeve he squinted at his watch. One in the morning. He'd been on the woman's trail for two hours. Devon was not going to be in a good mood when he got back to the apartment.

Holding his gloves in his teeth, he inserted a quarter and dialed her number. No answer. She must be with Hannah. He prayed to God she was with Hannah. Hanging up, he tried Rudy. Mandy grabbed the receiver on the first ring.

"Rude there?"

"No. He's not here?" He could tell her foot tapped in annoyance. "I wish he was. You, too. We'd all like our turn with you, boyo."

Jacob's chest contricted. "Who's 'we all'?"

"Hannah, Alma and me. I rounded them up after you and Sarge decided to chase floozies. Alma's brother went missing about the same time as you knuckleheads took off. We lost Roscoe to the search and rescue of Warren."

Jacob's heart thudded against his ribs. "What about Devon?"

"She left with one of the radio station's disk jockeys. A woman. Teddi, I think Hannah called her. Said she needed some space for a couple of hours, that they were going to Teddi's and she'd phone in the morning."

"Did you say anything to Devon before she left, Mandy?"

"No. Not for lack of wanting to, mind you, but since Rudy's involved, I held my tongue." Her fingers covered the mouthpiece. "In the top cupboard, Hannah, next to the cereal. We're making coffee, Detective Riker." A cobra would have spit the last two words out with less venom. "You're welcome to join us, providing you round up Devon and Rudy first. And Warren and Roscoe if you happen to stumble across them. We'll swap lies when you get here. But I warn you, Devon's feeling mighty mistrustful at the moment. You'll have to make your lie a convincing one."

A click of the handset conveyed her feelings on the subject of lies with perfect clarity.

"She's pissed," Jacob acknowledged, and laid his forehead against the cold plastic of the telephone casing.

He prayed that Devon was safe with Teddi Waters. Not that praying was sufficient to satisfy him. He'd have to detour by Teddi's home and make sure that Devon was there.

Frustration hacked at his senses. Except for waking up in bed next to Devon, this had been a spectacularly lousy day. He'd gone to Dugan earlier, hoping to strike a deal and had wound up leaving with no idea whether he'd succeeded or not. Dugan could be as ornery as a mule when it suited his purpose.

Then there'd been the murderer's latest note to Devon. Another threat that couldn't be traced. And now a strange brunette arrived on the scene, claiming to know him despite the fact that Jacob knew he'd never seen her before. Where the hell, he reflected, jerking his head up, had the woman gone? More to the point, who'd sicced her on him in the first place?

Someone who wanted him exposed as a phony. Jimmy maybe? But Jimmy Flaherty had vanished. Warren, then, or the idiot dentist?

Wind howled in freakish gusts around the corners of the phone booth. He heard it as a distant sound, only really becoming aware of it when the howl grew suddenly louder.

He felt it swirl in and blow the hair into his eyes. But the only way it could swirl in was if somebody had opened the door.

He wheeled but knew with a sinking feeling that he'd already forfeited the advantage.

The impact caught him on the side of his head, sending shock waves of pain and blinding white light back to front through his skull. A black fog followed the light as he dropped to the icy sidewalk. He glimpsed a shadow, possibly wearing a ski mask. Beneath it shone a pair of marbled eyes. No way to determine the color in the poor street light.

Jacob's cheekbone hit the concrete with a crack that echoed like a gunshot in his head. His attacker's hissed words wafted in like a vapor. "I killed the woman I loved once. Now I'll kill the woman you love and give you credit for it. A touch of ironic justice, Sydney Carton, in our own poetic tale...."

"RIKER, WAKE UP." On her knees in the snow, Devon darted a frightened glance into the darkness, then shook his shoulder again. "For God's sake, wake up, will you?"

At last, a low moan rolled out of him. Terrified and relieved, Devon shook harder. "Come on, Riker, please snap out of it. Whoever hit you probably isn't that far away."

His bleary eyes opened a fraction. "Devon?" His voice emerged as a croak. "What are you...?"

"It doesn't matter," she hissed, looking around again. There were people farther along the street but no one in the immediate area. No one visible, that is.

She caught hold of his arm as he endeavored to lever himself upright. On his knees, still bent over, he rubbed the side of his head. "Devon…" Oddly, his look of annoyed displeasure helped. "What the hell are you doing here?"

She brushed at his hair with short strokes, then, catching herself, pulled back. "I followed you."

The flash of pure anger in his face had to be a good sign. He wouldn't glare if he was seriously wounded. Still, mistrust continued to nag. "That was a stupid thing to do, Devon."

"I know." She glanced back then snagged his wrist. "I almost lost you outside the Kat, but I recognized your lead-footed driving style in the parking lot and caught up."

"Where's Teddi?"

"At home, I imagine." Her uneasy eyes scanned the shadows. "Look, this isn't a good place for a cross-examination. I know you have questions. Believe me, I have more. Let's get out of here first and sort the answers out later."

He winced when she helped him to his feet. As he gained his balance, the only sound he made was a muttered, "I can't believe I didn't see the bastard."

Emotions too divergent to separate clogged Devon's throat. "I saw him," she said steadily. "At least, I saw someone in a bulky black coat disappearing down the street. Then I saw you."

"Which way did he go?"

"Toward the river."

She watched his hand disappear inside his long coat, saw his eyes close in disbelief. "My gun," he said in a monotone. "He took my gun."

Edgy, Devon pulled on his arm. "You're lucky that's all he took. He could have shot you while he was at it."

"Or you."

"I waited until I was sure he'd gone."

Riker cast a wary look over his shoulder. "Why take my gun? He must have had a reason."

At the crosswalk, Devon checked both directions, then pushed him toward the all-night bar and grill. "You said he might be framing you. Maybe taking your gun was part of that plan."

It startled her when, at the curb, Jacob swore and spun, fists clenched, eyes sparking with fury.

"What?"

"The gun." His right fist curled and uncurled. "It isn't mine, Devon."

Fear made her sharp. "Whose is it, then?"

He turned to her grim-faced. "It's Rudy's old police special."

POOR GINA. He gazed down on her pityingly. The story played like a dirge in his mind.

Beautiful hooker, shot in cold blood by the man who called himself Detective Riker, the man Gina had so obligingly called Jacob tonight. Riker, né Jacob Price, had apparently not liked having his impersonation jeopardized. Of course, he'd have no trouble wriggling out of a tight spot courtesy of a lie or two, but seeds of doubt planted in the fertile soil of Devon Tremayne's mind would be difficult to uproot.

He blinked, regarded the stolen gun first, then Gina's motionless form. A shame really that she'd needed to die, but uppity women asked for punishment when they crossed him, and Gina hadn't wanted to do this favor. The absolute gall of it. How many favors had he done for her? Well, maybe not as many as she would have liked, but even one deserved a payback.

She'd paid him back in spades tonight, or would when his version of the truth came out.

Not yet, though, he thought, pocketing the gun. Not until Devon was dead and all the deaths could be pinned on Jacob Price.

He turned to Gina's apartment window. His view was blocked by her Christmas tree. The half-packed cardboard boxes strewn around the room indicated that she'd been planning to move. Uptown, no doubt, to an environment more befitting the whore of a state justice.

Without intending to, his gaze landed on top of the tree where a blue-lit angel hovered, wings spread, harp in hand.

The song burst out in his head, so unexpectedly that he clapped his hands over his ears. The words shrieked into his brain, sung, it sounded like to him, by a legion of gremlins. But it was the angels who sang, wasn't it? Angels did that, played their harps and sang.

He brought his head up. His eyes felt teary and red, fired with an emotion much deadlier than misery. Why, his thoughts screamed to a seemingly indifferent heaven, had the angel he'd loved sung for everyone but him?

Chapter Fourteen

Jacob's cheek throbbed, but no more than the rest of his body. He hurt everywhere, and, dammit, he still wanted Devon. A teenager would have better control, he thought in disgust.

He was almost cranky enough not to notice when she dragged him into the poorly lit bar and grill. The smell of greasy burgers and fries made his stomach clutch. The prospect of a sudsy beer settled it somewhat.

"Just a cola," Devon said when he asked her. She glanced at the scuffed linoleum, cracked orange vinyl benches and table crumbs as she blew on her fingers, smiled and added, "In a can."

Jacob's lips twitched. Admirable how she kept a straight face, really. This place couldn't be a reflection of her usual nightspots.

She was perusing the in-booth jukebox selection when he brought the drinks to the window table. Her eyes darted nervously between list and street—until he slid in, that is, then they bored directly into his.

"Explain Jacob," she said with meaning.

He winced at the arrow tip of pain that shot through his shoulder, and moved it tentatively. "Rudy explained that, Devon."

"He told me a story. I'm not sure I believe it."

"You think I'm the Christmas Murderer?" He sighed when she didn't answer. "You think it's possible."

Her gaze faltered. "No, I—" The breath she expelled fluttered her bangs. "I don't know what to believe." With impatient fingers, she flipped more jukebox pages. "You say you've never met Eden White."

"I haven't."

"She says you have. Rudy says you might have but wouldn't remember it." She propped her chin on her hands. Uncertain eyes tinged with accusation regarded him. "You disappeared before I was attacked, Riker, once in my office and again at the Holly Tree Restaurant. You appeared out of nowhere when I was trapped at the radio station. A woman popped out of thin air tonight, called you Jacob, came on to you then took off. Rudy had an answer for that, but then you took off, and so did he."

"So did Warren and Roscoe," Jacob pointed out.

"True, but Jimmy's missing, and I have no idea what to make of that. There's an angel pendant, an angel food cake and a woman named Angela who was not among the seven known victims of the Christmas Murderer. There's a man in prison who confessed to the killings—and then there's you."

Her tone softened on the last part of the sentence, but it didn't lessen the bite of her words. She didn't trust him. And right now, when he knew he should, Jacob didn't dare tell her the truth. Not after the weird episodes of this night. Even if she didn't strangle him, she would certainly evict him from of her life, and that would pave the way beautifully for the Christmas Murderer to kill her.

With fingers cold from handling the beer can, Jacob massaged his sore temples. There was him, all right, as she'd said. There was also Rudy's missing gun.

Devon's stare was relentless, as his would have been if a little man with a sledgehammer hadn't been banging away inside his head.

"You're not helping me understand this, Riker." She pouted a little and drummed the table with irritated fingers.

"Who are you? Why do you only let me get so close to you? Is it—" She hesitated, narrowed her eyes. "Does it have to do with your late wife?"

Jacob scrambled to remember her name. Delia Brightman. Death by heart attack en route to Minneapolis ten years ago.

He closed his eyes, willed away a sudden urge to blurt out the truth and substituted Laura's image for Delia's. "I loved her. She was—she died a long time ago, Devon. What I feel for you is different." Now there was an outrageous understatement. "It's overwhelming." He opened his eyes to her mistrustful stare. "It scares the hell out of me."

Finally, one truthful remark, and for an instant, it turned mistrust to doubt. Then she knit her brow and glanced back at the list of songs.

A country-pop tune played in a neighboring booth. Juice Newton. A song about angels.

He hated to see Devon's emotions being torn apart like this. It clawed at his heart. He captured her hand on the table between them and held it firmly, along with her gaze.

"I know it's hard," he said quietly, "but I'm asking you to trust me."

A frown pulled on her mouth. She glanced down and away. He saw her expression alter slightly. "Angel of the Morning."

He stared, unsure. "What about it?"

"The song, Riker. That's the title. It's also…" Her features hazed. "I can't remember. Something else. I almost caught it, but then it slipped away." She shook her head. "Maybe it'll come to me if I stop thinking about it. What were you saying before?"

He wanted to make love to her. He hadn't said that, but it had been on his mind since this morning. A smile grazed his lips, as he gave her fingers a reassuring squeeze. "Just trust me, okay? At least try to."

The suspicious light refused to die. It dimmed, though, and for that Jacob sensed he would have to settle.

"I'll try," she agreed. Her free hand rose to his cheek. "You're going to have a big bruise."

Her touch distracted him. Was it right that his lone sane thought in the middle of this godforsaken night, should be how desperately he wanted to find the nearest safe haven and start ripping her clothes off?

With extreme difficulty, he forced his mind back to the matter at hand. His, or rather Rudy's gun had been stolen by his attacker, undoubtedly the Christmas Murderer, undoubtedly for some unpleasant purpose. To shoot Devon? The prospect called up a shudder of revulsion that he hid behind a mouthful of beer. And yet, except for that deviation the other night, the M.O. of this killer was strangulation. He'd tried to stab Devon. As he'd stabbed another woman before her? Before any of his seven victims, including Laura?

The pounding in Jacob's head made organized thought impossible. He would see Devon safely home, swallow however many aspirins it took to counteract a whack on the head, then endeavor to reason it out.

With a quick check of the nearest booths, he slid out. "I've had enough of this place. Let's head back to the apartment."

"Mmm." Preoccupied, she worked her gloves onto her fingers. "The morning angel," she repeated, as the Juice Newton song began to fade. "What is it that's eluding me?" She noticed Jacob's outstretched hand, paused a beat, then lifted her gaze to his. "I really want to trust you, Riker."

"Then do," Jacob said without a flicker. "He'll have to kill me to get to you, Devon, and one thing you can believe— I'm not ready to die."

Her chin came up. "Most people aren't."

But even as she accepted his hand, it was someone else's voice that echoed in his ears. A raspy threat issued to him on the sidewalk just before he'd blacked out. A name within the threat.

"It was Dickens," he murmured. *"A Tale of Two Cities."*
Devon pulled her purse onto her shoulder. "Excuse me?"

"Whoever hit me made a reference to one of the characters."

"Sydney Carton?"

He glanced over sharply. "How did you know?"

She hiked up her collar as he opened the door to an icy blast of wind. "Carton was noble. He pretended to be Charles Darnay, knowing he'd die in Darnay's place. Don't murderers who are insane often think they're performing some noble deed when they kill?"

"It depends on the murderer. Apparently this one has a literary mind."

Devon halted so abruptly that Jacob bumped into her. He looked around, saw nothing. "What?"

"Roscoe." Her fingers caught and shook his coat sleeve. "His father's an English professor at NYU. He knows every book Charles Dickens ever wrote and every character in those books."

The touch of ironic justice his attacker had mentioned? Not for the first time in this case, Jacob's instincts fell flat. For the life of him he couldn't see where Christmas angels, "It Came Upon a Midnight Clear" and a Charles Dickens character intersected. Yet somewhere in the killer's mind they must.

Right at that moment, with the wind blowing in angry gusts and nothing but darkness and shadows surrounding them, Jacob would have given a great deal to be inside the killer's mind. His mad, agitated mind that wasn't going to be appeased until Devon was dead. Devon, seven other women, and—what else had he said? A cat on its ninth life?

ANGEL IN THE MORNING...

Why, beyond the song title, did those words sound so damnably familiar?

Devon knew that the more she agonized, the more elusive the answer would be. So she went to work on her feelings for Riker instead.

In her apartment bedroom with scented candles burning,

an old movie playing on the television, her mauve cotton sheets and coverlet turned down and her body begging for sleep, she sat on her queen-sized bed, hugged her upraised knees and stared out at the city.

It was after 3:00 a.m. Riker had seen her home, inspected her apartment from top to bottom, pressed an annoyingly chaste kiss to her forehead and muttered a curt goodnight. He'd also asked her to trust him again.

On the nightstand, Devon's phone hummed softly. She considered, then turned onto her stomach and reached for it. "Hannah." Although she'd been hoping for another caller, Devon wasn't disappointed. "You're still at Mandy's?"

"We got into the wine." Her sister sighed. "I feel fine, but two glasses is my limit and I've had three. Riker phoned a few minutes ago to say you were all right. Are you?"

Devon started to lie, recalled Riker's advice from the weekend and rolled on to her back. "Physically yes, but otherwise, not really."

"Are we talking about the attacks, or something else?"

Devon's eyes made out flickering angels' wings on the ceiling. "I think I love him, Hannah."

There was a pause before Hannah prompted, "But?"

Devon groaned. "I'm not sure I trust him. He keeps disappearing. And there was that woman tonight."

"What woman?"

"Rudy didn't tell you?"

"Rudy isn't here. Mandy's worried, but she says it's the cop in him. What woman?"

Devon explained briefly, rolled back on to her stomach and asked, "Is Alma there, too?"

"Uh-huh."

"And Warren and Roscoe?"

An uneasy edge crept in. Devon knew Hannah had placed a confidential hand around the mouthpiece. "Roscoe phoned about an hour ago. He said he hadn't had any luck finding Warren."

Devon judged her tone. "And that makes you nervous?"

"No, but it seemed to upset Alma. She, ah, drank a little more wine than I did. She started talking about the time she and Warren worked in New York. When her daughter died, she went into a depression for eighteen months. During that time, Warren was charged twice with sexual harassment."

"I thought the charges were dropped."

"They were, but it still didn't look good, which, I suppose, is what bothers her now. Not that I think Warren's involved in the attacks on you, but I have a feeling Alma's not quite so sure."

Devon's fingers plucked at the coverlet. "I'm not sure either. About anything. I don't imagine anyone's heard from Jimmy?"

"It's three in the morning, Devon," Hannah reminded gently. "But I know how you feel. He'll turn up soon."

If Devon had her doubts, she kept them to herself. One of the candles beside the TV crackled, and she glanced over. On screen, Katherine Hepburn was self-righteously dumping Humphry Bogart's gin stock over the side of the *African Queen.*

She made a determined effort during the next five minutes to keep her mood upbeat. No matter what Riker's opinion, worry weighed on Hannah like an anchor.

Having promised her sister again that she was fine and that all the doors and windows were locked, Devon hung up. She was in the process of extinguishing the candles when she heard the quiet knock on her door.

Her first instinct was to freeze. Her second was to cross the floor in silence and use the peephole.

Shadows bathed the corridor, but not so many of them that she couldn't identify her late-night visitor. Long dark hair, black coat, unfathomable eyes. "Riker," she breathed and, steadying her twitchy nerves, unsnapped the deadbolt.

His expression didn't betray a single emotion when he murmured, "I thought you might be asleep."

"Thought?" She let the door swing open in invitation.

He lingered on the threshold while the candlelight reflected in his eyes. The hot sweep of them across her scantily clad body might have made her blush under different circumstances.

"Was afraid," Riker clarified. He stepped inside and, with his booted foot, nudged the door closed.

He stood unmoving while the candles flickered wildly around them. The spicy scents of pine and hyacinth swam in the air. Devon's wisp of negligee floated about her ankles as a draft blew across them.

Riker stared through half-lidded eyes, his hands in his coat pockets, his features a near-perfect mask of imperturbability.

But something gave him away to her, a tiny glitch in his otherwise flawless armor. A muscle twitching in his jaw, a slight flare of his nostrils, or maybe it was just the simple act of breathing—not quite as steady as it usually was.

Questions, ever-present, flitted through Devon's mind only to be shooed away by a single, inescapable fact.

Stopping the thought, she reached for his hand. "I'm afraid, too, Riker, but not, it seems, of you."

His brows went up. "You mean you trust me after all?"

"I don't know." She brought her fingers to the faint bruise on his cheek and her mouth level with his. "I only know I love you. And that scares me more right now than the Christmas Murderer."

BLEARY-EYED, Devon ate breakfast with Hannah at Jerry's Deli the next morning. A perky redhead on Jerry's television predicted more snow while Devon spread cream cheese and strawberry jam on a whole-wheat bagel.

"You look awfully happy for a woman in turmoil." Hannah cupped a steaming coffee mug in her palms. "I wish I could find so much pleasure in uncertainty."

"No word from Roscoe?"

"Or Warren. Alma was beside herself when I dropped her off at home this morning."

Devon licked jam from her thumb, paused and frowned. "Well, everyone can't have disappeared."

"No, Rudy's back. He got in half an hour before Alma and I left. He looked…"

"Tired?"

"More than that. I'd say weary. It's the way I felt after Tony died, and I had to keep going through the motions of day-to-day life. Oh—" She interrupted herself to offer a compassionate reaction to the television newscaster. "There was a three-house fire in Germantown last night. What was I saying?"

"Rudy looked weary."

"Mandy's terribly worried about him. He didn't go to bed after he got home; just washed up, changed his clothes and drank three cups of coffee. He said he had to meet someone this morning."

"Riker?"

"He didn't say. Devon." Her normally serene face troubled, Hannah touched her sister's wrist. "I'm so scared for you. We didn't really get into it last night, but I kept thinking about all those women who've died. And then you left the club with Teddi. You have to be more careful. Let Riker and Rudy do their job. I've been reading up on the Christmas Murders. Four of the seven women were killed at midnight."

Devon swallowed her bite of bagel before it turned to sawdust. "I know that, Hannah. Believe me, I don't take foolish risks." Actually, she had last night when she'd followed Riker, but that had been an impulse, prompted by love and a nagging sense of doubt that refused to die despite the fact that she'd woken up beside him this morning.

Regret rolled like a wave through her mind. She sipped her coffee and glanced at the TV screen. What she saw there caused her hands to clench around the mug.

The woman's face, not that of the newscaster but rather the face of a brunette, stared out at her. She knew that face, had met the woman only last night.

"—Gina Bartholomew, a prostitute known to the Philadelphia police, was found dead in her downtown apartment at 5:00 a.m. this morning. She had been shot once at close range. Neighbors claim not to have heard the shot which killed her instantly...."

"Devon?" Alarm registered in Hannah's tone. "What is it? You've gone white."

Nausea churned in Devon's stomach. Gina Bartholomew. A prostitute, known to the police. Known to Riker, whether he remembered it or not, admitted it or not. Known to Rudy as well?

Aggression spawned by shock swept in to douse the sickness. She'd said her name was Eden White. She'd approached Riker deliberately to make that claim. For whose benefit? Hers? Riker's? Rudy's?

"I'm—" Devon found she couldn't swallow. Her cheeks felt waxen, her lips stiff. "I have to go."

"No." Hannah gripped her arm with surprising strength. "Something's wrong. Tell me. Please. I want to help."

Wanted to—or needed to? Devon had no idea which it was, and now was no time to debate the issue. She drew a deep breath, felt her tension ease and said, "That woman they just mentioned on the news. The one who was killed last night. I met her at the Kat. She said—she insisted that she knew Riker."

Hannah's face paled. "Killed last night! Oh, Devon, no, not another victim. How can he do these things? It's the same person who attacked you, isn't it?"

"I don't know. Maybe. Probably." She pressed her fingers to her forehead, willing clear thought. "Whatever else it is, you won't convince me that it's a coincidence." Her hands came down to fist on the table. "He knows something. He must. He just refuses to tell me what it is."

Baffled, Hannah asked, "Who?"

"Riker."

"Well, he *is* a cop."

"Yes, he's a cop. And Gina Bartholomew was a prostitute. There's a connection, Hannah, I know there is." She slanted a determined look at the TV screen. "And I'm going to find it."

DUGAN HERDED Jacob and Rudy into a relatively obscure corner of the detectives' room, whipped around and began to pace.

"You're off your nuts by a mile, both of you. I've got a dead woman who was seen talking to you last night at the Kat. I've got a .38-calibre bullet—"

"—but no weapon," Jacob reminded him evenly.

Dugan snarled. "I've got the legal counsel of a respected state justice panting down my neck, whispering discretion and action in the same breath." He waved his arm dramatically. "I've got homicidal pimps and pushers lined up in the corridor, drugs and guns missing from downstairs, a drive-by shooting on 10th Street and a bystander plugged with a semi-automatic during a convenience-store robbery. I've got all this crap to deal with, and you want me to turn a blind eye to your criminal role-playing? Hell, I should be holding the pair of you as suspects. A dozen or more people probably saw you take off after Gina Bartholomew last night."

"Have any of those people come forward?" Rudy asked.

"The investigation's only four hours old, Rudy. Give us time to make the rounds. There'll be plenty of finger-pointing by this afternoon."

"All in the wrong direction, Dugan." Jacob used a pen to stir the motor-oil coffee brewed in all cop shops. "Your instincts know that even if your brain refuses to see it. I want to catch a killer; I haven't turned into one."

"And you think you'd be better at doing that than the law-enforcement officers of this city?"

"It's the same guy, Dugan. He wants Devon. He's setting me up. He used Gina to do it."

"So where's your missing gun?" Dugan jeered. "If this is a frame, the gun should have been discovered, together with a full set of your prints."

Jacob resisted an urge to snap. "It's too early for that. He hasn't killed Devon yet. The gun'll surface, but not until the murderer's finished his plan." Which he wouldn't do, Jacob swore, until hell froze over and took him with it. Setting his cup aside, he regarded the surly cop. "It won't help anything if you arrest me for fraud. It'll only piss this guy off more, make him desperate, maybe even reckless."

A bushy brow elevated. "My point exactly. Reckless means we'll nab him."

"Yeah, right. You'll nab him—after he murders Devon."

Rudy inserted himself between the glaring men. "You've already got a corpse, Dugan. A fresh one and at least seven others before. You've been assigned to Gina Bartholomew's case. Your gut-cop sense has to tell you her case bisects the attacks on Devon Tremayne somewhere. Your men are working on Devon's problem, granted, but it isn't enough. You know it isn't. Let Jacob see this through. Watch him like a damned hawk, but forget about the deception angle for the moment. It's no skin off your nose, and it might save Devon's life."

Dugan hissed. A hand raked his woolly hair as he turned. "You're not asking me to bend the rules; you want me to tie them in knots." He scowled. "What did this woman say to you, Jacob? Exactly."

Jacob recognized the concession but said nothing to it—Dugan wouldn't appreciate the sentiment. He recounted the details concisely.

"So if not you, who *did* know her?" the cop demanded. Dugan accessed her computer record and the entries already made of her clients.

"Lawyers, cops, a chiropractor, three oral and two cosmetic surgeons."

Jacob bent over his shoulder. "Oral surgeons?"

None of the names he scanned belonged to Andrew McGruder, but then Gina Bartholomew's client list contained more than a few obvious gaps.

He read on until his sharp eyes caught something in the middle of her rap sheet. "You busted her, Rudy?" he said with a frown.

The older man's fingers curled. "Guess so. Don't remember it. Must've been donkeys' years ago."

"Eight donkeys," Dugan informed him. "She was twenty-six at the time, and already a pro. Her rap sheet goes back nine years before your bust. Look at the list of johns! What is this?" He scanned backward. "Her personal diary? Who entered these names so fast...?"

Jacob didn't care who, when or how. He didn't much care for the expression on Rudy's lined face either. Leaving the computer to Dugan, he regarded his uncle. "You do remember her, don't you?"

Rudy sucked in his cheeks. "Took me a few minutes but I pegged her quick enough."

"Funny she didn't peg you."

"Probably she did. I wasn't her assignment, was I? Whoever sent her wanted your apple cart upset, kid."

"How many times did you arrest her?"

His uncle squinted. "Couldn't say. A couple or three. Others busted her a lot more. I only worked vice for a few years."

Jacob held his gaze. "You were in homicide eight years ago, Rudy."

"Back off, boy," Rudy growled. "I was a good cop. Still am, dammit, on or off active duty. I backed you to Dugan, even tried to tail Devon for you last night. Is it my fault she drives like a crazy woman in that fancy car of hers, or that my old clunker hates fast starts these days?"

Jacob held up a surrendering hand. "All right. I get the message, Rudy. I was out of line. I'm sorry."

"You're twitchy's what you are." Rudy's scowl deepened. "We all are, Dugan included. But taking bites out of each other won't solve our problems. There's something we're missing, all of us, something we should be seeing but aren't."

"Something to do with Gina Bartholomew?"

"I doubt it. She's too new on the scene. It's in the M.O., has to be. No rape involved, he just kills 'em. Strangulation for the most part."

"And a probable stabbing," Jacob recalled. "He said he'd

used a knife before when he attacked Devon at the Wave. He also mentioned the name Angela.''

"It's a slow check,'' Dugan tossed backward from his console. "Manpower,'' he added at Jacob's look. "Our budget, the holidays and a nasty flu bug, versus a sharp rise in crime over the past six months. We're stretched to the limit.'' His gaze narrowed in warning. "Which is the one and only reason I'm allowing this farce to continue. No unnecessary risks, Jacob, or you'll be behind bars so fast your head'll spin off its bolt. Now, what was the name of the woman Devon's attacker mentioned?''

"Angela,'' Jacob told him. Picking up his cup, he let the rim rest against his mouth as he mused out loud. "Angel…''

Chapter Fifteen

Devon waved at the smoke from a score of cigarettes and at least one cigar. "So we're sitting in a billiard hall three days before Christmas, watching people play pool, drink themselves senseless and sing bad country carols because Tanya suggested that Brando's death might be linked to this place? I think we'd be better off going through Rudy's computer files looking for a woman named Angela."

"We'll get to that," Riker promised. He wove his gaze back and forth across the crowded room. "Cop," he said of a broad-shouldered, man with a buzz cut. "Rookie, I'll bet."

"Must've been the peach fuzz that gave him away. What about his buddy? He looks too shifty to be a cop."

"Could be undercover. Or just a playing partner." He nodded right. "Those three guys are lawyers."

She squinted through the smoke. "I'll take your word for it. I'm not sure I understand how this is going to help you find Brando's murderer, or what his death has to do with Gina Bartholomew's." Although she had a vaguely uneasy idea. "Gina lived several blocks from here."

"Her record says this was her turf until quite recently."

"Then shouldn't you be talking to people, asking them who knew whom and how well?"

He sent her an amused smile. "I'll get to that, Devon. Right now, I just want to watch."

"And I want to know how it's possible that Gina Bartholomew recognized you when you continue to insist you never met her.''

He rubbed his fingers over his closed left eye. ''You're not going to let that go, are you?''

''Not until I'm satisfied you're telling me the truth.''

''The truth.'' He sighed and it sounded impatient. ''Okay, the truth is, I think she was sent to the Kat last night.''

''Why? To make me doubt you?''

''Maybe. Partly. But also to throw me off the scent. To set me up. Devon, if someone you didn't know came up to you like that wouldn't you be tempted to follow him, find out what the hell was going on?''

''Of course I would. Anyone—ah.''

''Right. My gun—or rather Rudy's. The murder. It's all part of whatever setup he has planned. Maybe he's trying to spook me as well, I don't know. But I'll lay odds that he intends to pin more than a hooker's death on me.''

''Not a comforting thought.'' For either of them, Devon reflected.

She toyed, preoccupied, with her cider glass. Still no word from Jimmy, and Riker had been as skittish as a colt all day. Circumspect and moody. Tonight was an improvement, but there was still something he wasn't telling her—and other things in her own mind that she couldn't reason out.

The morning angel. Angel of the morning. The words had begun to haunt. If only they would...

A distant light flashed mid-thought. Very slowly, Devon's face cleared. '''Who ''morns'' an angel such as you.' He spelled *mourns* wrong.''

Riker dragged his gaze from the tables. ''Who did?''

''In the note I got yesterday morning, he spelled *mourns* without the *u* and put it in quotations marks. It must be significant. Morning angel.'' Frustration moved in on the heels of discovery. ''That's still not what my mind's trying to remember, though. Why won't it come to me?''

Riker traced a water ring with his finger. ''It must have

been a deliberate misspelling since he put it in quotes. I wondered about that when you showed me the note.''

''Well, I can't believe he's descended to giving us clues, can you?''

''I can believe a lot of things, Devon. Insanity leaves itself open to errors in judgment. It's possible he wants you to know who you're dying for.''

''Presumably Angela. Whoever she is or was, she must have been important to him.''

''She didn't live in Philly,'' Riker told her. ''Dugan ran every Angela on record. More than fifty women by that name have been murdered in the past twenty-five years, but none of the unsolved cases match up in any cross-check with the Christmas Murders.''

Devon spied a little man in gray and poked Riker's ribs. ''There's that guy who told us about Brando.''

''Pop.'' Riker slid out of the booth. ''Wait here, I'll bring him over.''

Devon couldn't imagine what an old pool-hall junkie might know that would help them, but Pop was a rather sad-faced man and appealing because of it. An aging basset hound with a quick smile and a crafty nature.

He trotted along beside Riker and slipped into the booth without a qualm. ''Thought you might be back,'' he said, smiling hopefully at Devon. ''We heard about Brando. Not a good end.''

Riker got right to the point. ''What's the word, Pop? Did he drown?''

The little man snorted. ''Brando? When ducks start drowning, I'll believe it. Not till. He did half of Erie once, before he got into the stuff. Bragged he coulda done the whole thing if he hadn't swallowed the water.'' A wink at Devon. ''Lake water wasn't so good ten years ago.'' He smacked his lips for Riker's benefit. ''Dry in here, don't you think?''

Devon pushed her untouched cider sideways. ''Will this do?''

He took a doubtful drink, shrugged and huddled forward

around the glass. "I think Brando was done," he confided. He tested the cider again. "I think he knew something and that's what got him done."

"Why do you think he knew something?" Devon asked.

"'Cause he was hurting, and when you hurt you do deals. No one would lend to him anymore. His old lady was bugging him to get off the stuff. But getting off's hard, and what do you do afterward?" He rubbed his thumb and fingers together. "Takes bread, or something like it. Brando was done for sure," Pop repeated firmly.

Devon saw the exchange of money below the table and smiled. A fifty this time. Must be a Christmas bonus.

"Who did he deal with, Pop?" Riker scrutinized the old man's face. "Do you have any idea?"

Pop stuck out his lower lip. "Maybe." He glanced at the bill in his palm. "Leastways I saw Brando here the same day you came asking for him. Told his buddies he was killing time, waiting for a score. A blue-line shot, he called it. Laughed when he said that. Hockey game was playing on the TV. Philly against the Islanders. The guys, they thought he was talking hockey shot, but I don't know. Brando had a funny sense of humor. Cops hated it. Called him a wise ass."

"Sarcastic." Devon grinned. "I'm like that sometimes."

"So are cops," Pop said with a sly smile at Riker. "You gotta give back what you get, whether you're scared or not. Brando knew that better'n most here."

Riker sent him a considering look, then said simply, "Gina Bartholomew."

Pop screwed up his face. "Rings a bell, but not a loud one. I'm not big on names. Better on faces. She a looker?"

"She was," Devon told him. "Someone shot her last night in her apartment."

Riker drew a computer photo out of his jacket pocket. Pop peered at the photo, then made a gesture of recognition. "Oh, yeah, I know her. Used to hang out here sometimes late on Sundays. Said that was her slow night for office dogs."

"Did you ever see her with anyone?"

"Once or twice." Pop's eyes twinkled. His fingers gave a subtle wag. When he was satisfied, he leaned back and raised his cider. "She liked 'em young—like you, detective. Young, strong, a bit cocky. Sometimes she got lucky, sometimes she got busted. Went for older guys once in a while, but not much. Professionals, most of 'em."

"Anyone specific?" Devon asked.

"Not that I saw. She just liked men. Flirted with them all the time. Used to sass the cops plenty whenever they came around, in or out of uniform. Usually they didn't bust her, but even when they did, she'd tease 'em. Too bad she's gone." His expression grew vaguely woeful. "She was kinda nice in her own way."

Riker cocked a curious brow. "Did she know Brando?"

"Probably."

"That's it? Just probably?"

Pop flashed his gap-toothed grin. "I come here to shoot stick, not to spy on people, Riker."

"Yeah, right." Clearly unbelieving, Riker fished in his jeans' pocket for a blank card. On it, he scribbled his apartment and cell phone numbers. "Call me if anything comes to mind while you're shooting your stick tonight, okay?"

Pop closed a shrewd eye. "Never know. It might do." He scooped up the card, fisted the money, grinned and hopped from the bench before Devon realized his intent. Her hand went automatically to her purse, but this time her wallet was intact.

"Interesting world, down here," she remarked with a blend of resignation and irony.

"It has its own peculiar brand of charm."

She rested her elbows on the table. "Did we learn anything valuable?"

"Not immediately, except that Gina and Brando knew each other."

"And they both knew the person who killed them. The Christmas Murderer." Devon visualized. "I can't picture Warren in the part. Or Andrew for that matter."

"Which is precisely why they'd be perfect for it."

Her gaze traveled around the smoky room. Silver balls twinkled dully above the bar. She saw Pop bite into a greasy burger and felt absurdly relieved. Better a burger than a bourbon. But no doubt that would come.

She sighed at Riker's expression as he watched her. "You can't change the world, I know. I can wish, though."

"Mmm, well, wish later." He drank up and pulled out his gloves. "We have work to do."

"I hate to ask." She secured her purse. "What and where?"

His eyes glinted. Surprising her, he caught her fingers and brought them to his lips. "Belated dinner, Devon. My place. Cold stroganoff and wine."

Warmth pooled in her stomach, flowing swiftly outward to weaken her limbs. "No more blood and guts?"

"It's almost midnight. I'll refrain if you will."

She smiled. "Be glad to."

Her mood only faltered for a moment when she glimpsed Pop at the bar. He was studying the shadowy area near the rear door. The door through which a man in a knitted hat, a green sweater and a bulky black coat had just passed.

"WHERE ON EARTH have you been!"

It wasn't so much a question as a shriek, and it made the hair on Warren's neck curl in protest. Bringing his bleary eyes into focus, he mumbled a sullen, "I'm allowed to have a life, Alma. You're my sister, not my drill sergeant."

She marched down the stairs of their sensibly furnished Chestnut Hill house in her blue flannel robe and matching mules. Head band holding her hair back, make-up creamed off, legs, he noticed through the flap, increasingly veined and fish-white. He contained a shudder but didn't have the nerve to head for the whiskey bottle he so desperately craved.

"It's 2:00 a.m., Warren," she barked. "You didn't come home last night, or to work today. I had to make up a story about you spraining your ankle. *Under the weather* would have translated to *hung over,* and I won't have the staff gossiping about you any more than they already do.''

Warren's head ached; his mouth and throat were parched, and sometime over the past twenty-four hours, someone had removed his eyeballs from their sockets and rolled them in wet sand.

''Well?'' Arms folded, Alma tapped her foot.

''I—'' He swayed precariously. ''I don't know.'' He blurted it out, hadn't meant to sound so stupidly defensive, yet for the life of him, it was true. For the most part.

Alma's flint-hard eyes stared through him. Then her brow furrowed and her neck craned forward. ''Good Lord, what have you done with your clothes?''

What had he…? Warren glanced down, then again in panic. Aghast, he held his hands out at his sides like a scarecrow stuck in a field. ''I have no idea. I thought I was wearing my tuxedo.''

''You can't tell a tux from those—'' Alma made a gesture of disgust. ''Thrift-store cast-offs? That overcoat looks like a sack and the pants are stained.'' She pointed to his knees, which did, in fact, appear to be caked with something. Dried mud, he hoped, but his stubborn mind refused to fill in the gaps.

''Was there a woman?'' Alma pressed.

''I don't remember.'' He did actually. Vaguely. There had been a woman—or was he assuming that because the sweater he currently wore carried a faint scent of perfume? ''I didn't do anything wrong,'' he maintained.

''I thought you couldn't remember what you did?''

''I can't.'' He knew he sounded whiny, couldn't help it. ''I'm not a monster, Alma. It's Christmas. I had a few drinks, missed a day of work. No one got hurt, not like…'' What? Something. Truth to tell, he couldn't recall much about that other night either.

He'd been in Seattle, at a conference. The party afterwards was a blur to this day. He'd seen his niece, Margaret at the hotel. She'd been upset, had come to his room, asked him to call her mother. But Warren hadn't wanted to talk to Alma. He'd pretended to call. No answer, he'd lied. They'd have a little drink, and he'd try again later....

Unfortunately, now as then, the events of later eluded him. The next he'd heard, Margaret had been dead. She'd hung herself. And he'd had to sober up fast in order to face the authorities.

Highly suspicious, Alma walked over to where he'd halted in the foyer. "You didn't hurt anyone, Warren? You're sure of that?"

Did she mean now or in the past?

Sweat trickled down his spine. "I'm not a monster," he repeated, his lame tone making him wince. "I had a lapse, Alma, a blackout."

She sniffed. "You smell like a brothel. Go upstairs and take a bath, for heaven's sake. You have dirt under your fingernails, and I hate to think about the vermin living in those clothes."

Warren wished, oh how he wished, he were a stronger man. The type of man who could stand up to a steamroller like Alma. How satisfying to take the same vicious runs at her ego that she took at his. Mow her down and shut her mean mouth for good. No wonder Jimmy had deserted his post. Alma could grind a man to a fine powder with nothing more than a glare and a few pointed words. He hated her now as he had for years—and he wouldn't have let her know that for all the money in the world.

One day, though, he vowed as he trudged dutifully toward the staircase, he'd show her a side she wouldn't dream he possessed. One day. After he'd figured it out himself. And when he did, Alma wouldn't order him around any more. For the first time in his life, he would be free....

JACOB DECIDED he must be dreaming. Two songs buzzed in his head. One a Christmas carol, one a pop song.

His eyes felt gritty from fatigue and residual smoke from

the billiard hall. The bedroom was dark, the sheets beside him warm but empty.

He woke in a heartbeat, vaulted from the bed then had to pause. Where was he? Not in his apartment, but in Devon's, floating on sex and microwaved stroganoff.

He dragged on his jeans, bringing her grandfather clock into focus as he stumbled squinting into the living room—4:40 a.m. Had she lost her mind?

He located her in the shadow of the illuminated tree. Since it was the only light source in the room, his eyes adjusted fairly quickly.

She sat cross-legged in a skimpy robe the color of ripe cranberries. Her hair was tousled, her eyes excited as she hopped up to grab his hand.

"Listen." She pulled him between two separate music sources.

"It Came Upon a Midnight Clear," he murmured as the choir sang.

"No, not that one." She stopped the cassette recorder. "I just wanted to hear about the angels. This other one is significant too, at least it is to me. Maybe to him as well, though I doubt it since he chose the Midnight Clear song."

Jacob frowned as he stared at her. "Are you sure you're awake?"

"Positive. Sit down, and I'll explain." She pushed him toward a chair, picked up the last note she'd received and handed it to him. "'Who ''morns'' an angel such as you.''' She quoted the second line. "*Mourns* is spelled wrong. I knew it must be significant, but I wasn't sure how."

"And now you are?"

"Don't sound so skeptical. If you expand *morns* to *morning,* you have, in a manner of speaking, a 'morning angel,' right?"

"It's a stretch, but okay."

She went to her knees in front of him, eyes bright as she fisted the denim that covered his knees. "You lived in New

York, Riker. Don't you remember the Angel of the Morning?''

Riker *had* lived in New York. Then again, so had Jacob, briefly, and he still drew a blank. ''I don't—'' he began, then opted for the truth. ''No.''

Her breath huffed out on an impatient note. ''She was the morning disk jockey on one of those mellow FM stations. It must have been close to twenty years ago.''

Jacob's expression closed down. ''Do you know this woman?''

''I was ten years old, Riker. But I remember hearing about her later in college. She disappeared one day.''

''Like Jimmy.''

Devon set her jaw. ''It turned out she'd been murdered. Her radio tag was Angel of the Morning, or the Morning Angel. I don't remember her real name, but an older broadcaster might. She must have been a real go-getter. She was quite young when she got her own syndicated series—some New Wave thing where she featured up-and-coming artists. I'm pretty sure the show was picked up here, in Pennsylvania, which is where I'd have been living at the time. Hannah might remember her better, although she was never really into New Wave.''

Jacob studied her still-energized face. He wished his brain would defog and catch up. ''So you think the Christmas Murderer was referring to this Morning Angel in the last note he sent you?''

''I think it's possible. Figure it, Riker. Angela—Angel— it does fit. We assume he murdered a woman name Angela at some point. But what if the murderer was never caught?''

Jacob let the idea sink in. ''I could run it through records, I suppose. You're sure she worked in New York?''

''Pretty sure. I took courses in broadcasting, Riker. Certain names tended to crop up—innovators, pioneers, that sort of thing. Angel had a prime morning slot at what was probably a male-dominated station back then. Plus, she pulled off a syndicated series. I'd call her a pioneer of sorts, wouldn't you?"

"Maybe," he allowed. "But no more than Alma. Her bio's full of media cudos."

"Behind-the-scenes cudos." Sitting back, Devon combed a restless hand through her hair. "I'm not trying to diminish Alma's accomplishments by any means, but on-air and in-syndication was tough even in the enlightened early eighties."

"I'll check it out," he promised, then let a reluctant smile tug on his lips as he reached for her. "Right now, though, there's something else I'd like to check out."

Devon grinned. "You cops are insatiable."

The gleam in his eyes could have been mistaken for lust. Jacob hoped she wouldn't recognize it for what it really was.

Guilt, love—and the pure unadulterated terror that he would lose her, not only to the lies, but also to a madman bent on murder.

ANDREW MCGRUDER opened his apartment door on December twenty-third and promptly screamed as a man toppled backward onto his welcome mat. Fortunately, he was a pathetic screamer. More fortunate that the man on his doorstep wasn't dead, merely sleeping.

"Well, *really.*" Indignation warred with uncertainty as Andrew nudged the recumbent stranger with his loafered toe.

He didn't expect the man to surge up like a sprung jack-in-the-box. He yelped when the man did precisely that, and flung himself back against the wall.

"Where am I?" the man demanded, whip-sharp.

Pressing a palm to his heart, Andrew located his voice. "You're on my floor. You were outside my apartment until I tried to leave for work."

The man swore and cast an accusing look over his shoulder. "Who are you?"

"Andrew McGruder. I—" he straightened, cleared his throat and strove for dignity. "I live here. Who are you?"

"Roscoe—" The man blinked, scowling. "What floor is this? Where's Dev—never mind. I must have come to the wrong door."

"So you decided to sit down and go to sleep?" Andrew who'd ventured off the wall, backed up a pace at the man's thundercloud expression.

"Roscoe?"

Heavenly angel, Hannah. Andrew closed his eyes as her face appeared through the staircase slats.

"What are you doing here?"

The man's lean cheeks reddened. "Sleeping it off, apparently."

"Sleeping what off? Go ahead," she instructed the man behind her. "Suite 302. Mrs. Makon. She's expecting you, or rather her pipes are." She returned her attention to Roscoe. Her eyes softened in sympathy. "You look terrible, Roscoe."

He adjusted his black wool overcoat, scraped a hand over his stubbly jaw. Andrew still wasn't sure what to make of the expression in his coal-black eyes and so wisely held his tongue.

"I played raquetball for three hours last night," Roscoe recalled, wincing. "The guy's name was Brad. Couldn't have been more than twenty-five. The sponsor's son. Carpet and flooring company. We hit a few clubs afterward. Shouldn't have done it. I don't know why I told the taxi driver to drop me here."

"Or why you climbed up to three when Devon lives on two," Andrew added, resentfully belligerent. He hated slick operators. All looks, no substance. Women were so easily hoodwinked.

Hannah's delicate brows came together in perplexity. "You were looking for Devon? Why?"

Roscoe jammed one hand into his pocket, lifted the other to his forehead. "I don't know." He squeezed his eyes closed. "Seeking shelter maybe. Were you home last night? I tried your door first, or thought I did. Judging from the way I feel, I must have been pretty tanked."

"You didn't look tanked when I woke you up," Andrew said, merely to irritate.

Roscoe shot him a nasty look, and he shut up.

Hannah linked her fingers. "I was home, Roscoe, but I drank a cup of Chinese tea before I went to bed. It has a mild sedative effect. I could have slept through your knocking."

"Yes, but how did he—" Roscoe's slitted sideways glance had Andrew finishing his sentence into his collar. "—get into the building without a key?"

Hannah waved the question aside. "It doesn't matter. You're here, Roscoe, and neither of us have had breakfast. If you want to talk to Devon, she'll be leaving for the station around nine, I think. I gather Alma's trying to instill some holiday spirit. Late in, early out. We decided to take the train to Mom and Dad's tomorrow night instead of this afternoon."

The two walked away.

Creep, Andrew thought, miffed that none of his shots had hit the mark, even more miffed at the fawn-eyed look of gratitude Hannah bestowed upon him.

Then again, Hannah didn't interest Andrew, never had. It was Devon he sought, and Devon he would have. Soon enough, he would make her understand that as clearly as he did.

Chapter Sixteen

"Happy holidays, all." In her bronze-tone living room, Alma raised a glass of eggnog. "Christmas Eve tomorrow, and Bob, Tim and Teddi already volunteered to hold the afternoon fort. Everyone else goes off the clock as of twelve noon. That doesn't include either Warren or myself, of course."

Devon joined in the toast, but kept her gaze fixed on Riker's cell phone. He'd given it to her before she and Hannah had left their respective jobs for Alma's pre-Christmas cocktail party.

"I'll call," he'd promised, "the minute I turn anything up."

"Ring," she ordered the phone, then gave it a frustrated shake and stuffed it into her purse.

Alma, misinterpreting the action, strode over to clamp a firm hand on her wrist. "What do you think you're doing, madame?"

"Leaving, if you so much as hint that I shouldn't."

"Stubborn," Alma accused. Her severe expression melted. "I'm only concerned about you, my dear."

Worried, too, that Warren hadn't seen fit to put in an appearance yet? Devon patted her plump arm. "I know. Thank you. I want Riker to call, and he hasn't, so I'm feeling cranky about it. No word from Jimmy after I left the station?"

"Not a peep. He—yes, Roscoe?" Alma inquired coolly.

"Shall we speak louder, or are the accoustics adequate for your eavesdropping needs?"

Caught red-handed, Roscoe gave his tie a perfunctory tug and his employer a curt smile. "I only want to help Devon with her problem, Alma."

"By prancing from stripper bar to stripper bar with Richard Egan last night?"

Devon's eyes narrowed. "Richard 'six-o'clock-news-hour' Egan?"

"He's a friend," Roscoe defended. "We were humoring a mutual client's son. Can I help it if the son likes stripper bars?"

"It's immoral," Alma began, her cheeks quivering. "Not to mention exploitive, and I don't know what else."

"Try fishy," Devon suggested. She glanced at Hannah near the hearth and arched inquiring brows at Roscoe. "Would you care to explain how, after visiting a few clubs, you wound up propped against Andrew McGruder's door?"

Roscoe smoothed his silky black hair. "We've been through this, Devon. I thought it was your door."

"You were coming to me because Hannah didn't answer."

"What would you have done in my place?"

"Ditched my buddies before I got buzzed and gone home to my own bed."

His soft eyes flashed with more temper than she'd ever seen him display. "Is that a warning, Devon?"

"It would be if I didn't think my sister could handle her own life. But," she released a weighty sigh, "she can, so no, it isn't. Just remember, I love her, Roscoe. Anyone hurts her, and all promises are off."

He eyed her levelly, but offered no response. Instead, he crossed to the carved walnut doors and let himself out.

"Most unusual behavior," Alma remarked in his wake.

"Just plain weird if you ask me." Deflated, Devon sat. "Do you think I'm getting paranoid?"

The laugh that rumbled out of Alma's chest surprised her. "I'm sorry, my dear," she managed after several seconds of choked amusement. She wiped a moist eye. "It's just that you're the very last person I would have expected to hear utter those words. And so seriously. You've been attacked, threatened and attacked again. Your young man, a trained police officer, has a welt on his cheek from a blow very likely delivered to him by the man who's after you. And you ask me if you're getting paranoid. Poor dear." Planting her hands, she kissed Devon's forehead. "Tired yes; paranoid never." Her face grew puzzled. "Is that your purse I hear ringing?"

In two quick moves, Devon retrieved the phone and flipped the mouthpiece down. "Riker?"

For a moment, she heard nothing. Then, slowly, it began. Scratchy notes, poor quality sound. A single, small speaker, her distant mind discerned.

She let the song play out. No words. No need. Any fool would recognize the melody at this time of year.

The raspy voice that covered the final notes made her skin prickle and crawl. "This is the last verse the angels will sing for you, Devon Tremayne." He warbled the words to the tune he just played for her. "The days move ever forward, and with them the years. Soon I will do the same, my dear and you will move no more..."

"GOTCHA," Jacob exclaimed. "Angel Barret, the Morning Angel. WABQ." He frowned. "That's the old Manhattan Q."

He slouched back in his office chair. It had been some kind of risk using the *Beat*'s computer today, but Dugan had been backlogged, Rudy was nowhere to be found, and Mandy had tacked a note to the front door that read simply and irritably, Gone shopping. Chances were good she hadn't meant for presents.

"Jacob?" Sadie poked her head inside. "Do you need anything before I go?"

He didn't look at his efficient, mop-topped assistant, but

answered absently over his shoulder, "No thanks. Take off, and you and Al have a nice Christmas."

"Hanukkah," she corrected.

A few ticks, then a plaid arm poked at the monitor. "Back issues of the *Times?* You on a story?"

"You could call it that. Ever heard of Angel Barret?"

"Nope."

"What about the Morning Angel?"

"No—well—maybe. It's going back some, though."

"Eighteen years," Jacob confirmed. "She died at Christmas time. This is the first article I've found on her."

Sadie tucked her brown curls under a woollen tam. "Cops know more. Why don't you pick Rudy's brains, or better yet, his computer's?"

"Because I'd have to B and E his home to do it."

"You've done that—"

"Button it, Sadie."

He heard the grin in her voice. "Hey, I'm only repeating one of Rudy's stories." Bending, she patted his cheek. "Happy Christmas. Bring your pretty new woman friend over for dinner during the holidays."

Jacob swung his head around, hoped he managed not to look startled. "You know about her?"

Sadie's grin widened. "I'm a reporter, remember? Oh, all right," she relented at his unpromising expression, "One of the guys in the bullpen spotted you going into the Kat with, quote, a looker, unquote. You never hit the clubs; I could count the dates you've had in the past few years on the fingers of one hand, and Steve said you were wearing a suit. Put those things together, it spells relationship to me. Strong potential for one anyway." She gave him a sassy grin as she pulled on her gloves and an airy, "Bring her by," then she was gone.

"Damn," Jacob swore and dropped back into his chair. This nightmare was primed to blow sky high. He had to figure out who the Christmas Murderer was and stop him before Devon learned the truth and booted him out on his lying butt.

Inspired, he scrolled for another ten minutes, checked his watch and swore again. No time now for a deeper search of the New York news. He should have called Devon an hour ago.

He tried the cell phone he'd given her and had to snatch the receiver away from his ear when a woman's voice, Alma's, he suspected, spit a furious, "Listen up, whoever you are. You're—stop it, Devon, I'm trying to help. You're nothing more than a sniveling little worm, telephoning threats, quoting Christmas songs. It's sacrilege, and you have no—Devon, stop it, I'm…"

"Hello?" Devon's voice came on the line.

Jacob judged her greeting. Flat. Annoyed. Frightened. "It's me, Devon." A concerned ridge formed between his eyes. "What happened?"

"He called me," she said calmly, "with another warning."

A sliver of fear, razor-sharp, whizzed along his spine.

"He said it was the last verse the angels would sing for me."

Jacob was already halfway into his jacket. "Are you still at Alma's?"

"Yes."

She sounded zapped, shocky. He didn't like it. "Stay there. Do you hear me? Devon?"

"I hear you… Riker?"

He wanted to leave. "What?"

Her breath hitched slightly. "He said something else. He told me—" She firmed up the quaver in her voice. "He told me that a dead rat is a good rat; a picture is worth a thousand words; curiosity isn't the only thing that can kill a cat on its ninth life; love and angels don't mix, and…" she drew a deep, steadying breath. "trained illusionists aren't the only ones who can make people disappear."

"RUDY?" Bewildered, Mandy followed the smell of cigarette smoke to the den. She spied the glowing tip and, with a hot pink fingernail, flicked on the overhead light. "What are you doing, sitting like a zombie in the dark?"

His chin rested on his chest, loosening the skin of his throat even more than usual. His head bobbed up at her entry.

Anger flew. "Are you okay, Rude?" Dropping her parcels, she went to her knees beside him. He looked like a ninety-year-old man. She touched his gray hair. "Is it Jacob, Devon, what?"

He shook his head. "It's everything. It's sick, Mandy, that someone, anyone, could be so screwed in the head."

She eased the cordless phone from his tight fingers and set it aside. "The world's full of sickos, Rude. You can be a cop and try to round them up, but you'll never be rid of them."

His eyes met hers, flat and tired. "He's gonna do it soon; every gut instinct I've got is screaming that at me. Dugan's busy, doing the drill with a possible suicide; Jacob's digging and Devon's a sitting duck at Alma's cocktail party. It's a crock, I tell you."

There was something more here, Mandy decided. Something raw and unpleasant, gnawing away at those gut instincts of his. She prodded a little, squeezed his calloused hand. "What's in your head, Rude? I can't quite see it."

His free hand crawled around his neck. "Neither can I. Something, though. Jacob's tracking someone who used to be called the Morning Angel. Ever heard of her?"

Mandy searched her memory. "No bells on that one. Sorry."

Rudy tapped the nape of his neck. "I got a light going off back here. She's someone, or was. But not recently."

"You could use your computer. Well," she amended. "Jacob could." Determination set in. "Hell, why not?" She stood, took hold of his wrist. "Let's give it a whirl ourselves. We may be pathetic hackers individually, but who knows what we might accomplish together? You game?"

Rudy's eyes darkened briefly, then an odd sort of smile stole across his lips. "Yeah, sure. Why not?" Rising, he reached for the iron poker on the hearth beside him. "I'll get this fire back to speed while you boot up the computer." His fingers clenched around the smooth handle. "Maybe one of us'll get lucky at that."

How COULD IT only be 7:00 p.m.? Unbelieving, Devon stared at the dashboard clock. Time must be standing still.

A chill swept through her, and she rubbed her arms under her coat. "Where are we going?" she asked Riker as he skidded his Blazer through a snow-covered intersection. "Not to the apartment apparently."

"No, not there." He glanced over. "Are you sure you're not in shock?"

"From a telephone threat?" She angled her chin. "Absolutely not. I'm sick of this nightmare and, I'll admit, terrified down to my bones, but I'm also mad as hell at whoever's behind all of it."

And that was precisely as far as she was prepared to go in terms of thought and of conjecture. Riker hadn't been with her when the Christmas Murderer had telephoned. The murderer had called her on Riker's cell phone. Who, besides Riker, had known she was carrying it? Anyone who cared to know, that's who. He'd handed it to her outside the apartment building this morning. Half the city could have seen the exchange if they'd chosen to set up a watch.

So there was no reason for her to acknowledge the tendrils of suspicion twisting around in her stomach. No reason at all.

Devon used her strong feelings for Riker to keep the worst of her mistrust firmly at bay. She scanned the snowy streets and endeavored to identify the neighborhood.

"This is where Jimmy lives." She recognized one of the corner signs. "Why here?"

Riker maneuvered his vehicle over a patch of rutted ice. "Because he disappeared, and I want to know why."

"Angel," Devon murmured. "Angela. I wonder if Barret's real?"

"What?"

"People don't always use their given names in radio. Often don't," she amended. "It's a privacy thing."

"Not for you."

She shrugged. "I'm not a private person. I'm also not listed in the phone book and my computer's not hooked up to the Internet. Waters isn't Teddi's last name."

Riker approximated the location of the curb. "I hadn't thought of that," he admitted.

"There was no reason for you to. Besides, I doubt if it's significant."

"It could be on an official level. She'd be entered by her legal surname in the police computer files. I used the *New York Times* to track her down. I should have had—well, let's say I should have gone the official route."

Preoccupied with the crumbling old house before them, Devon nodded. "I think Jimmy told me once that his place was split into three units. It doesn't look like any of the tenants are home."

Riker followed her gaze upward. "That'll make it easier then, won't it?"

"Meaning you don't have a warrant."

He braved the storm, then stuck his head back in, collar upturned against the shrieking wind. "Do you want to wait or come?"

"I'll come."

"I thought you might."

Counted on it more like. Tempted to pull out her hair, Devon took Riker's hand instead, hopped into the snow and accompanied him to the front of the converted house.

He went to work at once on the lock. "Piece of cake," he said from his knees. "Keep an eye out, okay?"

Devon's teeth chattered as she hopped discreetly from foot to foot. Her mind moved in spurts from question to question, dark thought to darker thought.

She loved Riker, that was not a question. But, God help her, what if…?

"Got it." He nudged gently, and the door squeaked open. A cold, dark hallway greeted them. Lights helped, but weren't sufficient to dispel the gloom.

"This place could use some help from the Home Pro." Devon wrinkled her nose in distaste. "Why are rental houses always so depressing?"

"Because the owners live in Germantown and don't have to see them every day. Jimmy's mail box says he's on two."

Two minutes and another picked lock later, she stared in dismay at the stained carpet, faded furniture, gouged tables and split seat cushions.

"I don't think it was tossed," Riker said, his gaze circling the living area. "He's a slob, though."

Devon wandered over to the desk. "He came back here the day he ran out of my office. These station faxes are dated and initialed. No picture, though."

Riker flipped through a stack of file folders. "Picture of what?"

"Whoever that man was he showed me."

"What? Oh, that."

Leaving him, Devon drifted into the kitchen. Dregs of coffee in a cracked mug; coffee pot, half full, in the machine. Both stone cold.

Dirty dishes littered the sink and countertops. The herbs in their window pots looked healthy if a little sparse. The fridge was partially stocked and included a Cornish hen which he must have been planning to eat on Christmas Day.

A flurry of guilt pangs attacked. Devon had no idea whether Jimmy had family in Philadelphia or not. She should know, should have asked.

"Anything?" she inquired, returning to the living room.

"Nothing I can tell."

Devon replaced the rosary beads she'd discovered next to Jimmy's answering machine. No messages, she noticed and felt another twinge. Did Jimmy have friends, or had he withdrawn into himself when the young woman he'd loved had died?

Not a cheerful thought, she decided, stuffing her hands in her coat pockets. "We're wasting our time here, Riker, to say nothing of invading Jimmy's privacy. I think we should go."

"I agree." He never had removed his gloves, she noted. Neither had she. A reflex action? Devon wouldn't put much past her subconscious mind at this point.

"Alma says I'm not paranoid," she told Riker when they were back in his Blazer. "I'm not so sure about that. I'm having trouble trusting people. Any people," she added with a meaningful sideways glance.

No offence registered on his shadowed face. "It's an understandable reaction. I've been feeling like that myself lately."

The admission jarred. "Toward Rudy, you mean?"

He concentrated on the road. "I've known him forever, Devon. He was a good cop, still is. But I wonder sometimes where he is, what he's doing, even what he's thinking."

"And you feel like slime for doing it." Devon understood the contrary emotions, all too well.

She flicked at her bangs. "Where to now?"

"Home for you." Riker held up a hand to forestall her heated protest. "I'm only going to Rudy's. You're better off with Hannah tonight. Dugan—we've stationed a uniform outside the apartment. I'll feel better if you stay there," he added, well aware that the emotional angle would make arguing her case impossible.

"I suppose Hannah and I could take turns helping each other pack." Devon's shoulders sagged. "All right."

When they arrived at the apartment building, Riker left her in the warm Blazer and jogged through the snow to an unmarked car. She saw the cop inside grin and punch his arm. Nice that someone could find humor in a situation like this. She wouldn't care to spend her evening sitting in a cold car, staring at a windblown street. Maybe she'd sneak the cop some sandwiches and coffee after Riker left.

"Houdini couldn't get in," Hannah insisted five minutes later. "Everything's locked tight."

Riker kissed Devon in the hallway, not gently as she'd anticipated but in a somewhat desperate fashion. He fingered a strand of her hair as his troubled eyes stared into hers.

"I love you, Devon." Another, briefer, kiss. "Remember that."

He was out the door before she could open her mouth to reply. With a sigh, she pressed a brooding palm to the door frame. Damn her suspicious mind. Why couldn't she shed those last niggling doubts and simply love him the way her heart longed to? Why did life refuse to cooperate?

She lingered in the hallway, allowed her gaze to travel up the softly illuminated staircase, past her floor and Andrew's to the upper railing where Riker currently resided.

She'd been inside his apartment, had decorated his Christmas tree. No secrets lurked there waiting for her to find them. Only an unopened bottle of burgundy that they'd forgotten to bring downstairs last night.

She hesitated, considered, then called to Hannah. "Do you want some wine?"

"I'd love a glass." Hannah appeared, tying on her Christmas apron. "I was going to cook us some risotto. I thought we could watch *A Christmas Carol* like we used to when we were kids."

Sidetracked, Devon smiled. "Do you have almond cookies?"

"Always. Where's the wine?"

"It's—" She glanced upward one last time, then hunched her shoulders and made her decision. "I'll get it." Maybe she was a cat at that.

She climbed, lead-footed, despising her intentions. She had a pass key to all the apartments. She glanced sideways on three. Maybe she should check out Andrew's place while she was up here.

Riker's rooms were cool and smelled of latex paint. Drop sheets adorned at least half of the floor and furniture. She gave his punching bag a passing swack, then crossed to the kitchen and switched on the light.

It was bright white and more than adequate for her needs. Feeling decidedly disloyal, Devon balled her fists, pushed her recriminations aside and dug in.

She found nothing unusual on the coffee or end tables, nothing of significance in the stack of papers on the dining table. Only two empty soda cans, a candy-bar wrapper and photocopied reports on the Christmas Murders to date.

Pressing the heels of her hands to her gritty eyes, she re-thought her motives. Love and underhanded searches did not mix for her.

She'd spent enough time in Riker's bedroom to know that he kept little there of a personal nature. Socks, underwear and sweaters in the dresser. Jeans, shirts and jackets in the closet. And one black suit.

She smiled faintly, running her fingers over the fine wool-and-silk-blend fabric. He actually did own a tie, a narrow black affair with a subtle Celtic design woven through it in her favorite shade of blood-red. Irish-American, born to an addicted mother; adopted at age thirteen into a family of eleven other adopted children. Must have been a madhouse at Christmas time.

Her eyes swept across the closet floor. Boots, sneakers and a shoebox tied with white string.

Pictures of his late wife? Devon mused, aware of yet not quite ready to deal with the sharp tweak in her midsection.

Delia Brightman. She couldn't forget the woman's name. It had sounded familiar when Jimmy had mentioned it and did again now as it flashed through her head.

Kneeling, she drew the shoebox forward and untied the knot. If it was too personal she would stop. Invading privacy was one thing; shattering it was something else again.

Devon lifted the lid with tentative fingers. Nothing jumped

out, so she peered inside—and released a huge breath when she spied a collection of old news clippings.

Setting the lid aside, she examined the top clipping.

Laura West, né Price, later confirmed as the Christmas Murderer's first victim, had been a beautiful young woman at the time of her death, the great-niece of Ewen Mahoney-Price, a ruthless but shrewd racketeer from the twenties and thirties. Laura had been survived by her great aunt, Ida Price, her brother, Jacob Price, and her uncle, Rudy—

Devon broke off and snatched the paper around to better light. "'—her uncle, Rudy Brown,'" she read out loud, "'a sergeant with the Philadelphia Police Force....'"

A strange sort of nausea settled in as she reread the words. Closing her eyes, she set the paper on the floor. When her knees threatened to shake, she collapsed beside the box and let her mind go.

Why hadn't Riker told her? Why hadn't Rudy? Why would they keep a secret like this?

She halted there, on the fringe of the most dreadful and frightening answer possible. A person might very well keep a secret like that if it meant hiding a much more horrible secret—the secret of a serial killer.

Chapter Seventeen

"Come on, Rudy," Jacob said through chattering teeth. "Open the door."

He hit the bell again, used the icy brass knocker and finally resorted to his fist. Eight o'clock. The inside lights blazed, the shopping note was gone, but no one answered. Mandy must be in the bathtub.

Although he was tempted to pick the lock, Jacob's conscience scotched the idea. Mandy's car stood forlorn and snow-covered in the driveway. If he could pop the hood, he might get lucky and locate the spare house key she kept there for emergencies.

It took a full ten minutes to get the faulty hood latch to give. By comparison, ferreting out the key's hiding place was a piece of cake. Only Mandy, Jacob reflected, sucking on a cut forefinger, would drive a piece of junk strictly because the cotton-candy seat covers matched her favorite lipstick.

Ernie Ford was singing Christmas gospel when Jacob finally wedged the back door open. "Anyone here?" he called into the murk of the kitchen. "Mandy? Rudy?"

No answer.

Tearing off his remaining glove with his teeth, he headed away from the rear stairwell. If Mandy was soaking in a hot tub, she wouldn't appreciate him barging in on her.

Warmth and wood smoke wafted toward the back of the

house. Jacob followed it to its source, which just happened to be Rudy's den.

The lights burned brightest here. The computer screen blipped green where the cursor had stopped. There was a chair toppled backward, a poker lying on the hearth and what looked like spots of blood on the blue-gray carpet.

Jacob dropped to his right knee and tested one of the spots. Sticky, almost dry. Frowning, he brought his fingers away and sniffed. It was blood, a small puddle on the floor next to the computer desk and then several drops of it as the person bleeding apparently moved away.

Although there was not a sufficient amount to alarm him, he tracked it to the front door. Another small puddle, smeared, then the drips seemed to lead to the foot of the stairs. Which meant—what?

He eyed the front door, then the staircase. "Mandy?" he shouted.

No lights shone on the upper landing, but he checked it anyway. At the bedroom door, he knocked and called her name again.

No response; no water running; no sound whatsoever coming from inside.

Already edgy, Jacob's stomach gave a fierce wrench when something solid and furry rubbed against his leg.

A quiet woof from below had his breath blowing out in disbelief. "Thanks a lot, Buddy." Bending, he scratched the beagle's soft, floppy ears. "You almost gave me a heart attack."

Buddy woofed again and ambled off. Accepting, Jacob shrugged the matter aside and returned to the main floor. If Buddy wasn't concerned, he probably had no reason to be either.

Because blood was not a thing he cared to look at, he angled the computer screen away from it and shifted the chair appropriately.

"What the hell?" As he sat, he found himself staring nose to screen at a column of numbers. Old tax records? The name at the top read *A. E. Baltimore*. It didn't mean a thing to him—or likely to Rudy either, he decided with a hint of amusement. His uncle and Mandy defined the term *computer illiteracy*. Rudy knew only the basics; Mandy had learned how to update her checkbook. Beyond that, they relied on Jacob or Mandy's twelve-year-old grandson to get in and out of their files.

Rubbing his thumb and fingers together in anticipation, Jacob took up the challenge. Devon was safe with Hannah, and Mandy had probably cut herself on the fireplace hardware. She knew her neighbors well enough that borrowing a bandage could easily lead to coffee and several hours of local gossip.

His warmed fingers flew over the keyboard. Ernie sang on behind him. He thought he heard the phone, but since the cordless handset on the end table wasn't ringing, Jacob assumed he was hearing things.

"Angel Barret," he murmured. His dark eyes fixed on the moving screen. "Okay, darlin'. Let's see who you are, and what, if anything, Manhattan's Morning Angel has to do with the Christmas Murders."

THE PAIN HAD STOPPED attacking in waves. Now it attacked all the time. And with it, looming in the back of his head, the song. Taunting. Teasing. Tormenting. He hated it. He hated her.

He breathed deeply, felt himself in the darkness, growing stronger. It would end after tonight. A midnight clear, then Christmas, then freedom. She would not return. Cats only had nine lives. Surely angels could have no more than that.

The hands of his watch crawled slowly forward. Must do it now. Elimate the guard, infiltrate the building. He could do that no problem. You dealt with rats every day, grew up watching them come and go from your home, you learned their tricks. Five minutes tops, and he'd be in.

He'd been paying close attention today. Of those who mattered, he knew who was where. To facilitate the frame, he'd have preferred to have the times nailed down, but as long as Jacob had no alibi, the plan would work. And he would have no alibi. Watchful eyes coupled with beeping devices in his pockets assured him of that.

Quick knock on the door, slash of a knife over soft, shocked flesh, suffer the piercing scream and run. Out she flew. All was well.

Skulk in the dark for a time. Wait out more minutes. Follow the trail. Jacob was bright but oh, so predictable. And trusting of locks and dumb uniforms on surveillance. First rule of protection, Jacob. Know the enemy. See through his eyes.

A snicker escaped him as he left his vehicle and finished his two-block journey on foot through a welcome curtain of snow. He was good at this, really quite proficient after so many years of doing it. In some ways it seemed a shame to end the matter.

"Hello, darling…"

Out of nowhere, her velvety voice came to him. The words scraped across his soul, as painful now as they'd been then. He smelled wet wool, felt his muscles bunch in that tiny enclosed space. How dare she! He'd come all this way to surprise her, and she'd called another man darling. *His* Morning Angel, not someone else's. How could she do this to him, rip out his heart and stomp on it? Well, he'd put a stop to that soon enough.

He'd begun to shiver in the dark space. What if she didn't listen? Who ever listened to him? One small voice in a crowd. She might laugh, or worse, be kind and try very sweetly to brush him off.

No, no, he must be clever. In a crowd, clever worked. It would work even better with Angela.

Blurred memories rolled across his mind as he trudged, head downbent, through the snow. He spotted the unmarked car, checked his devices, approached carefully, casually. Mustn't alert the dumb officer.

Snow pelted him, icy flakes, like the ones at Angela's funeral. He'd stood at her gravesite, showed sorrow and horror. Nothing faked about the emotions. Then a hand had touched his arm. His head gave the same convulsive jerk now that it had in the cemetery.

"I'm Angela's cousin," a whisper-soft voice had said. "You must have worked with her at the Q."

Was it a trap? He'd almost panicked, but something in her gentle eyes had dissolved his fear, and much of his anger. No trace of the Morning Angel here. Nothing to remind him of her treachery. He'd fondled the rosary beads in his pocket. Prayer worked, it really did. No one suspected him of murder, and now, this gift. A new woman for him to love. A worthier one. And he would love her well....

The uniform directed his gaze at the apartment building as he'd been instructed. Sorrow scratched at his subconscious mind. What had this young cop done to deserve death?

No, he couldn't care. It had to be done. The man paused, rubbed his forehead. More innocent blood spilled. Please, God, he begged. Let this be the last of it.

Teeth gritted, he reached into his coat for the gun he'd stolen from Jacob. Tap on the window, look helpless.

"Yes?" The glass rolled down. The officer's eyes came up. "Is there a problem?"

He saw a heart explode in his mind, his beloved's heart. Angela's voice covered the image. "Call it a payback," she'd said once over the airwaves. She'd understood some things, if not all.

The scratch of sorrow stung briefly, then was ruthlessly obliterated. "No, officer, no problem."

The cop craned his neck. "Wait a minute, you look..."

The shot caught him in the throat. Didn't even have to be silenced in the storm. Garbage can lids lifted by the wind made as much racket in alleyways.

Hands sweating and shaking, he switched off the cop's radio, then moved swiftly to the shelter of the nearby shrubbery and watched for inquisitive neighbors. His gaze rose to

Devon's window. No light there, but she was in the building. Alive for now.

Unfortunately for her, she would not be alive much longer.

MORE CLIPPINGS, more victims' names. Devon skimmed the yellowed pages. None of the other Christmas Murder victims had relatives she knew. Only Laura West.

She rubbed her arms and struggled to rationalize. Did it compromise her safety because Rudy was related to the first confirmed victim of the Christmas Murderer? What had Riker said less than an hour ago? Rudy had lived in New York once. Briefly. Had he known the Morning Angel who'd worked at the now defunct Manhattan Q?

She spread the clippings around her like pieces of a jigsaw puzzle and continued to dig.

She unearthed a picture of Laura West, buried halfway down the pile. There was no apparent order to the storage of the articles. Why would Riker clip newspaper accounts when he had access to the police reports?

Devon's nerves refused to steady. Angel Barret had died eighteen years ago, Jimmy Flaherty had disappeared less than a week ago. Were those two events somehow connected?

Warren had worked at a Manhattan radio station for several years. Maybe Andrew McGruder had pulled teeth there once. Roscoe had definitely lived in New York. His family still did. Had Jimmy been familiar with that city? Why hadn't she gotten to know him better?

Her head swam with unanswered, unanswerable questions. She lifted her gaze to the unshaded bedroom window. Hannah would be waiting for her downstairs. She should go, forget about the shoebox. Surely it couldn't be relevant to her predicament.

"Damn you, Riker." She hissed out a spiteful breath. "You knew, and you didn't tell me. Why didn't you tell me?"

The snow danced beyond the frosted glass, teasing her like

tiny fairies. Something hovered on the fringe of her brain, a fragment of memory.

She swiped the hair from her eyes and delved deeper into the box. More articles. Another picture of Laura West. Laura who'd been survived by her Uncle Rudy, her Great-Aunt Ida and her brother Jacob.

Jacob...

A different image flickered and held. Gina Bartholmew, alias Eden White. She'd called Riker *Jacob*. Coincidence? Or something worse?

She pictured Riker's somber eyes, sincere, intense. "I love you, Devon. Never doubt that, no matter what happens."

A water pipe made a clunking sound that sent her heart rocketing into her throat and brought her, jittery as a cat, to her hands and knees.

When nothing in or out of the shadows stirred, she released her tightly held breath and relaxed the muscles in her neck.

Her gaze fell on the open shoebox. So close to empty.

Her hands slid forward. Two more articles about the Christmas Murders emerged, then another newsprint photo.

She stared at it. It wasn't a picture of Laura this time, or any of the other seven female victims. This was a man, bearded. His features were partially obscured. His hair, a mass of shoulder length curls and waves, flowed loosely about his shoulders.

The words beneath the photo fuzzed. Blinking, she brought them into focus.

The moment she did, she wished she hadn't. Her mind bobbled, rejected, then finally absorbed. God help her, she knew who it was. Faced with this photo, the Christmas Murderer could only be one man.

"ABOUT TIME," Jacob muttered.

A new name rolled up. Not Angel Barret after all. His eyes narrowed. Same last initial, different surname. His fingers tensed. A damned familiar surname.

The ringing telephone was real this time, though the handset remained silent. Feeling for it, Jacob shifted the Ring Off button and punched Phone. "What?"

"Jacob?" Mandy sounded shaken. "You're there. Is Rudy?"

"No. Why?" Fear jittered in. He needed to get to the apartment. Digging out his keys, he started for the door. "Where are you?"

"At the hospital."

That slowed him. "What happened?"

"I don't know exactly. Rudy—I went to make us a snack. The phone rang and next thing I knew, Rudy was shooting out of the den like a missile. He wouldn't tell me where he was going or why; he just left. I heard his bike roar off, then a few minutes later, someone knocked on the door."

In the kitchen now and impatient, Jacob paced. "Get to the point, Mandy. Bare bones."

Annoyance superseded fear. "He cut me. Is that bare bones enough for you?"

Jacob swore. "I'm sorry, Mandy. I have to get to Devon. Who cut you?"

"I don't know." Tears moved in. "A man in black. He slashed my shoulder. He might have been going for my throat, but I jumped away and slammed the door on him. I was bleeding. I started to go upstairs, then I thought of Millie Hart next door. She's a nurse. She took one look and drove me straight here. I thought—" her voice quivered. With shock, or something else? "I thought Rudy might have come back by now. I'm worried, Jacob. He's been acting funny. Moody. Withdrawn. Then he up and charged out of the house. His bike's no good in the snow. He could have an accident."

Could but likely wouldn't, not on the street at any rate. Desperation set in. Angela's name flashed neon-bright in Jacob's head.

"I have to go, Mandy. Are you all right? Can you stay with Millie tonight?"

"Yes, but..."

He cut her off, tossed the phone onto the counter. When had Rudy left? He should have asked. 8:20 now. Pray to God the cop assigned to Devon was good.

He ran to the Blazer and skidded it into the snowy street. He shouldn't have left her. Damn, damn, why hadn't he considered this angle? Because he'd been too caught up in the lies, that's why.

Ida had lived her life by lies. Laura had died from them. He'd used lies, hoping to bring a killer to justice—and in the nature of all deceptions, had wound up leading that killer to Devon's front door.

THE PHOTO CRUMPLED in Devon's terrified fist. The caption underneath had already burned itself into her mind.

Detective Joel Riker of the Philadelphia Police Department. Riker, whose face, though blurred, resembled, no, *was* the face in the picture Jimmy had tried to show her.

Devon started to shiver. She wanted to beat her head on the wall in fear and frustration. The man she loved was an impostor. Not Riker at all, but someone else. Jacob Price, brother of Laura West.

The shiver degenerated into a bone-chilling tremor. Had he killed his sister? Killed the other women? Had he tried to kill her?

Devon's legs trembled as she forced herself to her feet. Vertigo threatened to set in, but she couldn't allow that. Wouldn't. This was his place. He had a key. He could return any time and—what? Strangle her? Stab her? Shoot her?

No, dammit. She refused to believe that, simply could not accept that the man she'd come to love with all her heart was a cold-blooded serial killer. Nobody was that good an actor.

But what if she was wrong?

The water pipe clunked again, and with the sound, Devon's state of temporary shock broke. She bolted from the bedroom across the half-renovated apartment and out into the hall.

Below her, a door opened and closed. Stealthily? She couldn't be sure of anything at this point.

Crouching, she wrapped one hand around a railing post and peered downward. She saw a shadow, indistinct, moving toward the stairs. The treads creaked slightly as the person descended.

Andrew? Possibly. Didn't matter. She had to get away, get to Hannah.

Hauling herself up, she plunged down the stairwell. Whoever had been ahead of her was gone by the time she reached three.

"Devon?"

A blond head materialized, startling her so badly that she barely muffled a scream. "Hannah!"

"What? Are you all right?"

Heart thudding, Devon grabbed her sister's shoulders, spun her around and pushed.

"What's wrong? Devon, what are you doing?" Confusion blended with fright, but it was fright that won out.

Devon heard the street door open, felt the blast of wind that funneled up the stairwell.

"My place," she hissed. "Quickly."

Fumbling for her key, she shouldered the often-stubborn door open, shoved Hannah inside and slammed it.

"Devon, please, what's going on?"

She flicked the deadbolt. Funny that her door should suddenly seem so flimsy.

She backed away from it. Did she hear footsteps on the other side? Ice pellets rapped against the window like the spray of machine-gun bullets. She swung her gaze to the pane, spied the frozen terror in Hannah's face and crossed to her.

"What...?" her sister began, white-lipped.

"It's Riker." Shoulder to shoulder, Devon pried her fingers from the crumpled newsprint photo and pressed it flat. "This is Riker, Hannah, the real Riker. Detective Joel Riker of the Philadelphia Police Force. It was—I found it upstairs in a shoebox, along with a bunch of clippings about the Christmas Murders.''

"But who—'' Hannah's voice deserted her as the horror of the lie sank in. Huge brown eyes appealed to her sister. "Then who's the man we've been calling Riker?''

"I don't know.'' Devon pushed the tumbled hair from her eyes. "Jacob Price, maybe. Probably. Oh, God.'' She whirled, let the picture flutter to the carpet. "I have to call the police. Detective Dugan.'' She stopped her hand partway, curled her fingers. "But he'd be in on it, wouldn't he? Maybe he's not a real cop either? Rudy was, though. The desk sergeant knew him the night I phoned from the Wave.''

"Devon!'' Hannah backstepped into her arm. Her eyes were glued to the far wall. "There's someone on the stairs.''

Devon barely made it to the door before heavy fists began to pound it down.

"Open up, Devon. Do you hear me? Open this door!''

"Rudy!'' Hannah breathed the name over her sister's shoulder. Her fingernails bit in. "We're trapped!''

"Devon!'' Her name was a coarse bark, spit like an army command.

Devon's overtaxed brain ground into a functional mode. She swung Hannah around and pushed. "Use the bedroom phone. Call Roscoe. Tell him to find a police officer. Tell him Riker's not Riker, and Rudy—'' Hysteria threatened to bubble up. "Just tell him to get over here with help.''

Hannah opened her mouth, then promptly closed it again and fled.

Rudy used his fists like mallets. Devon could scarcely hear his shouts above the weighty pounding.

She'd only turned on one light. It glared at her, seemed to expose her somehow to the maniac in the corridor. She ran to extinguish it, then jumped swiftly backward.

"Devon…!''

His growl broke off abruptly. The hammering ceased. Devon held her breath and her stance, ridiculously afraid that if she moved the horrible noise might begin again.

The silence grew deafening. Ice and snow continued to pelt the windows. She thought she heard Hannah's frantic whisper in the bedroom, hoped she did. Any help would be good help at this point.

The seconds stretched out agonizingly. Still no sound came from the other side of the door. It must be a trick. He couldn't have gone away.

She dragged in a deep breath, lightly pressed fingers to the carved wood panels and said clearly, "It won't work, Rudy. I know the truth."

The explosion of wood and metal together with the choking stench of gunpowder caught her completely off guard. Smoke and sawdust blew up to blind her. A vicious inward thrust sent her sprawling to the carpet.

Stark light from the corridor revealed a silhouette, larger than life to Devon's reeling senses. It breathed hard, its chest and shoulders heaving as it stood, legs spread, on the threshold. One hand held a gun, the other a length of green silk scarf.

"It's me, Angel," the silhouette said hoarsely. "I've come to kill you for the last time."

Chapter Eighteen

Devon stared at him. She knew now what a startled deer must feel when it got caught in the headlights of an oncoming vehicle.

The Christmas Murderer made a jerky motion, and with it, Devon's courage galvanized. To hell with deer and headlights. She wasn't about to let a homicidal lunatic kill her, not before she put up the best fight she could.

Clambering to her feet, she yanked the foyer bench between them. With a single lithe kick, he booted it aside, lunged and sank his hand into her hair.

"Lying bitch," he swore. To Devon's ringing ears, it sounded like a sob. "It was all lies from the start. You slept with someone else." Her head snapped back as he gave her hair a vicious tug. "I hate you. Do you hear me, Angela? As much as I loved you before, I hate you now. So you can just stop coming back. Stop it, and leave me alone."

He clamped his other hand across her windpipe. His bitter words came directly into her ear. Her brain bobbled. The voice, the touch, even the scent of him was wrong. But it must be him, because it wasn't Rudy. No, too young, too agile and much too strong to be Rudy.

She didn't know what to call him. Her fingers came up to claw at a gloved hand. The pressure hurt. She couldn't breathe.

"Riker, please," she gasped, willing back the black spots of unconsciousness.

"Shut up," he ordered and shook her. His grip tightened. She kicked and it tightened further.

"Riker…"

"I said shut up! There's nothing you can say to stop me. It's too late for begging."

She was going to choke. That was one of two thoughts that floated hazily in Devon's mind. The more tantalizing thought drifted away, too far away for her to grasp it.

She tried to ram his stomach as she'd done before, but he was quick and blocked her elbow with his. Pain arrowed up her arm and into her teeth.

The action skewed him slightly to the side. As he turned, Devon spied a tiny movement in the bedroom doorway. She also succeeded in catching a quick, distorted glimpse of the killer's face in the glass face of her grandfather clock.

His long hair was caught back in a ponytail, but strands of it had escaped to tickle her cheek. His face was long and narrow, hollow-cheeked with misery. Terror battled relief. Her vision wavered. She knew that face. Did she know that face?

She coughed, squinted, blinked. "Riker…" Her lips moved soundlessly. The black spots became a black blur. "Oh my God… Riker!"

HE COULDN'T believe it; he'd lost his keys.

Jacob swore, glanced at the motionless form in the cop car across the street and the battered motorcycle behind it, bared his teeth and gave the door a mighty kick with his foot.

It took five well-aimed attempts before the wood frame splintered, another three before lock separated from frame, allowing him to shove the thing aside.

The Morning Angel's name resounded in his head. Angel Barret, born, Angela Brightman. Brightman. As simple as that if they'd only discovered it earlier.

He took the stairs three at a time. It was Devon's face he

saw in his mind's eye—but not her bony fingers he recalled. They'd once seized his in a cold, bruising grip.

"You killed her, boy. It was your fault, not mine." Mean brown eyes had burned with denial. "You confused her. Laura was mine from the start. You should have been like us or you should have gone away and left us alone. You made her doubt her values, boy. You made her fight with me. She ran out, and the next morning, she was dead. She was dead, and you caused it. You killed your baby sister. And now you've killed me, too...."

No, Jacob thought grimly, he hadn't done either of those things. But he knew who'd done one of them.

The bastard would not do it to Devon.

"RIKER!"

It was a desperate croak, an accusation, a truth Devon could see now despite the blackness that threatened to engulf her.

"Smart and beautiful," he said with sarcastic pity. "But a poor illusionist."

She fought him with every scrap of her strength. Joel Riker, the real Riker, cop and killer twisted up into one tormented ball. Her fingernails tore at the skin of his wrists. He made garbled sounds of pain and, lifting her from the carpet, whipped her around like a cloth doll.

The blurred fury sprang at him like a small dog. Devon glimpsed a blue ceramic vase, caught a flash of blond hair and snatched her head sideways.

"Leave her alone!" Hannah swung the vase with all her might.

It would have made contact if Riker hadn't ducked swiftly and thrust Devon away from him. The base of the vase grazed the side of her head as she stumbled forward. With a shocked. "Oh!" Hannah dropped her makeshift weapon and ran to catch her sister.

Devon heard Riker breathing like an enraged bull. She

fought for balance while Hannah held onto her and whispered white-lipped, "He cut the phone lines."

"And bugged the vehicles of your would-be heroes," a leashed but otherwise perfectly modulated male voice added scathingly.

Devon scuttled around on her backside while Hannah knelt behind her. Her mind spiraled. Her vision remained blotchy and unsure. "Bugged?" she repeated slowly.

His shoulders hitched. He snatched up the scarf, then reached with deliberate calculation into his coat. "As in monitored, Angela. Nothing sophisticated, just a few miniature devices planted in strategic places so that I could—" He stopped, glanced into his palm, swore. A second later, a small black box hit the wall. "Piece of crap." His eyes darted back and forth, then landed on her and focused. His agitated breathing slowed. "Doesn't matter." He advanced on the pair of them. "I'll handle him."

Devon had difficulty making her lips move. "Who?"

His eyes blazed, actually lit up in a way that altered their color, deepened it, polished it to a marble-bright sheen.

"Back up," she whispered through her teeth to Hannah.

Hannah responded instantly, her gaze riveted to Riker's contorted face.

"My alter ego." He continued to advance. "My Sydney Carton." Bitterness spewed from his lips and eyes. "Jacob Price, Angela. Your latest lover."

"I'm not…"

She got no further than that. What was left of the door crashed open behind Riker, hit the wall and bounced off.

"Drop it, Riker," Jacob growled.

Did he have a gun? In the garish glare of light from the hall, Devon could only see his extended hands.

Riker moved like a cheetah, down and sideways. A bullet zinged off the stereo stand. He had a gun, all right. Devon pushed at Hannah. "Get into the bathroom," she ordered, "before he—"

Riker seized her so unexpectedly and so savagely that it

took Devon several seconds to understand what had happened.

"Ever the protector." He squeezed her up tight to his body. His neck muscles formed rigid cords. A knife—Devon had no idea where it had come from—slid like a straight razor across the soft skin of her throat. "You drop it, Price," he snarled, "or I swear by all the saints, I'll carve her up in front of you."

He'd do it in a minute. Devon let the fingers that had risen instinctively to his hand rest without pressure on his strong wrist.

Jacob faced him, appeared to calculate the odds. Jacob, not Riker. Not a cop at all. The cop was the killer. Devon's mind trembled. The world had slipped into a freakish alternative dimension.

Jacob's hands fell. The gun hit the carpet. "Let her go, Riker," he said without inflection. "She isn't Angela."

Something rumbled in Riker's chest. Anger? Anguish? "What the hell do you know?" he snapped. "Your own sister played host to Angela's vengeful spirit. My Morning Angel. Mine. Not some other creep's who didn't even love her." His breath hissed out, poured hotly over Devon's cheek. "You don't know what it is to love, Jacob. To love and to hate at the same time. To be fed one lie after another. To be treated like a complete and utter fool."

"You're wrong." Jacob took a cautious step forward. "I know exactly what it feels like."

So did she, Devon thought, but her glimmer of spite gave way swiftly to renewed fear as Riker's grip shifted on the knife.

"So your Morning Angel jilted you," Jacob went on. He could have been talking about the fate of the Phillies for all the urgency in his tone. "You did better than Angela in the end anyway. You married her cousin. Did Delia remind you of Angela?"

"Delia!" Devon gasped the name softly, then sneaked a look at Riker's strained profile. That's why the name had sounded so familiar. Angela Brightman had been the Morning Angel. Delia Brightman had been married to Joel Riker.

Jacob eased closer as Riker began to sweat. "I read about her, Riker. Manhattan's Morning Angel, with a voice like honeyed velvet."

"And the soul of a viper," Riker shot back. "You didn't know her. She was insidious, crawled under a man's skin and festered there. I loved her, and she lied to me."

At a subtle sign from Jacob, Devon steadied her breathing. Divert his attention, right. How? "You married her cousin Delia, Riker," she managed shakily. "You must have loved her very much."

His laugh resembled the cry of a wounded seal. "I loved her, and she died. A heart attack at twenty-five. No one has a heart attack at twenty-five." His mouth took an ugly turn. The hand holding the knife gave a jerk that drew blood.

Devon swallowed her terror, and refrained from moving.

"People die." Jacob attempted to draw his attention. "Many of them for reasons no one can explain."

"Bull." Devon felt Riker's heart pumping hard and fast against her spine. "I can explain it. Angela killed her. Delia and I had just moved to Philadelphia. I heard Angela on the radio. I knew it was her come back to torment me. But I waited. I told myself it didn't matter. What harm could a ghost do to me?"

Jacob's eyes impaled his. "You killed her, didn't you?"

"Who?" A lost wail this time as his emotions played leap-frog. Devon ordered her watery knees to support her and prayed for a chance. Any chance.

Ice pellets skittered down the window. Did she hear Christmas music? Carollers?

Jacob held tight to his even tone. "Did you kill Angela because she lied to you?"

Riker's broken bark of laughter froze the blood in Devon's heart. "Kill her? Of course I did. They found her, finally in her own basement, under the stupid linoleum floor that I'd laid down for her. Stupid cops. I fell apart, and they read it

as torn apart. They only questioned me once. Once, and then
they never talked to me again. So I went to her funeral, decided then and there to ditch my career in broadcasting and
become a cop. God knew, I could do it better than the ones
assigned to Angela's case. I met Delia at Angela's gravesite.
I married her. I buried her. I knew, I knew that her death was
Angela's doing. And I knew, finally, that I'd have to kill her
again.''

Laura West. The name drifted eerily through Devon's
head. Riker had murdered Jacob's sister. The tragic irony,
the horror of it, was that he'd subsequently been assigned to
investigate her death.

The knife sliced deeper. Jacob's fingers curled into fists.
Devon felt a trickle of blood slide down her throat and sucked
in a quick, panicky breath. ''W-why 'It Came Upon a Midnight Clear?''' she blurted out.

The distraction worked. The knife froze. ''A midnight
clear,'' Riker repeated, then more forcefully, ''A midnight
clear. Damn that song.'' One hand rose to clap over his ear.
''Damn that song to hell, and her with it!''

Devon seized her opportunity. Clamping her hands to his
forearm, she shoved the knife from her throat. His strength
was impressive, might have been insurmountable if she
hadn't managed to sink her teeth into his wrist.

They were still embedded when she saw the bullet that
was Jacob's body hit Riker with a full flying tackle.

Devon stumbled, then quickly righted herself and ran for
the vase Hannah had used…and smashed in the process, she
realized a frustrated moment later.

A thump sounded in the corridor. She snatched her head
up. Jacob and Riker were gone. How on earth had they disappeared so quickly?

Spinning, she rushed to the bedroom, flung open the
door—and had to dart to the window to prevent Hannah from
crawling onto the frosty ledge.

''Riker—Jacob's dealing with him.''

''He's—'' Hannah's distraught eyes widened. ''Devon, your neck! You're bleeding!''

She'd forgotten about that. She fingered the cut, then shook herself, grabbed her brass reading lamp from the night-stand and headed doggedly back through the apartment.

''Riker's cell phone is in my purse,'' she shouted as she ran. ''Beside the sofa. Phone Detective Du—oh, my God!''

The name splintered as her foot caught on something large and unmoving on the outer threshold. No, not something—someone. Lying face down on the carpet in a seeping pool of blood was the body of ex-Philadelphia Police Sergeant, Rudy Brown.

JACOB'S FIST SMASHED into Riker's face. A lucky but effective blow. Riker stumbled on the lobby carpet, used the newel post to save himself and let out an animal snarl.

But Jacob was on fire, furious and past caring about the cop's deteriorated state of mind.

''You tried to kill Devon,'' he shouted and landed another uppercut. ''You did kill Laura and six other women. Seven if you include Gina Bartholomew.''

Riker assumed a wary crouch, wiped a trickle of blood from his mouth. ''She was a whore, too good for me now, she said. Angela probably had a chat with her in transit.''

He moved swiftly and caught his opponent with an elbow to the ribs. Jacob's breath whooshed out but pain didn't deter him. He brought his own elbow up into Riker's ear.

Stunned, Riker staggered into the mailboxes.

A cold blast of wind proceeded an indignant, ''What on earth is this?'' from the outer door.

Bad timing, Jacob reflected as Riker launched the pair of them into Andrew McGruder's flabby chest.

The dentist flailed helplessly beneath them. Jacob twisted Riker around, sandwiching him. ''Hold him,'' he ordered, and too stunned to argue, Andrew did. Briefly. No sooner had Jacob fisted his black coat than Riker thrashed free of his captor's ineffectual grasp.

Jacob cursed and rolled in the opposite direction. On his knees, he saw Riker looking upward, judging the distance. Was he going to try for the stairs?

"You murdered Jimmy, didn't you?" Jacob's rough demand was designed to sidetrack, and it made Riker blink.

"What? Jimmy? Oh, the kid." He pressed a hand to his forehead, refocused. "Yeah, I did him." His hand snapped down, his eyes burned. "I had to do him. He'd have told her about us."

"There's no us, Riker."

A sly smile crept across Riker's mouth. Not moving, Andrew watched them square off. "Oh, there's an us, all right, Jacob. Working toward separate goals, it's true, yet united by deception. Brando made you right off. Bad move on your part. He was a junkie. All I had to do was get him some stuff. It goes missing all the time from the cop shop. It was strong. I thought he'd OD for sure. He almost did, but he sold too much of it—some promise he'd made to that dancer girlfriend of his. I had to—" his voice quavered, then ruthlessly firmed. "I had to drop him into the river. Drugs and nature did the rest."

His features hazed. His gaze strayed upward again. He was losing him, Jacob realized.

"You don't know," Riker went on, his tone eerily soft. "I didn't know myself how big a monster Angela could be. She played that song while she talked to her lover on the phone. And there I was, hiding in her front-hall closet with her Christmas present in my hand. A beautiful gold pendant. A Claddagh—a heart cupped in a pair of hands. Irish. A symbol of my love."

Jacob had worked himself to his feet but remained in a crouch. "You broke into her house?"

"To give her her present. We'd agreed at the station not to do presents that year. But I loved her. We went out for drinks. I told her she was everything to me. And you know what she did?"

Though he had a pretty good idea, Jacob shook his head, made a subtle warning sign to Andrew not to budge.

"She laughed. She patted my cheek. She told me crushes were cute." His muscles bunched at the memory. "That did it. I'd show her that I meant it." His lips thinned. "My Morning Angel. She kept playing that song, kept talking to him. A midnight clear—which is exactly when it came to me. I waited and sneaked out of the house. That night, at midnight, I finally realized what I had to do." His head came up. His eyes glinted. "And I'm going to do it again. Now!"

He sprang up with such speed and intensity of purpose that Jacob almost missed the move. But he was young and quick, and he'd connected more times with Riker's body than Riker had with his.

He took off as Riker did and managed to snag the other man's ankle. His fingers closed and yanked. Riker howled, kicked free and began to scramble upward.

"I think…" Andrew started.

"Stay down," Jacob shouted.

It took him till the top of the stairs to catch the bottom of Riker's coat. One foot came out in a lethal jab, but Jacob was prepared and dodged it.

"Not Devon," he grunted through gnashed teeth. "You won't kill the woman *I* love."

Giving Riker's trapped foot a mighty wrench, he flipped him over. Riker surged up, hands extended. No protection to the solar plexus. Jacob balled his fist and plunged it hard into the cop's stomach. Riker doubled, struggled for balance, then lost his footing and toppled awkwardly down the staircase.

Breathing hard, Jacob simply sidestepped and watched. Riker knew how to fall. He was out cold at Andrew McGruder's upturned feet, but nowhere close to dead.

And as he turned to face Devon's wrath, Jacob wondered idly how he felt about that.

Chapter Nineteen

"Riker's in the hospital under twenty-four-hour guard." Dugan slapped his file folder closed. "He won't be going anywhere for a very long time." He glanced at Jacob. "I, on the other hand, have a great deal of explaining to do to my captain."

Devon had been smoldering for hours. Now, as midnight approached at the police station, she slid her first resentful look at Jacob's unrevealing profile. When his head started to turn, however, she tore her gaze away and asked quietly, "How's Rudy?"

"The old hard head?" Dugan snorted. "He'll be singing Weird Al Christmas carols by morning." He sobered. "I'm sorry I can't say the same for your friend, Flaherty. Uniforms found his body in a storage locker Riker rented by the river. Corpse was frozen stiff. Not pretty."

"Death never is," Jacob muttered.

Devon rubbed her weary temples. "Did the officer assigned to watch the apartment building have a family?"

"Parents. A girlfriend. No kids. He was green but good. Riker just knew the right buttons to push. It isn't your fault what happened."

She stared at a distant spot on the floor. "It feels like my fault."

"It isn't," Jacob repeated. He waited until she slid her reluctant gaze to his. "It's mine and Riker's."

Dugan made a cranky sound. "Well, hell, you might as well toss my name into the mix, in that case. And Rudy's. Brando's, too, if you want to go broad on this. He ratted to Riker."

"He was an addict," Devon defended.

Dugan shrugged. "So was Riker's mother, but he never touched the stuff. We make our own choices, Ms. Tremayne."

"You don't know how her addiction might have affected him in the womb, Detective. His adult brain hardly functioned in a reasonable capacity."

Another shrug. "He hid his defects well."

Devon speared Jacob with her eyes. "Lots of people hide lots of things well. I can't decide if that's a good or bad quality."

Jacob stared at her solemnly, and, possibly flogged himself inside.

With a flick of his wrist, Dugan indicated a stack of paper. "Coombes'll be undergoing a full psychiatric evaluation for his problems—and I'd say he's got more than a few of those."

Devon was silent for a moment, then she took a deep breath and finished it off. "Does anyone know how Riker found that Jimmy had his photo?"

Dugan's lip curled in contempt. "Riker had a line into the whole police system, Devon. My guess is he discovered your friend's snooping and kept an eye on it. Some things you were allowed to know; some things you weren't. If Flaherty was a good hacker—"

"He was."

"Then he must have snagged the photo before Riker could stop him. So he stopped him another way."

"He might be insane, but he was on top of most things," Jacob noted sourly.

"He was that." Dugan glanced at his watch. "12:13 a.m. Christmas Eve. I don't know about you people, but I'm whacked. What say we—yes, Benson?"

"Sir." The uniformed woman who stuck her head through the door of the interrogation room moistened her lips, gnawed on the lower one, then straightened as her training kicked in. "Sir, we've just received a report from the hospital where Detective Riker was being held."

Devon caught it. So did Jacob. Dugan stated it, tersely. "*Was* being held?"

The officer faltered slightly, then continued. "He's dead, sir. Someone got in—strangled him in his hospital bed."

"YOU LOVE THE MAN, Devon," Hannah reminded patiently. "Love and forgiveness go hand in hand."

"Not for me they don't. Red dress or green?" Devon held both above her half-packed suitcase.

"Green. And yes they do, even for you. Especially for you. You're the most forgiving person I know." Shrewdly, Hannah switched tacks. "He did it for his sister in the beginning. Riker—" she shuddered lightly. "—murdered her. Wouldn't you use any means at your disposal to catch the person who killed Daria or Sylvie or me?"

Devon threw both dresses on the bed and made an impatient motion. "You know I would. But he could have confided in me, Hannah. Maybe not at first, but later."

"Later he was in love with you. He was afraid he'd lose you."

Devon's eyes narrowed in suspicion. "Is he upstairs? Did he put you up to this?"

"He's with Rudy, and, no, I put me up to this."

"Rudy." His name rolled out on a vaguely wistful breath. "Now there's a story. Jacob's uncle. A real cop, really retired. I wonder who'd have been arrested for Gina Bartholomew's death if Rudy's gun, which Jacob was carrying, had surfaced as planned?"

"Does it matter now, Devon?"

"No." She squared her shoulders in an attempt to shed her mood. "Mandy said that mystery phone call Rudy received probably came from Riker. Rudy thought it was a tipster calling from the billiard hall. Riker must have wanted him out of the way, so he arranged a fake meeting at the hall. Except that Rudy stopped here en route to see if he could find Jacob. He saw the officer dead in his car, and figured the Christmas Murderer was inside. Or so Dugan says.''

"Thank heaven Riker didn't kill Rudy." Hannah almost contained a delicate shiver. "I wish I hadn't missed him with that vase."

"Strong and bloodthirsty." Devon's mood began to lift. "I underestimated you badly, Hannah." She took her sister's hands, sat beside her on the bed. "I'm sorry for that. Love is a lot of things, not the least of which is blind. I'm a prime example of the failing."

"No, you're a wonderful example. Joel Riker's prime."

"Was prime," Devon reminded. She squeezed her eyes closed. "Strangled by person or persons unknown. God, I can't believe how muddled I am. I actually feel sorry for him. And I'm mad at Jacob."

Hannah smiled. "That's because you love Jacob. Otherwise you'd feel sorry for him, too. Sorrier for him than for Riker."

Devon slanted her a canny look. "Wisdom, too. You'd better watch it, or you'll turn into a saint."

"Just as long as I don't turn into an angel."

"Too late for that," a man's voice remarked from the doorway. "You already are one."

Damn the man's nerve. Devon's eyes flashed upward. "I should have known you weren't a cop, Jacob. You're too good at breaking and entering to be official."

Hannah smothered a grin. "I'd better go and pack." Devon heard her cautionary, "Her temper's still running on high," as she passed Jacob in the bedroom doorway. Out of spite, Devon launched a slipper at Jacob's chest.

He caught it neatly. "Lousy shot, Ms. Tremayne."

"I wasn't aiming at Hannah."

He tossed the slipper aside and advanced, an undisputed

threat in his black leather and jeans. "In that case, you're a great shot."

She stood, holding her ground. "I'm a lousy judge of character."

"No, you're not, and neither am I. As a rule." He paused, let his gaze move away. "I missed Riker," he said softly. "By a mile."

Something stirred in Devon's heart. Her expression melted slightly. "The police missed him, too, Jacob. Rudy, Dugan, everyone. And the ones who knew anything at all paid a high price for their knowledge. Brando, Gina, Jimmy—" she flinched at the last name. "Riker killed all of them. And eight others, including your sister. I don't know where Casey Coombes fits in."

Jacob didn't crack a smile. "No one does yet, but his book deal's deader than Marley's ghost." He started toward her again, stopped less than a foot in front of her but didn't remove his hands from his jacket pockets. "You have a right to be angry, Devon."

She refused to stroke his face or to touch the dark hair that tumbled onto his forehead. "I know I do. I am—I think."

Amusement flitted briefly across his mouth. "You're not sure? I'm encouraged."

She toughened her stance. "Don't be. I can be a tediously thorough thinker when I choose." She spun from him, arms folded at her waist. "You lied to me, Jacob. I hate liars."

"So do I."

"You have a strange way of showing it."

She heard the thunder of distant memories in his tone. "My great-aunt was a liar, Devon. And my sister. The truth seldom suited their purpose. I fought with Laura the night she died. I thought our constant fighting somehow made it my fault that she died. I didn't pay enough attention to her as a child. It was all lies anyway, so why bother? I had my own life to deal with. And she had Ida."

Devon stole a quick look back. "Your great-aunt."

"Another liar. She blamed me for Laura's death. Of all

the lies she told, I chose that one to believe. I don't believe it any more.''

She felt his hand brushing aside the silky layers of her hair and fought a tremor of desire.

''I never meant to hurt you, Devon. I only wanted to absolve my feelings of guilt. I felt I owed Laura something for not caring as much as I should have over the years. I knew a long time ago how strong an influence Ida was on her, and I didn't do a damned thing to stop it. Self-preservation, I suppose. I escaped the moment I could. For all her flaws, Ida was one hell of a powerful woman. I could have handled the power. It was the manipulation that drove me out of her life.''

''I have trouble picturing you being manipulated.''

His fingers grazed the soft skin of her neck. ''Picture an eight-year-old child and a very old, very opinionated, very vocal Russian woman.''

''Really?'' She couldn't resist turning. ''I thought you were Irish?''

''I didn't share blood with Ida.''

But he had with Laura. Meltdown all but complete, Devon reflected with a resigned sigh. How could she stay angry when she knew she would have done exactly the same thing in his position? Still...

She managed one last reproachful stab. ''You could have considered trusting me with the truth.''

He rubbed his thumb over her chin. ''I did consider it.''

''What stopped you?''

His eyes glinted. ''We made love. I fell. Men in love don't always think with their brains.''

That did it. Laughter climbed into her throat. Her palms pressed lightly against his chest as his arms closed around her. ''One thing about you, Jacob. You're hell and gone removed from Sydney Carton.''

A smile tugged on his lips. ''I love you, Devon. Is that a noble enough declaration for you?''

''No.'' She brought her mouth up to tempt his. ''But it's close enough for this ex-Christmas Angel.''

Epilogue

"I told Hannah we'd leave for our parents' place at five," Devon said to Jacob as they drove toward Tanya's dingy riverside apartment.

"We'll make it." He sent her a wry smile. "If I'm pulled over for speeding, I'll flash my fake badge."

Devon, who'd been counting presents—two for Pop, two for Tanya, one for the woman who'd taken Tanya in—flopped back in her seat. "I didn't hear that." She cast a look at the seat between them. "Your phone's ringing."

"It's in your purse."

Devon made a face as she drew it out.

Alma's voice greeted her. "Devon, my dear, I've just received the oddest note. Someone slid it under my front door. I don't know when. Possibly this morning sometime."

Devon stopped fiddling with the bows. "A note?"

"Let me read it to you." Alma cleared her throat. "It says: 'Angels and others deserve to have their revenge. The thin blue line broke. So did I. I am not an angel.'"

"It's a confession," Devon maintained ten minutes later as she and Jacob climbed the stairs to Tanya's apartment. "I don't know why it was delivered to Alma, but that's what it is. Whoever killed Riker wants his or her statement aired on the Wave."

"It's a reasonable assumption." Jacob gave Tanya's door a tap. "What was that about a thin blue line?"

"'The thin blue line broke.'" Devon's brow furrowed. "I've heard that somewhere before."

Tanya was tucking her red hair under a dramatic black wig when she answered the door. Her eyes widened when she spied Devon. "You came," she said simply. "I didn't think…" A wary veil dropped over her features. "Why are you here?"

"Presents." Jacob studied her. "You look—different today."

"I got a job." She jerked her head. "Over at the Midnight Club. Dancing." Her eyes glinted. "I got the news about Riker. The real Riker, that is. Bastard cop. Heard all about the capture first-hand." She cocked a brow. "I was bailing out a friend at the time. They made me wait. Suddenly, all hell broke loose. It was a circus, and I had a front-row seat."

"You know that Riker killed Brando?" Jacob's tone was questioning.

Her breath hitched, then settled. "Yeah, I know. About him and you. You had Pop fooled, Mr. Big Shot Magazine owner, and me. But not Brando. Then again, my Brando he'd been around the block. He hated blue liners, really hated them, but he knew that sometimes a person's gotta take advantage of an opportunity."

Blue liners… The blue line broke…

Devon handed her the presents with great deliberation, "I imagine security was awfully tight at the hospital where Riker was being held," she mused out loud. "I wonder how someone managed to sneak past the guards on his room?"

Tanya fingered a shiny red bow. "Diversion maybe. Probably. Wouldn't be hard to create one in a hospital. Just takes an inventive mind."

"Anger breeds inventiveness." Devon flicked a glance at Jacob's impassive face. "From what I've observed." She regrouped and smiled. "So, the Midnight Club? Sounds interesting."

"It is, so far. The manager and I get along pretty good. Well," Tanya moved a shoulder, "except for one thing."

"He wants you to dye your hair black?" Jacob guessed.

Tanya's eyes came up, rock steady. A defiant challenge fired their depths. "He wants to bill me as the Midnight Angel. I told him no way. I am not an angel...."

Amnesia…an unknown danger…
a burning desire.

With

HARLEQUIN®

I N T R I G U E®
you're just

A MEMORY AWAY

from passion, danger…and love!

Look for all the books in this
exciting miniseries:

THE BABY SECRET (#546)
by Joyce Sullivan
On sale December 1999

A NIGHT WITHOUT END (#552)
by Susan Kearney
On sale January 2000

FORGOTTEN LULLABY (#556)
by Rita Herron
On sale February 2000

A MEMORY AWAY…—where
remembering the truth becomes
a matter of life, death…and love!

Available at your favorite retail outlet.

HARLEQUIN®

Makes any time special ™